THE CHRONICLES OF DARKNESS

The Box of Infernos

Published in 2013 by FeedARead Publishing

Copyright © Matthew Head.

Characterisation and continuity consultant – Stephanie Shapland

British Library C.I.P.

A CIP catalogue record for this title is available from the British Library.

For all my friends, everywhere.

Into the desert, one, two, three.
Is anybody watching, can you see?
Although no eyes appear to show, there are always the eyes of the shadow below.
If you find it you should hide, for there's terrible fear of the fear inside.
The lid is locked and the lock is sealed, pray the fear is never revealed.
There'll be suffering, there'll be loss.
Fear the Box of Infernos.

Childrens rhyme from the Negev desert, circa 1020 B.C.E

Prologue

It is said by some that all of creation can be divided into good or evil. Light or dark. Right or wrong. True or false. Those who say this say it as a comfort to themselves, as they are undoubtedly the ones who will claim to be good, light, right and true and it makes their lives just a little easier if they can believe that those adjectives really apply to them.

It is said by others that all of creation can be classed together - that every being is a combination of good and evil, that there is in fact no true good and no true evil in existence. Those who say this say it also as a comfort to themselves, as it means they can sleep better in their beds believing that there is no true evil lurking in the world, or perhaps in the shadows of their own bedroom.

It's an unfortunate truth then for both of those groups of people that they are both wrong in their beliefs. There is pure good, there are beings of pure light in existence. And there is pure evil, and rest assured there are many beings of pure darkness in existence. But then there are also creatures who straddle both camps, which are impossible to class one way or the other.

The beings of light are predominantly the angels who sing and blaze in the higher realms, radiating love and beauty. They live their lives in what we as humans have decided to call heaven but that isn't to say that they don't make their presence known still in our world from time to time. They aren't the only beings of light however - there are the Witches of the Veil who pass through worlds offering help and kindness, and legends also tell of ancient beings that swirl in the deserts of the east of the world - always happy to show love and friendship to any who need it.

The beings of darkness can be loosely tied together with the common term of demons, however this broad term does their numbers an injustice. There are many creatures of hate and lies - soul dwellers, ghouls, the Children of Despair, the Ar'karnak, the shadows, malignant fairies - the list can continue almost indefinitely as the dark realms have spawned infinite monsters in the time since the dawn of creation. Higher up than simple demons there are also the primordial beings of chaos and hatred that have long been forgotten by our world although that is not to say that they have forgotten us.

It might seem on the face of it that the beings of darkness outweigh the beings of light, but then it must be remembered that a single match shines brightest when surrounded by the pitch blackness and that a single truth if properly wielded can topple a whole tower of lies.

Still there is another group to look at, the beings that fall in between. Those gloriously grey beings that refuse to be either the deepest black or the purest white. Humans. People. Grey is often seen as a boring, drab kind of colour but in the case of humanity it shines brilliantly. Many people in the world would resist being painted with the grey brush - some may claim to be pure good, some may well claim to be pure evil. But whatever you may think of an individual you must remember the truest truth there is in the whole of the world - they are all grey. They are all somewhere in-between. No person is wholly right ever, everyone has their own faults and everyone makes mistakes and does wrong from time to time. And equally no person is wholly wrong ever, behind the most wicked people you will always find some glimmer of good - a shadow of the person they once were perhaps or an indication of some terrible event which once turned them down darker paths.

The greatest strength of humanity is its ability to comprehend and exhibit the emotion we'd loosely call love. Love binds people, binds families, binds friendships together and holds them close. It pulls you close to people and keeps you with them and through that it can be a source of great joy and great happiness. But despite being the greatest strength love can also perversely be the greatest weakness of a person too. For many it never becomes an issue because their lives are too ordinary. But for some who find themselves dealing with those creatures who dwell purely in the darkness then love can twist and turn. Before long it can lead to terrible choices, awful deeds and heartbreaking consequences.

So then, we can see that there are beings of true light, beings of true darkness and beings of the in-between. All are important and all will play a crucial part in the story which is about to begin before the final move is made and we see whether creation ceases to exist or if it will continue to flourish in all its diversity. For there is one more truth to impart.

Something is coming.

Chapter One

The balmy late August night air breathed hot waves through the open window into the dark flat. The two figures stood there facing each other from opposite sides of the room.

"So, you're Jewish?" asked the deep, cockney voice by the window.

"No."

"Your name sounds Jewish."

Isaac Jacobs was well aware that his name sounded Jewish. "Yeah I know." He was growing uneasy. It was late at night, he didn't know this person, he didn't even know this city very well. He should go. This had been a mistake, coming into a stranger's house after just happening to walk past and see a dirty flyer for psychic abilities in the window. "Look, I'm not even sure that I should be here. I'd better go." He turned and headed for the door. If he could find the door. Would it kill this guy to turn on the lights?

"What do you want, Isaac Jacobs?"

Isaac paused and turned back towards the young man leaning against the window. "I want to help. That's all."

"Help with what?"

"Help with the things that no-one else helps with."

"Ahhhh." The young man leaned forward slightly. "You've lost people to them."

Isaac grimaced. He didn't want to remember. "Yes."

"Who?"

"Friends."

"I'm sorry." The young man sounded genuinely sympathetic.

Isaac stayed silent. He didn't want to remember.

"And so now you want to help others? Fight back a bit?"

"Someone has to."

"It's dangerous. Here especially. This city's old, older than anyone cares to imagine. All kinds of nasties lurking round here."

"I know." It wasn't that Isaac loved danger, he didn't. But now that he knew the things he knew, and had seen the things he had seen, how could he just ignore it and do nothing at all? He guessed that some people probably could, some people could convince themselves it was all just a fairytale, but he just couldn't. He couldn't. Not now.

"Well then, if you're sure, I guess I could help you get started." The young man walked from the window towards a beaded curtain hanging in a doorway on the other side of the room. He stopped when he got to the doorway, which Isaac presumed led to the kitchen. "There's a library in the old children's hospital on the other side of the city. It's all closed down and abandoned now of course, has been for more than forty years."

"Right, so do I need to go there or -"

"If you want to help. The council are trying to knock it down and build a leisure centre or something, but the builders keep getting scared off. Ghosts apparently. Of course that's not the official line, according the council it's just too old and interesting to demolish at the moment." The young man smiled knowingly at Isaac. "Why don't you go check it out?" He moved to go through the doorway and out of sight.

"Wait!" Isaac called out.

The man stopped again, barely turning round.

"Should I come back here after I've been there? Or come back in a few days? I don't even know your name!"

"You don't come back here. We're not friends okay? I'm just helping you get started." His voice sounded strict. "Oh," he grinned, his tone of voice suddenly lightening, "and you can call me Pete."

That was five months ago. That was back when Isaac had first come to the city of Monks-Lantern. Now, as he crouched next to Gabbi Gurtpasha behind a large bin in an alleyway, he couldn't help but think how far he'd come in five months. He hadn't seen Pete since that night, but he certainly owed him a debt of gratitude for helping him out that one time.

Isaac had come to Monks-Lantern for university, to study religious studies and ancient history. Monks-Lantern university was renowned for being one of the best institutes for religious studies in the south of England - and whilst the ancient history department wasn't renowned for anything it was a subject that interested Isaac. Things that were old, things that were really, really old fascinated him. He supposed part of that fascination had come from where he had grown up - the county of Wiltshire near the town of Marlborough. He used to love visiting places like Stonehenge and the Avebury circle when he was younger, marvelling at how these things that were thousands of years old were still there - still standing, still important and still a mystery.

He had been brought up by his parents, Richard and Violet Jacobs. He didn't have any brothers or sisters and so being the only child it would have been expected that he would have been doted upon and lavished with affection. No such luck. His parents were never cruel to him, and he never wanted for anything - they lived in a large detached house and he never went without at Christmas or on birthdays. But still despite that good life his parents were always somehow absent - his mum was a lawyer, his dad an architect - they both spent a lot of time away from home on business.

Shortly before he came to university they decided to up sticks completely and move away to Italy. They sold the house near Marlborough and bought Isaac a terraced house in Monks-Lantern - number twenty Elsbridge Hill Road - a generous gift but one which Isaac suspected was more of a guilt-payment than anything else. Of course, if absentee parents were his only problem then life would be fairly simple. However for Isaac life hadn't been simple in quite some time.

"Is this guy going to show or not?" Gabbi asked, sounding impatient. "It's gone midnight and I am freezing!" She wrapped her arms tightly around herself as much as she could and shivered emphatically.

"It'll show up." Isaac said optimistically. "Just give it a few more minutes. And your hair should keep you warm, you've got enough of it." he joked. Gabbi had long, wavy raven hair, almost to her waist.

"Oi!" Gabbi laughed. "Cheeky."

Just then a dark shape appeared out of the gloom at the far end of the alleyway.

"Finally." Isaac muttered.

The figure was large and bulky, and walked slowly but with a sure step. As it got closer Isaac could see it was covered in tattered and torn clothing. To anyone on the street it would probably have looked like a particularly shabby homeless person. Isaac knew different.

He leapt out from behind the bin and pulled Gabbi up with him. "Demon!" he shouted, trying not to let the cold night air stop his voice from sounding authoritative.

The figure stopped and glared at the pair of them. It was too dark to make out a face in detail but Isaac saw the eyes. Dark eyes, flickering with fire. It stood about ten feet away from them, and before Isaac and Gabbi had interrupted its journey it had been heading for an empty building on one side of the alleyway.

It snarled at them from behind its teeth. "What do you want clay child?"

"Oh a cup of tea would be lovely, just one sugar in each -"

"Do not play word games with me!" the demon hissed. "I was there when your language was born."

Gabbi gave the demon a disparaging look. "Yeah, you and every other smelly demon out there!"

Isaac looked at her. "Smelly?" he mouthed.

"What?" she shrugged. "He smells."

Isaac shrugged back and then turned his attention once more to the monster before them. "We want information. People are going missing. Tell us what you know."

It gave a gravelly, hoarse laugh. "Why? Why would I speak helpful words to you?" it hissed.

Isaac knew the demon wouldn't give up information easily – they never did. From his jeans pocket he pulled a small and thin glass bottle of holy water. "Because if you do then we won't banish you." He shook the bottle teasingly in the demon's direction. "You know what this is, don't you? A good slosh of this stuff and the right words from me can send you back to whatever hell you crawled from."

It laughed again. "You mortal things aren't capable of doing anything to me!"

"Aren't we?" Isaac said as convincingly as he could. "That body you're walking and talking in was a human being before you jumped behind the wheel. There's a chance he's still alive in there, somewhere. Just try and stop us from saving him."

The demon sneered at them, looking viciously from Isaac to Gabbi and then back again.

Isaac tensed himself, he felt like the demon was about to leap at them in attack. He reached behind and grabbed Gabbi's hand.

Instead, the demon turned on its heel and ran with a lumbering step back down the alleyway.

"Typical!" Isaac cursed, slipping the holy water back into his pocket. "Come on!"

Still holding hands they took off after the demon. It wasn't running fast, so they should have been able to –

"Look out!" Gabbi screamed as the demon knocked over several of the large bins to block their path. The bins rolled, rubbish spewed out onto the ground.

Isaac managed to stop his feet just before they reached the hazard, otherwise he would have fallen headlong into the mess and taken Gabbi with him. They circled round the newly formed rubbish heap and continued the chase. The demon turned a corner, down another small alleyway that ran behind a pub. Isaac and Gabbi followed it round the same corner – but much to Isaac's dismay the demon was nowhere to be seen.

"Crap, crap and crap again!" Isaac cursed, kicking another bin in frustration.

"Well, we can always try again tomorrow I suppose." Gabbi sighed. "At least we didn't -"

The demon jumped down from somewhere high above, landing right in front of them! It turned and whirled round, knocking into Gabbi and send her flying to the ground a few feet away with a scream.

"Gabbi!" Isaac yelled.

The demon growled at him. "Clay children break so easily."

Isaac punched the monster in the face as hard as he could. His fist stung immediately but the demon did stagger back in pain. Isaac quickly followed up his attack with a sharp kick to the demon's ribs, causing the creature to groan and clutch at the wall of the alleyway. "Yes. Fire children seem to be pretty flimsy too." He got the bottle of holy water out again. "Or should that be pretty easily extinguishable?"

Gabbi got up from the ground and joined Isaac in front of the demon.

Isaac looked sideways at her. "You alright Gabbi?"

"Fine thanks darling. You know me, tough as old boots."

"Goodo."

The demon righted itself, standing up to its fullest height again in defiance. "I will never help you. You'll bleed and drown along with this ageing earth." it spat. "But I do know what you speak of, I hear whispers in the night."

"And what do those whispers say?"

"Something is coming."

Isaac felt a chill run down his spine which wasn't caused by the cold. "What something?"

The demon leant in closer to them. "Fire will never help clay."

Isaac frowned. "Well then. Time to put the fire out."

Isaac stepped back a few paces, Gabbi with him. He hurled the bottle of holy water at the demon's feet, where it smashed and created a puddle on the ground.

"Unclean thing! I order you to leave this human guise and return to the dark realms!"

"By what authority?!"

"By the authority of all that is holy! By the authority of God the creator and all the higher beings you will leave NOW!"

The demon roared from within the human shell. The air around them crackled and hissed, like reality itself might have been fracturing open. The mouth of the body the demon was in opened wide, wider than a mouth should have been able to open. Then a dark mist, the demon in spirit form, swarmed from the mouth, swirling and screaming down towards the puddle on the ground like angry smoke.

"You may not pass go, and you certainly may not collect two hundred pounds." Isaac muttered under his breath. He turned to Gabbi who was shielding her face somewhat, fearing some kind of explosion.

The last of the black swarm disappeared into the ground where the puddle was, and instantly the air became normal once more. The body that the demon had been dwelling in slumped to the ground lifelessly. Both Isaac and Gabbi rushed to the ground next to the body but it was useless, whoever this had been died a long time ago. Isaac sighed and hoped the poor man hadn't suffered too much.

"No information." Gabbi said, her soft voice heavy with disappointment, "Maybe we should have asked it more questions."

"It wasn't going to tell us anything. Besides, I didn't like what it said about bleeding and drowning. Sounded like two very un-fun activities to me." Isaac sighed and looked down at the body of the man. "Poor man. I wonder who he was."

"No I.D." Gabbi had quickly checked through any pockets. "One less demon though at least. And it went quite easily in the end."

"Yeah I guess. Still it will probably find a way back." Isaac said, fumbling in his pocket for his mobile phone. "Evil never stays gone for long."

Chapter Two

Monks-Lantern was not a normal city. Not by any length. Of course, if you asked ninety-something percent of the population whether they thought it was a normal city, they'd say yes. And it was true, it had a lot of characteristics of a normal city. Isaac often thought to himself how easy it would be to perceive just the city that was around him and not look any deeper. He could well understand how people thought it was normal. If he hadn't had the experiences he had, then he would most likely view it as a normal city too.

There was the university of course, which was very normal. The students weren't always a beloved percentage of the population, particularly not on a Saturday night, but they were normal enough. U.M.L as it was known was very popular and it drew people in from not only all over the country but from all over the world. Walking from lecture to lecture Isaac often heard numerous languages, so many he sometimes thought he'd be able to learn a language or two just by walking around the campus. He knew French and German pretty well, enough to get by at least, and through his courses he had become somewhat familiar with Latin and Greek, although the Greek was the ancient kind and so wouldn't get him very far in Greece today. One of his old friends used to speak Gaelic, his old friend Lee. Still, he was gone now.

And then there was the city itself. Monks-Lantern boasted everything you could want - it had good communication links, with trains and buses going to London and beyond. There was an airport not too far away so that was pretty good, and in the city centre itself there was plenty to do. It was a beautifully picturesque city, quintessentially English, full of cobbled streets, narrow lanes and half timbered buildings. There were pleasant walks to be had along the River Els which ran through the very heart of the city, or strolling in the well manicured parks or exploring the old forests to the north.

The main feature historically and the main tourist attraction was the cathedral. It was huge, not to mention stunningly beautiful - sitting within its own walls on a wide expanse of green grass, its main tower reaching high up into the heavens - visible from far away as you approached the city. The building as it stood now had been built in the twelfth century, but Isaac had read in a book about the history of the city that the site that the cathedral was on had been a mystic or religious site of one kind or another dating as far back into history as records went, even before the Christianisation of England.

Alongside the ancient cathedral there was plenty of modernity in the form of shops. There was the Holy Grove Shopping Centre, an indoor shopping mall which Isaac frequently took advantage of whenever his finances would allow him, and sometimes even when they didn't. Money wasn't exactly growing on a tree in his back garden, but then Isaac figured he probably had it better than a lot of students, seeing as his parents, as well as buying him a house, frequently sent him cheques with a brief note attached saying something like "make sure you're keeping well." Isaac often thought it sounded more like something you would say to a doddering old relative than to your twenty year old son, but he was happy to receive the money nonetheless. He made sure he had enough for food and enough to pay bills, and then the rest of the money would either go on clothes or DVDs or when he had time, going out. There were some great nightclubs in Monks-Lantern, including Bubble-Gum, which had an adult sized ball-pit and jungle-gym inside. Not always the best idea when you're more than a bit drunk, but fun nonetheless. Definitely fun.

Yet despite all this apparent normality - life for Isaac Jacobs was anything but normal. Something existed in his world which didn't exist in most other people's worlds. The supernatural. The other-worldly. Isaac knew that almost anywhere in the world had some supernatural occurrences - every town had a ghost or two, and every village had had a demon roam its streets at some point in history. Yet Monks-Lantern seemed to have more than its fair share of paranormal phenomena. Why that was Isaac couldn't be sure, but he suspected it might have something to do with the mystical history that the city had, and just how old it was in general - as Pete had told him before. It was one of the oldest settlements in England, and archaeologists had found lots of Bronze Age and Stone Age remains in the area - so Isaac was sure that a city that was that old was bound to have racked up more than a few supernatural beings over the centuries.

Sometimes he wished that it didn't exist in his world, just like it didn't exist in the majority of people's worlds. Then he could have a completely normal life in a normal city. But it did exist, and if he was being honest with himself then most of the time he was glad that it did. However much pain it had caused him, and however horrifying it could be, he was glad he knew so that he knew to fight back. It was only occasionally when things got really bad that he wished for blissful ignorance - the majority of the time he was pleased to be in the know.

Luckily for him, he wasn't alone in it either. He had friends. Four really good friends that he'd met soon after coming to Monks-Lantern; Gabbi Gurtpasha, Billie Stamford, Laura Henley and Ben Pokely. He loved them all very much and even though they'd only met five months ago he felt closer to them than he did to anyone else in the world, closer even than he felt to his parents. They had bonded instantly and all moved into the house that Isaac's parents had bought him. They had all had supernatural experiences of one kind or another, and they all saw the abnormal side of the city in which they lived.

Another aspect of his life which put him in a minority group of society was his sexuality. Isaac was gay, he had been for as long as he could remember. He had tried fancying girls in his early teens, but it just hadn't worked at all. It always felt forced. All his friends knew, he never hid it from them, or from anyone really. He'd taken his time in telling his parents but he had done eventually. They seemed quite apathetic about it – his coming out to them was neither a celebration nor a disaster. That didn't bother him, as long as he wasn't disowned he wasn't particularly worried – after all it wasn't like he was super close to them.

So Isaac Jacob's life wasn't particularly normal. But it wasn't particularly awful either. As terrifying as the supernatural could be sometimes, he had his friends with him to help fight it - and he wouldn't change that for the world. He wouldn't lose them - not again. He often thought that he led a difficult life but not at all a completely unbearable one. One of the only things that seemed unbearable to him now was the thought of being alone again. He had been alone for a time, before he came to Monks-Lantern. And he had managed. He wasn't particularly happy during that time but he'd managed. But now that he had friends, now that he had people who cared and people he cared for it was impossible to think of not having them. In many ways he was luckier than he could have ever expected to be. If someone had told him five months ago that he would be where he was now, he wouldn't have believed them.

Five months ago of course he had been in that dark flat with Pete. And then it was off to the library in the old children's hospital. That night was the scariest night he'd had in nearly five years. Even now, five months later, he still had nightmares sometimes about what happened there. The only fortunate thing about the experience was that it was how he had met Gabbi. Gabbi had been doing the same thing that he was doing, investigating the haunting that had kept the builders away, and from that encounter onwards they were instant friends.

Gabbi, like Isaac, was relieved to find someone who shared her beliefs. Her parents were from Pakistan originally, but her mum had sadly died from a heart attack when Gabbi was only a year old. Herself and her dad subsequently moved to England, to the small town of Cowbrook, which wasn't far from

Monks-Lantern. Her dad ran a small spiritualist group there in their house, and she had told Isaac about how she would listen in on the meetings when she was younger, enthralled by the tales of angels and spirits that she heard. Her interest grew from there, and when she expressed her interest in the supernatural to her dad he nurtured it and gave her information, cases and accounts to read about. Isaac felt a twinge of jealousy when she'd told him this - he would have loved for his parents to have taken an interest like that. Gabbi had hated the student halls she had been assigned to and it was only a week after meeting Isaac that she moved into his house on Elsbridge Hill Road - it was an attractive prospect after all as she could live there rent free because Isaac's parents had already bought the house outright.

From there Isaac and Gabbi had met Billie, Laura and Ben through their religious studies classes. In-between lectures conversations invariably started and Isaac and Gabbi had overheard the three of them discussing supernatural experiences they'd had. Other people in the class smiled and reacted politely and then either moved away or changed conversation, but Isaac and Gabbi started talking to them and they were soon good friends too.

Billie had befriended ghosts in her cottage at home, and then defended them from some kind of malignant force. Her parents didn't share her beliefs at all, and they fiercely ridiculed her for having such delusional thoughts. As a result Billie didn't talk to her parents much either, just like Isaac.

Laura had had a friend who became possessed by a demon but who was thankfully exorcised before any serious harm was done, and also a friend who dabbled in witchcraft. Laura kept that side of her life secret from her parents, and so she still shared a happy relationship with her mum and dad, albeit a distant one – they were retired and spent much of the year staying with relatives in Canada.

Ben didn't have much of an interest in the supernatural at all until just a year before he came to university, when he was the victim of a vicious poltergeist whilst on a holiday with his football team mates to Ibiza. His younger sister had apparently been the one with an interest in weirder things, but she'd tragically died from a brain tumour when she was only sixteen and he had been seventeen. As a result of the recentness of Ben's experience, he came across as quite skeptical of supernatural phenomena, and whilst he believed in the other-worldly goings on just as the rest of the group did he very often questioned and challenged it more.

They all began talking and very quickly became friends, all of them, just as Isaac and Gabbi had. By the end of September they were all living together in Isaac's house, and it was as if they had been friends for a long time. It was far more than Isaac could ever have hoped for.

Although Isaac shared everything with his friends, he was never very graphic with them about the more painful parts of his past, not through distrust of them or anything malicious, purely because they were painful thoughts and talking about them didn't help at all. They were memories, they weren't going to go away. So he liked to keep them as quiet as he could in the back of his mind. He told them what had happened, he just didn't go into much detail with it at all. Besides, pretty soon they were all investigating their own supernatural occurrences and there wasn't the time or the need to be going over past events. By the time Christmas had come they had been dealing with ghosts, demons and spirits for quite some time, and they had well and truly become a little force with some reputation in the darker community of Monks-Lantern.

They were making ripples. Ripples that would move. Move and get bigger.

Chapter Three

"Are you certain they didn't see you?"

"Yes Imperator. I'm certain."

The room was dark, lit only by the light of the moon shining through the window and a small lamp on the Imperator's desk. The man eyed the Imperator carefully as he spoke. There was an air of comfort and warmth about him that you could almost mistake for genuine kindness and compassion if you weren't careful. He had known of people to misinterpret the Imperator that way. He hadn't known of them after they'd made that mistake.

"Good. And the demon, was it one of ours?"

"No sir. Just a passing spirit I should imagine. It had stolen the body of a homeless man."

The Imperator laughed dryly. "The homeless man becomes a home himself. Nevertheless, even if it wasn't one of ours, it could have known something. It didn't reveal -"

"It said nothing that could lead those students back to us." He surprised himself by interrupting the Imperator. He winced slightly, expecting a backlash, but it never came.

"Good. Very good. You know how important our work is. We must remain hidden until the time is right." The Imperator stood up from his desk chair and walked over to the window, gazing up at the stars. "We've been hidden for millennia now. Hidden for so long." The Imperator turned and smiled at him. "But don't worry. For soon the things that are hidden shall be found. And the things that have been locked and sealed away shall be unleashed."

Isaac wrapped his cold hands around the hot mug of tea as Gabbi passed it to him. They had phoned the police as they always did when dealing with exorcised corpses, and left an anonymous tip that they had found a body. To begin with Isaac was concerned that they would get visits from the police, that they could somehow be traced or something, but it never happened - thankfully.

"So," Gabbi said, brushing some of her long raven hair out of her eyes, "no luck yet again. I hate to say it but this isn't looking too good."

They were sitting in the kitchen, perched on a couple of stools that stood against the worktop. Isaac suspected that there must have been an extension put on at some point, as their kitchen did seem to stick out further than their next door neighbour's one did, and in the bit of extra space they had as a result of that they'd squeezed in a small dining table and chairs. The fittings were quite modern too - Isaac's dad had seen to that when they bought the house. There were large French patio doors at the end of the room that led out into the garden, which was in a very bad state. It was clear that whoever had lived there before had been a keen gardener, as there were remnants of flower beds and a vegetable patch and there was even a small overgrown pond hidden away amongst the long grass and untamed shrubs at the bottom of the garden. Isaac often had montage images of him cleaning it all up and making it nice for summer. So far it hadn't happened.

"No I know." Isaac sighed and sipped his tea. The garden was a mess, and so was their attempt at investigation. And the tea was searing hot. "If anything does know anything then it's not telling us. Two people a month going missing, going back ages and we can't find anything out about it." Every time it was the same situation. Someone went missing, and a brief and emotionless article appeared in the local paper, playing the entire situation down. And it was always someone visiting the city, not a permanent resident. No-one with an address, no-one with ties. Isaac had phoned the paper and asked if they had any more information, but they didn't tell him anything. Letters and emails to the police remained unanswered.

"How far back did Billie and Laura look the other day?"

"Three years. Three years ago people were still disappearing at the rate of two people a month."

"Blimey."

"Yep. That's a lot of people." Isaac sipped his tea again. It was still incredibly hot, but it felt good on such a cold January night as it was.

"What are we going to do?" Gabbi asked plaintively.

Honestly Isaac had no clue. They had dealt with plenty of supernatural stuff before but this had a feeling of being part of something bigger about it. It felt like they were just scratching the surface of whatever was going on. It had only been because of Gabbi's keen eye that they had started investigating the disappearances in the first place - every day they looked through the papers to see if there was anything that sounded like it might have some supernatural aspect to it and she just happened to have noticed that over time there continued to be these disappearances that no-one seemed to be caring about. It had all seemed too unusual not to have a supernatural edge.

"I don't know. Not right now anyway. Maybe if we brainstorm it with the guys tomorrow, we might be able to come up with some kind of next step." Isaac smiled, and Gabbi smiled back.

"Okay." She slid off of the stool she had been sitting on and walked over to the biscuit tin, picked out a custard cream and shoved it in her mouth.

Even with a mouthful of biscuit Isaac thought Gabbi had a glamorous look about her. She had an air of natural beauty that was quite rare to see in people. She was slender without being stick thin, and clothes seemed to suit her incredibly well. Isaac stood up too and went and stood next to her by the biscuit tin, picking out a bit of shortbread for himself. They were almost the same height, with Isaac being slightly taller at about 6ft. He popped the biscuit into his mouth but as he did it broke up and he ended up with crumbs all over his lips and round his mouth. Shortbread was messy.

"I love biscuits." he declared with his mouth full.

Gabbi laughed, looking at his crumb covered face. "I can tell! Think I should call you Mr Biscuit-Face."

"I'm not Mr Biscuit-Face!" Isaac said laughing, still trying to chew and swallow the shortbread. When he had finished his biscuit he put the lid on, Gabbi grabbing one last custard cream just before they were sealed away.

She shoved this in her mouth too and then leant across to give him a biscuity goodnight kiss on the cheek. "Goodnight darling." she said.

"Night night Gabbi, sleep tight."

"You too." she replied, as she headed out the door and headed through the living room for the stairs, "Sweet dreams."

Isaac switched all the lights off and then headed for his own room, which was the only bedroom downstairs and would have once been the front room when the house was built. It also happened to be the biggest bedroom. This meant he could fit a double bed in the room, which he was grateful for. Nobody minded really though, as everyone in the house was single. Isaac just liked having the extra space. Ever since he was eight and got to sleep in a double bed for the first time whilst on holiday in Germany, he'd loved it. The holiday itself had been rather boring, his dad had been meeting constantly with the best of Germany's architects. Thinking about it, it had been much more of a business trip than a family holiday. Still, the double bed had been nice.

Isaac quickly undressed and got into bed. The sheets were cool and he shivered, wrapping himself up tightly in the duvet. He was exhausted - mentally as well as physically, having spent most of the night waiting for a demon in the cold, then having that demon yield no information which was of any use to them. The last thing he thought before sleep was that he needed to do some food shopping tomorrow as he was almost out of food in the freezer. After that the world melted away.

Chapter Four

"Oh Tom you're being silly!" The fourteen year old Isaac lay on the daisy strewn grass, squinting in the sunlight, the warmth of the summer sun tingling his skin. He giggled and rolled over to see Tom splashing about in the stream and wearing some waterweed as a wig, whilst doing a comical impression of one of their teachers at school.

"So what if I am?" asked Tom, laughter in his voice. He staggered out of the stream, pulling the waterweed off of his head, revealing his short brown hair with blond highlights. They had come to an idyllic piece of countryside not far from Isaac's house for a picnic. Isaac saw it as everyone's view of a perfect summer's day, there was absolutely nothing not to love about it. Their only company were several cows who were grazing on the lush grass, occasionally looking up at the two teenagers whilst chewing, as if they were entertained by Isaac and Tom's antics. Tom pulled a towel from his backpack and vigorously dried his hair, before throwing the towel on the grass and then laying down next to Isaac. Tom was well tanned compared to Isaac, which could be put down to his frequent holidays in the sun. Isaac was lying on his front now, with his legs bent at the knee, rotating his sandaled feet absentmindedly in the air. Tom started picking daisies and dropping them onto Isaac's back.

"Issy?" started Tom, almost cautiously. They had been best friends for nearly a year now, it was unusual for Tom to sound so uncertain when he spoke.

"Yeah?" replied Isaac, trying to sound as laid back as possible, although secretly he was slightly worried as to where this was going.

"Do you believe in like ghosts and demons and things?" The question came out of Tom's lips quickly, as if it were something he had been holding in his mouth for a long time which had to be spat out.

"Oh, erm -" Isaac had no clue what to say, he hadn't given it much thought and that hadn't been the question he had been expecting. Although he had never told Tom he was gay, he felt sure that Tom knew it, and he felt more than sure that Tom was gay too. Sometimes the way Tom would look at him, he could tell it meant something more. "What you mean like on TV and stuff?" Isaac asked, trying to keep the conversation light.

"Not exactly - like in real life." Tom had stopped picking daisies and his voice now sounded serious with a twinge of what Isaac was sure was fear. Isaac sat up and looked Tom in the eye. A single cloud passed across the sun casting a cool shadow over them.

"Tom, are you okay?" Isaac reached out and touched his friend gently on the arm.

Tom looked at Isaac's hand and gave a small smile. "Yeah, of course I am." The cloud left the sun and brilliant sunlight poured over them once more. "Come on, break out the sandwiches – I'm hungry."

The dream merged and drifted, shapes contorted and colours changed. Time was moved.

"Hey guys what are you doing in here?" Lee Mcdarmagh stood in the open door. It was dark in the room but light outside on the landing, so his short dumpy figure appeared like a black silhouette in the doorway.

"Oh…n-nothing." Isaac started, giving a knowing look to Tom. Isaac was now fifteen, sixteen in four months.

"Yeah, we were just having a chat." confirmed Tom, "We're ready now."

"Good," said Lee in a morbid voice, "Because we're all set up downstairs. Isaac are you sure your parents won't be home tonight?" Lee switched on the bedroom light and Isaac could see he looked deeply concerned, fear etched on his pale freckled face - the gravity of what they were about to do obviously so great that he couldn't help but fear interruption.

"Yes, they've gone to this Italian housing fair or something, it's up in Leeds." Isaac said, hoping that would calm Lee somewhat.

It seemed to do the trick - Lee nodded and then stepped back out onto the landing and headed for the stairs.

What Isaac and Tom had in fact been discussing was much more than just a chat. It was the discussion Isaac had expected just over a year ago, on that perfect summers day.

A lot had changed since then of course. They had become close friends with some other boys - Lee Mcdarmagh, Toby Tamer and Matthew Arnley. The five of them together had become very good friends, and the thing that bound them was their interest in the supernatural.

After that initial mentioning of demons by Tom on that day by the stream, Isaac had become more and more interested. Curious at first, as to why Tom

- 18 -

had brought it up and then genuinely interested. It came out after several months of probing on Isaac's part that Tom's mum had been killed by a demoniac - a man possessed by a demon - when he was just nine years old. Isaac had always been aware of Tom's mum's death but he always thought it had been a very human murder. Grim certainly, but human. However, Tom had seen it happen. He never professed to know why or how he could see the demon in the man, but he could. He had described the moment as being the scariest of his whole life, and the first time he told Isaac the whole story he had broken down in tears. When Isaac had asked what he had seen when he saw the demon within the man, Tom just replied "Darkness." He had, of course, tried to tell his father but his dad didn't believe him, and so it had been with great bravery that Tom had confided in Isaac.

Since becoming friends with the others they had become something of an investigatory group, seeking out supernatural occurrences - although it was never anything that serious, and most of the time their "cases" had very natural solutions. A werewolf they had once investigated turned out to just be a feral dog and reports of a ghost in a nearby village church turned out to simply be a homeless man who took shelter in the roof space from time to time. Tonight, however, would be different.

They had decided for better or for worse to summon a demon into their presence and to attempt to destroy it, or at least banish it so it could never enter this world again to do damage. Isaac had been fully onboard to begin with and had helped Matthew research the correct rituals online. He had a keen enthusiasm to begin with, to experience that which he had become increasingly fascinated with over the past year. But as the time drew near he had become nervous. His research had shown that summoning demons was not at all child's play and he knew that they were all barely more than children. In the cases he had looked at, people had died - he'd read how in America twelve frat boys had been found brutally murdered after they had tried to summon a demon to help them win their varsity trophy. Isaac was certainly in no hurry to die, no hurry at all. He had called Tom into his room that night to discuss his fears - but Tom had got there first with a topic of his own choosing.

"Are you gay?" The question had come out like his question over a year ago - quickly - as if it had been trapped for a long time and was now free.

Isaac didn't see any point in lying. "Yes." he replied, tentatively but firmly.

Tom, who had been standing until now, sat down on the bed next to Isaac. He appeared to be both relieved and at the same time somewhat deflated.

Isaac looked round the room, waiting for Tom to make the next move. His room was quite large, and he had always liked the fact that since that trip to Germany he'd been allowed to have a double bed, although it had only been in recent times that he had realised he would like someone to share it with. He looked at his bookshelf and noted how much his library of books had changed, at one end of the shelf it was all Roald Dahl Novels and children's history books, and then suddenly there was *A field guide to Demons and Ghosts* and *On the origins of Exorcism*, amongst others.

Tom, at last, broke the silence. "I am too." He spoke as if he were a small child who had done something wrong and when Isaac turned to look at him he saw that his cheeks had flushed a deep red and his eyes were wide open, as if by blinking he would lose courage.

Isaac was not sure what to say, whether to admit that he had known or not. He didn't want to in any way make Tom's obvious bravery immaterial. So he stretched out his hand and held Tom's own. With his other hand he reached out and turned Tom's head towards his own, as it had been facing straight down at the floor. Then he smiled.

"It's ok," he said, quietly and warmly, "I'm hardly going to judge you am I, being a big gay myself." Tom chuckled a little, but Isaac could tell he was still uneasy. "What is it?" he asked, trying to sound as patient as humanly possible, although in reality he was anything but.

Tom's face turned once more to the floor and seemed to contort with all the stress of two years worth of emotions. Then, grimacing, as if forcing a truth that did not want to willingly come, he spoke. "I love you."

Isaac unintentionally recoiled slightly, no-one had ever said this to him in this context before. The words, although familiar, seemed alien. He was suddenly confused, completely speechless.

"And now I bet you hate me." Tom spluttered, his voice beginning to choke. Still Isaac remained speechless, he wanted to speak, goodness knows he wanted to speak more than anything, but he couldn't. "I can't help it, when I think of you I'm happier than when I think of anybody else. I keep thinking back to that day last summer, when we were by the stream, I wanted to kiss you so much that day, but I was terrified." Tom seemed to be suffering with the opposite of what Isaac was suffering with - whilst Isaac's words wouldn't come, Tom's seemed to be flowing uncontrollably from his mouth. It was clear from his rather shocked expression - shocked at his own honesty. "Please say something." begged Tom, his voice sounding more scared than Isaac had ever heard it.

Finally his tongue seemed to be free and Isaac spoke, although his words were still uncertain. "I don't know what to say Tom, I mean, I mean you mean so much to me, you really do, and I…" Isaac trailed off and without really thinking much about it he moved forwards and kissed Tom on the cheek. Tom turned and he looked as if he were searching Isaac's eyes for some hint of anger or some unseen lie but he didn't appear to find any. The next instant, without it really being planned at all, their lips met and Isaac felt a cool wave of excitement and thrill course through him. He had never kissed another man before, nor anyone for that matter, and he liked it. He leaned further forward and they toppled back onto the bed, staying like that for what must have only been minutes, but to Isaac it seemed much longer. When he felt Tom's hand feel and rub his groin through his jeans he momentarily experienced another crashing wave of thrill but this one crashed and receded quickly. Isaac sat up. Something was not right. This experience, however carnally pleasurable, was not right. He suddenly knew, he knew more than anything he had known up until that point that he did not love Tom, not in the fullest sense - not in the way that Tom deserved. But his respect for Tom, as a close and true friend was as full as it could be. Tom looked unsurprisingly confused, and attempted to reach out once more to Isaac but Isaac pulled away completely.

"I'm sorry," he started, "I'm so sorry."

"You led me on?" Tom's voice wavered, slowly moving from upset to angry.

"No, I thought, I thought it was right, but it wasn't…when you touched me, I realised…I'm so sorry Tom!"

"When I touched you?" Tom was definitely angry now. "My touch repulsed you? I thought you were gay? What, now you decide society's right and it is wrong after all?!"

"No, I don't think being gay is wrong, I just don't think I should be with someone intimately if I don't love -"

"If you don't love them. Like you don't love me." They sat staring at each other, saying nothing, until Lee Mcdarmagh appeared in the doorway. Once he had gone Tom stood up to leave. "Come on." he said darkly, with all traces of love or friendship gone from his voice.

"No, Tom wait!" Isaac suddenly remembered why he had called Tom up to his room in the first place. "I don't think we should do this, I've been researching, I think it's dangerous - we could get killed!" Isaac leapt from the bed, hoping to impress upon Tom the seriousness of the matter.

Tom considered him for a moment, then spoke. "I don't think, after what has just happened, that you are of any authority to decide whether actions are a good idea or not. These things killed my mum! I saw it! And now I have a chance to make at least one of the bastards pay and I will not pass that by!"

"But Tom, these things are more powerful than you know, you could be killed -"

"I don't give a toss about me and now, thanks to your behaviour, I don't give a toss about you, or anyone else. I'm doing this, with or without you!"

The right hander caught Isaac off guard. He fell back towards the bed, clutching the left side of his face.

"In fact," continued Tom, pausing at the door whilst holding his fist which was obviously stinging from the punch, "Make it without you. I never want to see you again." He left and Isaac heard his footsteps creak along the wooden landing and then down the stairs. The ritual was being held in the study, at the back of the house. Isaac picked himself up and took a look around his room. He realised it wasn't his anymore, not really - it belonged to a young, innocent boy with no knowledge or care about things that lurked in the dark. That certainly wasn't Isaac anymore. He could hear some raised voices from downstairs, but they weren't distinguishable. Isaac walked over to the wardrobe and opened it, pulling out a large duffel coat. He pulled it on and then slowly yet firmly walked from his room and along the landing towards the stairs. He felt dead inside. Everything safe and warm about his life was gone -Tom, his best friend, was gone and about to do something more dangerous than anything else in the whole world. Tom's words echoed in his brain and tore through him, jagged and sharp. He walked slowly down the stairs, and without looking back towards the study, walked straight to the front door. He opened it and stepped outside, a cool September night blowing into his face. Still in a state of shock from the events in his bedroom, he stepped down the few stone steps that led into the front garden and then his feet crunched on the gravel drive. There was a tree by the front gate that was V shaped, he'd liked to sit in it when he was a child, and watch the sheep in the field across the road from his house. He headed straight for it on auto-pilot. When he reached it he pulled himself up with ease into the gap between the split trunk, and pulled his duffel-coat tightly around him. He gazed across the road and saw that the sheep had gone. Only then did the tears come. But he cried silently. Even though internally he was being torn apart in more ways than he would have thought possible, externally he was calm, almost corpselike, the silent tears running down his cold cheeks. He stared vacantly into the middle distance, sitting there in his tree for what seemed like a very long time.

A cloud passed across the bright September moon and that's when he heard it. The silence was ripped apart. A blood-curdling scream pierced the night, followed by more screams of voices he recognised. His tongue paralysis from earlier in the night now seemed to grip his entire body. Tom had said he never wanted to see Isaac again. He should do what Tom said. The screams continued, mixed with tortured cries for help.

He heard a voice - which he recognised as Toby - screaming. "Get rid of it Tom! For god's sake get rid of it!"

Inside him now there was an internal battle being fought. The Isaac of thirty minutes previous wanted to run in and help, although what he would do he wasn't sure. The Isaac of now was almost content in his youthful hideaway, content to stay and let the night run its course. Tom had said he never wanted to see him again. He should do what Tom said.

"But Tom also punched me," he said, very quietly to himself. "I don't have to do what he says!" With that he steeled himself for pain and terror and leapt out of the tree. He turned back towards the house and noticed that he lights were flickering on and off, making it look like some demented Christmas decoration. He started sprinting back across the lawn towards the house, when he saw something which made him stop dead in his tracks. The lights flashed on to reveal thick red bloody handprints smeared on one of the ground floor windows. Someone had tried to escape. They had failed. "Tom -" he muttered, and started forwards again towards the house.

He reached the front door and flung it open, caring not what was on the other side, he just knew he had to help. But he was flung backwards by an invisible force, back onto the driveway. The gravel bit into his face as he landed with a crunch and although every inch of him felt splintered he got up immediately and ran at the now open door. He realised what had happened as soon as he reached it. Lee, in his paranoia about being disturbed, had included in part of the ritual an incantation which would prevent anyone from entering the house for the duration of the ritual. Isaac had read about such things when he had been researching the ritual himself with Matthew. He lifted a hand and pressed on the open doorway - it felt as solid as a brick wall.

Then it happened, the thing that would haunt him most. He looked inwards as far as he could and to his right. He saw Lee laying there, sprawled like a rag doll on the floor. Broken. Empty. Dead. To his left he saw a bloody arm protruding from the slightly open kitchen door. He recognised the watch on the wrist as Toby's. Then like a scene from a horror movie at the cinema, it unfolded, unstoppable before his eyes. Matthew stumbled backwards out of the dining room door to the right of Isaac. His eyes were fixed straight ahead of him on something which was still out of sight to Isaac, still in the dining room. He was staring so much at that thing that he didn't notice Lee's lifeless body on the floor. He tripped backwards, and when he looked to see what had been the cause of his fall he gave out a scream, a scream full of fear which you would rarely see in an otherwise macho sixteen year old boy. He shot a look back up to the dining room door, made a noise which sounded like a wounded animal and crawled on all fours away from the door. Isaac could see that he was bleeding from his stomach. Unable to help, Isaac stepped back, hoping against hope that he would not be seen. He watched from his position a few steps back from the open door and then he finally laid eyes on what Matthew had been staring at this whole time.

A grey monster, about seven feet high, walked through the dining room door and out into the wide hall. Isaac felt his stomach turn over with fear. The creature had no eyes and no ears, yet it seemed that it could see and hear perfectly well. It had two slit like nostrils in the centre of its elongated face which oozed a black tar. A very protruding jaw accommodated the most fearful thing about this demon - its mouth. It was huge, and from what Isaac could see it had several rows of dark, bloodstained teeth. The mouth was arranged in a kind of horrific smile. Its arms were longer than that of a human but looked strong - and its four fingers had long, sharp, iron like nails on the end of them. Its legs, like the arms, were long and powerful and its toes exhibited similar nails to that of its fingers. Isaac could see that its back was somewhat serrated and hunched. The demon advanced on Matthew like a wild beast on its prey. It stooped low and let out a scream just as blood curdling as the one Isaac had heard from the tree.

Matthew was now on his back, trying to move further away from the demon. He turned his head briefly and that's when their eyes met. He looked Isaac straight in the eyes, a penetrating stare, which conveyed utter fear, isolation, and unwilling acceptance of his fate. Isaac opened his mouth to say something, to try and help in some way, but before he could the creature was on Matthew, tearing at him with its talons. Blood spattered on the floor. The screams stopped after only a few seconds.

Isaac let out a small gasp of horror and the demon jerked his head up from the now still corpse with such suddenness that it made Isaac physically jump and scream slightly. It looked straight at him, even without eyes it was looking straight at him. Raising itself up to its fullest height, it opened its putrid blood filled mouth and spoke.

"Small child." Isaac was shocked that he could understand it, he hadn't expected such a monster to speak English . "You think to control me? You are human, and tiny. You are foolish. I cannot be controlled, I do my master's bidding! And he is untameable, as the raging waters! You will die here this night and the darkness shall have you forever!" With that the demon sprang forward, arms outstretched.

Isaac was rooted to the spot, the demon's words ran through him and he was terrified. He lifted his arm to feebly shield himself, but he knew it would do no good. He would die, like Lee and Toby and Matthew - and Tom. Isaac wondered where Tom's body was, if his end had been quick. Then his question was answered as Tom leapt into sight, knocking the demon off course, sending them both careering into a potted palm standing against the wall. Tom was on his feet first, the demon crouched on the floor and looked up eyelessly at its assailant, making a growling noise between its gore drenched teeth.

"You shall do no more damage here tonight foul creature!" Tom bellowed, with such force that the entire house seemed to recoil at his words. "In the name of the true God and all the higher beings I command you to leave here and to go to the dark places!"

"You cannot banish me, small thing!" the demon hissed. "You speak of those above, but I speak of those below and by their authority I remain! Words of Messiahs and Saviours are old now in this ancient world and I do not fear them!"

"You will fear what I have knowledge of!" Tom commanded, and for the first time the demon paused and appeared confused.

"What?! What prayer or magick do you have to banish me?"

"I have no prayer, and I have no magick. But I have a name. Yours!"

The demon let out another blood-curdling scream. It sounded furious. Tom stood there resolutely, blood dripping from his face and his clothes torn and ragged. "How?! How do you know my true name? None know it!" The demon was screaming its words now. Isaac too wondered how Tom had gotten hold of the name, but at that moment it didn't matter - it only mattered that he had.

Tom appeared to be remaining calm. He didn't give the demon the courtesy of an answer. "Verk'an-gorek!" he shouted, his voice commanding, as if scolding a small child for some wrongdoing, "I order you by the power of your own name to go to the dark abyss, the realm of dust and bones and to never return! Leave!"

The demon Verk'an-gorek rose off the ground to his full height and pointed a bloody iron claw at Tom. "This world will drown in the deep, and you will drown with it!" The air crackled with warmth around them all, lightening seemed to fizz and snap through the atmosphere. Tom leapt back to protect himself.. Isaac heard what sounded like a loud sucking noise and then with a sudden bang, an otherworldly clap of thunder, Verk'an-gorek disappeared from sight in front of him. The noise stopped, and the world seemed to return to normal. But of course it wasn't. It hadn't been a nightmare. Three of his closest friends were dead, and Tom despised him.

Without saying a word Tom walked past Isaac and out into the open air, wiping the blood from his bleeding lip. He was hobbling and Isaac had the urge to grab him and try to help him, but he knew that would be a mistake. Isaac turned, his eyes closed. He didn't want to see Tom walk out of his life but equally he didn't want to see the bodies of his friends lying in his house as evidence of the murderous savagery of that night. So he sat, eyes closed, head in hands, on the front step. He heard the crunching of Tom's footsteps become quieter until they were completely gone. And from behind closed eyes he cried.

Chapter Five

Isaac woke with a start and sat straight up in bed - the past had caught up with him again. He touched his eyes and was surprised to find real tears. It'd been a long time since he had cried about what had happened.

The brilliant sunlight of a cold late January day blazed through his window. He gazed across the room to the long mirror hanging on the opposite wall by the door. He scrutinised his reflection; bleary eyed, dark brown hair gone wild out of its usual side parting and a pale complexion. The dream had certainly taken its toll on him, he'd need to wash and straighten his hair now before he headed out anywhere he thought, remembering that he needed to do some food shopping. He checked his alarm clock and saw that it was nine in the morning - he'd got eight hours sleep. He was sure he must have dreamt of more than the past - those dreadful memories couldn't have taken up eight hours of dreamtime could they? He thought deeply for a moment, but couldn't remember anything else.

He quickly pulled on some boxer shorts and a dressing robe and then slouched out of his room and headed towards the kitchen. Billie and Laura were there, both looking a great deal better than he was.

"We're making breakfast." said Laura, scraping some butter out of the tub. "Want some?" she smiled and waved the buttery knife at him suggestively.

"No, thank you." Isaac replied, affording her a small but genuine smile.

"What's up?" asked Billie, taking a bite out of the slice of cake she held in her hand. Crumbs flew everywhere.

"Cake is breakfast now?"

"It is for me!" Billie giggled.

Isaac smiled again and collapsed on one of the stools. Even sitting down on a stool he was taller than Billie. Laura was pretty tall, only an inch or two shorter than Gabbi Isaac reckoned. Billie was the blonde of the group and she always kept her hair straightened so it went down just past her shoulders. Laura had brown hair, the same sort of chocolate colour as Isaac's, and she always kept it up in a neat ponytail, only allowing a few strands to fall down over her face at the front.

"So come on," Billie continued, "You don't look too good. What's up?"

Laura looked across at him too as she continued buttering toast. Laura had the most emotive brown eyes, which spoke volumes all on their own. Isaac could tell she was concerned too.

"Oh, it's nothing really. Bad dream."

"About what?"

Isaac hesitated for a moment before answering this next question. He wanted to tell them, but at the same time he didn't want to have to just repeat to them exactly what happened. "About the past." He hesitated a moment longer. "The night my friends were killed."

Billie reached out and stroked his arm. "Oh, sorry Isaac." she said. "Are you okay?"

"Yeah I'm fine. Just need to jump in the shower and sort myself out and I'll be bright as a button."

"Yeah if I'm ever feeling a bit down in the morning a nice hot shower makes me feel better." Laura said. "I'll leave you some toast in case you want some after okay?" she looked at him and smiled.

He already felt better, just having his friends around him being supportive helped a lot. "Thanks Laura, that'd be great."

"No problem!"

"Right!" he announced, getting up off the stool. "I'll go get in the shower then." He turned and walked out of the kitchen.

Laura called after him. "Oh Isaac, what did you find out last night?"

"Nothing." he replied, turning and facing them in the kitchen, "If it did know anything it wasn't going to tell us. We banished it."

"And the man?" asked Billie.

"Dead." Isaac sighed, "Already dead."

He headed upstairs and went straight for the bathroom, only to jump back in momentary fright as Ben walked out of it dressed in just his pants, which didn't leave much at all to the imagination. Isaac didn't know where to look.

"Alright mate?" Ben asked, scratching his head through his short crop of dark brown hair. Ben was a footballer through and through, and this was entirely reflected in his physique. Whilst Isaac got plenty of exercise through his activities with the supernatural alone, Ben actually went out and sought more - he regularly went to the gym on campus and the sports science course that he took along with religious studies often involved practical sessions. As a result he was well toned and athletic looking, which along with his well defined but still boyish face made him quite a handsome chap.

"Oh, morning Ben." said Isaac, catching his breath after his moment of surprise. "You made me jump a bit just then. Are you all done in there?"

"Yeah, sorry, it's all yours. The girls up?"

"Billie and Laura are downstairs. Gabbi's probably still in bed. We got home quite late."

"Any luck last night?"

"Nope."

"Shit."

"Yep. I think we had all better have a talk about it later."

Ben nodded in agreement. "Well," he said, looking down at himself, "I should go and put on some proper clothes, don't want to give them a fright when I go downstairs."

Isaac laughed. Fright wouldn't have been the word he would have used. If he knew Billie and Laura, a pleasurable shock would have been a more apt description. "Yeah if I hear screaming whilst I'm in the shower I'll know what you've done!"

Ben laughed too and then headed along the landing to his room, whilst Isaac went in the bathroom and got in the shower. He spent a good twenty minutes under the water, keeping his eyes closed and trying to empty his head of everything. He would need to be calm and collected if he and the guys were going to be able to figure out their next move.

Chapter Six

The shower did Isaac a world of good and by just after ten he was dried and dressed in jeans and a dark green long sleeve jumper. He straightened his hair out into his usual side fringe which was long enough that it almost covered his left eye. Gabbi was also up by that time and soon everyone was sitting in the living room with a chat show on the TV that Billie and Gabbi were particularly interested in. The living room was shabby chic, or at least that's how Isaac always viewed it. The sofa and armchairs were green and floral and wouldn't have looked out of place at all in a black and white photo. There was a random collection of furniture in the room, including a coffee table and a large bookcase with glass doors that Isaac particularly liked. The ornaments were very random, like the furniture, and mostly consisted of brightly coloured or flowery things that Isaac had seen and liked. Nothing in the room matched, but it all seemed to fit together rather nicely.

Isaac grabbed one of the remaining bits of toast that Laura had made earlier, cold by now but still tasty, and sat and waited until the show was over so that they could have a talk about what their next move could be. At half ten the show came to an end and the conversation moved round to what had happened the previous night and what it all meant.

"So really," surmised Ben, "we're no better off than we were before."

"But we can't give up." said Gabbi. "Just a few days ago there was that disappearance in the paper. The second one this month. The pattern's still continuing."

"And we know it's been going on for at least three years. Two people a month. No fuss, ever." Isaac stopped talking for a moment and bit his bottom lip. He often found that helped him whilst he was thinking. "Was that as far back as the records went? Three years?"

"No." Billie said, "Well, I don't know. We didn't go back any further." She suddenly sounded as if she realised she had made some stupid mistake.

Laura too looked a little guilty. "Sorry Isaac, we should have kept looking back - we didn't think."

"No don't be stupid, don't apologise." Isaac didn't blame them in the least for not looking back any further. Searching newspaper archives was an incredibly boring and time consuming task. "I think we were all just keen to try and find out what's going on now rather than what's happened in the past. Still, since last night's attempt to find out some information was a complete failure maybe we should go back to the archives and see just how far back this goes."

Billie nodded hurriedly in agreement. "We can look this afternoon." she said enthusiastically.

"We all can." offered Gabbi. "I've got nothing to do today." Ben nodded in agreement.

"No me neither." concurred Isaac, "Although I do need to go to the supermarket quickly. But I can easily get that done before lunch."

"Great, so a research afternoon then!" said Laura, attempting to make it sound exciting.

"Hooray!" shouted Billie, throwing her arms up in the air, joining in the task of making a very dull activity something to get excited about. Everyone else in the room laughed, Isaac included. Gabbi then headed upstairs for a shower, whilst Ben went to his room to play computer games for a while and Billie and Laura stayed watching the television. Isaac sat with them for a few minutes, before dragging himself up and out the door to the supermarket to do the shopping he so desperately needed to do.

He was gone about an hour and as usual he was sure that he had just spent money that should have bought him a months worth of food on stuff that would last him no more than a week. The bags were very heavy and the plastic dug into his hands as he made his way back up Elsbridge Hill Road to the house. Isaac cursed the fact that he hadn't yet learnt to drive as he walked along. Wheels would certainly be better then feet. He knew that Ben could drive but he also knew that Ben didn't have a car and so was unable to help with supermarket runs.

He got back in to find everyone much as he had left them, although Gabbi was now out of the shower and had joined Billie and Laura in the living room with the TV. Lunchtime came and went quickly and soon they were all sitting round in the living room with their laptops in front of them, with several small piles of newspapers and folders on the coffee table in the centre of the room. With their combined efforts it didn't take long at all to pinpoint exactly when the disappearances started. It was Laura who found the answer.

"February four years ago!" she announced.

"That's the earliest set of disappearances?" asked Isaac.

"That's the earliest disappearance. There was only one that month]. Then in March there were two." she looked up at Isaac. "It carries on like that up to now."

"Only one that month though, are you sure that's involved?"

"The article sounds very similar to all the others. Here listen." Laura read aloud the article about the first disappearance:

Ivor Petrovski, a visiting exchange student to Monks-Lantern, has gone missing. Mr. Petrovski was expected to return to Russia next week but he has not been seen by friends or the people who he was staying with since last Wednesday evening. Officials do not suspect foul play in his disappearance, more that Mr. Petrovski simply returned home ahead of schedule.

"It does sound just like the others." Gabbi agreed, once Laura had finished reading.

"Right so that's good." Isaac said, "We know exactly when these disappearances started."

"And that's not all we know." Laura said proudly.

"It's not?" Isaac was relieved at the possibility of more news. Although it was good to know exactly when the people started going missing, it was hardly a firm lead to anywhere new.

"I've been checking the police website as well. There's hardly any information at all on the disappearances but there was one thing I noticed which I think slipped through our net the first time we looked."

"What is it?"

"They were all investigated, albeit very briefly, by the same guy. Inspector Ackley. Every time he seems to have been the one who conducts a short investigation and delivers the verdict of the disappearance being "not suspicious" or "not involving foul play.""

"So then he could be the one responsible for keeping it all quiet, keeping it downplayed and out of the public eye." This was exciting news.

"Exactly."

"How did we miss this before?" asked Gabbi.

"I guess sometimes it's difficult to see what's right in front of you." said Isaac. It was true, they had all been looking for something bigger, all the time not thinking to just check who had conducted the investigations. "Well then. Yay for us. We've finally got our lead."

Isaac phoned Monks-Lantern Police headquarters that afternoon and asked to speak to Inspector Ackley on a matter of personal business. He wasn't quite sure what the business would be if he got through to the Inspector, whether to confront him with what they had found out or whether to try and bluff him with some fake story. It never came to that however as the posh female voice on the other end of the phone told him that Inspector Ackley had gone away on holiday and wouldn't be back for a fortnight. Whether or not that was true or not, Isaac couldn't be sure. It could well have been a cover, but he decided to believe it nonetheless, thinking that he would be running the risk of going beyond simple suspicion and entering the realms of paranoia if he started questioning everything that he heard.

Everyone decided that their best next course of action would be to somehow speak to Inspector Ackley, so they all waited patiently for two weeks until he was supposed to return. The weeks went quite quickly, there was uni of course to keep everyone occupied, although no-one had any actual work due in for a little while. Isaac had found as the year had gone on that university work interested him less and less, mostly because he was becoming more and more interested in their supernatural investigations. They also managed to squeeze in a night out at Bubble-Gum as Isaac was determined to not let the often doom and gloom of their situation permanently affect their personalities. As keen as he was to get to the bottom of whatever was going on, he certainly wasn't going to let it turn his life into a nightmare. Not a complete nightmare anyway. He still had to have fun when he could. As mid-February approached, a few days before Inspector Ackley was scheduled to return, there was another disappearance reported in the paper, although this one didn't mention anything about a police investigation. Obviously Ackley would have this case in his inbox when he returned.

The Friday arrived when Inspector Ackley was meant to be back behind his desk in Monks-Lantern Police HQ and Isaac and the others planned to visit him after their evening lecture that day, which was one that they all shared for their religious studies course. It was called *Eschatalogical trends in religion: ancient and modern* and it was also the one that they most enjoyed, not only because it was genuinely fascinating but also as the course content very often became relevant to their rather abnormal lifestyles - something which Isaac was sure was not one of the course aims listed in the prospectus.

Professor Robert Archington took their Eschatology lectures, and Isaac found him to be the most engaging professor he had, and preferred him to any of the teachers he'd had at school. Professor Archington was the archetypal old professor - he oozed knowledge and wisdom. He was quite an old man, certainly in his 60s although Isaac had never heard his real age. He was of average height and was broad shouldered and quite broad in general, although he wasn't fat. He wore small delicate glasses which seemed to accentuate his already sparkling eyes and much of his neck and jaw was covered by his thin, but nonetheless respectable, white beard. Isaac always thought he was a man who could talk indefinitely and never repeat himself, that he contained so much information, that there was so much inside him - so much behind those small twinkling eyes.

They were the first ones in the lecture theatre that Friday. It was a large airy room with deep purple coloured folding seats arranged in an amphitheatre style. Professor Archington was half buried in his worn black leather briefcase when they entered.

"Ah!" he cried, looking up as they took their seats about halfway up the rows, "Someone has turned up after all!" He didn't disappoint the stereotype that day, wearing a full tweed suit and chequered shirt.

They all chuckled, albeit rather forcibly, with Billie adding quietly "Of course we turned up!"

"Suck up!" whispered Gabbi, and they all quietly giggled as more people entered the room. Within a few minutes most of the seats were filled, leaving empty only those where the student was either sick or, more than likely, lazy.

Professor Archington cleared his throat and started to speak, and the remaining chatter soon died down.

"So welcome again everyone, I hope you have had an enjoyable week and managed to fit some reading into your hectic schedules." He drew out this last word and gazed around the room, seeking some kind of affirmation.

Cindy Lackness was nodding enthusiastically and Isaac had a sudden urge to strangle her with her own scrunchie. He exchanged annoyed looks with Billie and Laura and then buried himself in writing the date very slowly at the top of his notes. He hadn't done the reading, it had looked particularly long and rather tedious that week. He wasn't too worried though - Professor Archington rarely checked.

"Isaac Jacobs!" Professor Archington announced, as if calling the next man forward for the firing squad.

"Bugger." Isaac whispered almost silently.

Professor Archington looked towards Isaac and smiled. "Please could you tell us what you know of Bilkes's theory of Extended End-time?" Professor Archington was obviously aware that Isaac didn't have a clue. Despite his marvelling at Archington's incredible knowledge, Isaac did not favour this characteristic of Archington at all - his ability to make you feel ten years old.

"Well," Isaac started, praying he might just be able to bluff his way through, "he basically talks about the idea of the end-time, the end of the world...being...extended." He looked bashfully at Archington but tried as hard as he could to exhibit some confidence. He should have done the reading, he knew he should have, but when you lived your life investigating the supernatural in reality, to read about it just seemed rather pointless sometimes - especially when were neck deep in investigating mysterious disappearances. He and the others did research all the time for their investigations - he saw the point of that, he found that interesting. But reading these essays and discourses that were assigned at uni just seemed so lacking in purpose and half the time when Isaac did read them he read them and disagreed. He thought it was like the difference between historians and archaeologists, or geographers and explorers. One set was in a room, reading about these things and theorising about them, and the other set was out experiencing them. Isaac was definitely an explorer, not a geographer. Even when he had several weeks of not much happening on the supernatural front like the two weeks he'd just had, he still found himself thinking about it a lot of the time, which didn't leave much time at all for reading the gigantic and boring text which Professor Archington had assigned.

"Very thorough." Professor Archington said, dryly, although he gave Isaac a small smile. "Extended End-time or Extended Eschatology is the theory that the end of the world, as we know it at least, began many, many years ago - if not beginning at the beginning itself. It's focused on the idea that the world is heading somewhere, that there is some final destination where the world will be left in the control of either God or the Devil and that the whole of our history is simply leading up to that point."

Jeremy Cuson cut in from somewhere above Isaac and the rest of the group. "But doesn't biblical prophecy say that the world will end up as God's kingdom, that peace shall have the world and the devil will be destroyed?"

"It can certainly be interpreted that way."

"And if the world has been ending forever, how does the theory explain the fact that the portents of the end of the world are written as future events?"

"Well Bilkes makes it clear that although the world has been ending forever, as you say, it doesn't mean that towards the end of the race the competitors wouldn't kick things up a bit, so to speak. Bilkes would call the prophesied end time in the Bible the "End of the End."" Archington paused, checking that everyone was understanding him.

Isaac saw his gaze head towards him and so nodded thoughtfully.

"Now as for your other question concerning the certainty of Biblical prophecy," Archington began again, "that's only a matter of opinion. I'm sure that if there were some dark side wanting control of the world, then they would consider the earth fair game until completely defeated. I believe an expression containing something about a fat lady and singing would fit in well here." The class chuckled. "I mean if you, Jeremy, were told that there was some ancient prophecy that said that you would die today, at, let's say at my hands -"

Everyone in the room laughed, and Archington even chuckled a little too, but he got quickly back to the point.

"- if it was written that you were to die today at my hands, are you honestly telling me that you wouldn't try and avoid me? Or try and kill me first so that you may live?" Jeremy didn't reply and Professor Archington obviously took it that he had pushed the student to a position of being stumped.

The whole class seemed to be rather deep in thought, and the Professor's speech certainly interested Isaac. He got the impression that Professor Archington wasn't much of a geographer either. Isaac wondered what he would do if there were such a prophecy about him. For all he knew there could be. It would be just his luck if there was. Were his friends prophesied to die on that night five years ago?

The rest of the lecture seemed to pass silently, Archington was speaking but Isaac wasn't really listening. He looked from time to time at Gabbi's notes next to him and he could see from what she had written that he wasn't missing anything interesting. It seemed Professor Archington had got his interesting points out of the way at the start of the lecture. His bottom was just starting to go numb when he was sucked back into reality by the sound of bags being unzipped and books being stacked up. The lecture was over.

Chapter Seven

"That was interesting I thought." Laura said as they made their way through town to the Police HQ. It had just gone seven and it was already completely dark.

"Yes it was." Isaac agreed, "Apart from the bit where I looked like an idiot."

Ben laughed as Isaac spoke.

"Yeah yeah keep laughing, I know for a fact you didn't read it either!"

"Nah I know." replied Ben, still chuckling. "It was funny though!"

"If Professor Archington knew what extra-curricular activities we do I'm sure he wouldn't mind the fact that I don't always do the reading." Isaac said, not sure whether he was trying to convince the others or himself. "I mean I always do essays on time. It's just next to demons and disappearances and also trying to have some kind of a life, reading always takes a bit of a back seat."

"I understand." said Gabbi, "It's like that for all of us from time to time." She offered him a smile.

"So what are we going to do when we get to the Police station?" asked Billie. "Just ask for Ackley?"

"I think so." Isaac said "I think maybe if we say that we've got some kind of lead on these disappearances and then see what he says. See if he's interested."

"And what's our lead?" Laura asked.

"Well if it comes to us actually having to tell him anything we'll just say that we've figured out that there are always two a month."

Billie spoke up again. "Wouldn't he already know that?"

"Yes but that's not the point. We're trying to find out if he is even interested in taking this case further. If our suspicions are correct then he won't even want to know what our lead is."

"And that will confirm that he's involved in covering it all up somehow right?" asked Gabbi.

"Exactly."

"Well then," said Ben, "Let's hope he's there."

They got to the station a few minutes later and as soon as they walked onto the forecourt Isaac grabbed Gabbi by the arm and pulled her round behind a large police van, and she in turn pulled the others with her.

"Isaac what're you doing?" she asked, sounding confused. Ben and Billie also looked confused but Laura had seen what Isaac had spotted as he approached the station.

"That's him." she said, indicating towards a man standing half in shadow at the entrance to an alleyway to one side of the building. "I recognise him from the photo on the internet."

"Yep." said Isaac, "And look what he's doing."

At the entrance to the alleyway Ackley was standing talking to someone, someone who was standing more in the shadows but was still just about visible. He was robed and hooded whoever he was and as much as Isaac squinted through the darkness he couldn't see a face. All he could make out were outlines.

"Is that a monk?" asked Billie. There was a monastery just outside of the city and sometimes the monks could be seen walking about through the city centre or sitting in one of the parks.

"No I don't think so." replied Isaac, "He looks more sinister to me."

"Or like he's just come off the set of any satanic movie ever made." Ben said dryly.

Isaac couldn't help but smirk. The outfit did look very much like that.

"Can we get closer?" asked Gabbi, "They're talking but I can't hear, it's just mumbling."

"Really? You can hear mumbling?" Isaac was amazed, he couldn't hear anything.

They all crawled forwards behind the van, and then quickly along behind a low wall which led to a dead end right next to the alley where several large bins were kept. Isaac thought that they must have all looked ridiculous had anyone seen them but amazingly the whole area was deserted. The station wasn't in the city centre really, so he guessed it wasn't that odd that it should be quite quiet this time of the evening. Obviously Ackley and his friend were confident enough to be meeting in the semi-open location that they were in. They all crawled up as far as the bins, which left them only a little way away from the conversation. Isaac had to listen hard, but he just about heard everything.

"Have you given your report yet on the latest missing person?" It was the hooded man who spoke. The voice sounded ordinary enough.

"Give me time, I only just got back from France today!" Ackley sounded wheezy and gruff. So it wasn't another cover up. He really had been in France.

"We don't have all that much time. You know we're close now, the quota is almost full. We can't afford any mistakes."

"No I know, don't worry it will get done."

"Good. The Imperator will be pleased to hear that."

"I'm sure he will." Ackley sounded sarcastic. "Just make sure that when this is over I get what you promised me. Then I never want to hear from any of you again."

"You'll get your thirty pieces of silver, have no fear about that."

"Don't call it that. You make me sound like a traitor."

"Aren't you?"

Isaac could tell without seeing the hooded man's face that he must have been smiling as he spoke.

"Our power is everywhere Inspector, it seeps out of the earth like water from sodden ground."

"Why are you telling me that?"

"So you don't fail. Succeed for us and yes, you shall be rewarded. Fail, and-" the voice paused.

"And?"

"Remember what I've told you. We can't be escaped. There's a purpose to all this beyond what you can see. A much bigger picture. You mustn't fail us."

"I won't."

"Good. We understand each other." With that the hooded figure turned and walked into the inky blackness of the alleyway.

Ackley stood there for a moment and then shook his shoulders, as if shaking away some unpleasant thoughts. Isaac and the others hit the floor as he turned and walked past their hiding place - thankfully they were unseen. They heard a car door slam from across the forecourt and then an engine start followed by the sound of the vehicle driving away.

Isaac stood up and brushed his jeans down. "Well that was interesting." he said. "Did everyone else hear that?" Everyone nodded or said yes as they themselves stood up from their positions on the floor.

"So what now?" asked Laura, "Do we follow Ackley some more?"

"I don't know. Seems to me like he is more of a lackey in this than anything else. As much in the dark as we are."

"That's what I thought listening to what he said." Ben said. "Plus with an ominous threat like he just had hanging over his head, I doubt very much he would be about to spill everything he knows to us."

"So what now then?" asked Billie, "Please say it involves going home, I'm hungry!"

Isaac laughed. He hadn't eaten anything that day really except a bag of crisps, so was feeling quite hungry himself. "Yes I think going home sounds good." he said.

"And the bigger picture he mentioned?" asked Gabbi

"Yes that was worrying. I'd quite like to find out more about that robed guy and his Imperator."

"Yeah what does that mean?" Billie asked, "Is it latin?"

"Yes it's Latin for commander, or leader. So whoever these guys are, they've got a boss who's probably spearheading this whole thing."

They headed off back towards Elsbridge Hill Road, theorising about who the robed guy could have been. Ben stuck to his movie set hypothesis, adding that it might be a secret army of pissed off horror movie extras who had finally decided to rise up and take the world for their own. Isaac laughed, as did everyone else, but he also couldn't avoid thinking that whatever these robed guys were involved in was actually pretty nasty and more than likely was only going to get worse.

The Imperator paced the floor of the dimly lit room. He had told Elias to come straight back and report after he'd spoken with the Inspector. How easily bribed that man had been - humanity was indeed weak. It just went to show that the whole concept of a moral compass was a complete lie, humanity had no central morality, no real definition of right or wrong. If the human race did then it would be impossible for the Inspector to turn the other cheek as he was whilst knowing what he was ignoring, no matter how much they were paying him for his silence. Just then there was a hurried knock at the door.

"Elias?" The Imperator called out.

"Imperator." The familiar voice of Elias came from the other side of the door.

"Enter."

The door opened and Elias stepped sure-footedly into the room, greeting the Imperator with a curt nod of the head. He pulled his hood down, his swarthy skin glistening in the warm light from the lamps in the room. "I spoke with the Inspector."

"And? Does he continue to be a well behaved puppet?"

"He does. He seemed anxious, however. Worried about his reward."

"He'll be paid, for all the good that will do him." The Imperator paused for a moment. "Humans."

"Everything is going according to plan." Elias smiled thinly, notes of smugness in his voice.

"Guard your tone, Elias." The Imperator said sharply, "Things progress as we desire, yes - but we progress along a knife's edge. One slip and we could plummet." He eyed Elias coldly. "Everything must happen so precisely. Thankfully we have power on our side. This city doesn't know it but it bows to my will. The police, the media, the council. They all dance to our tune without even knowing it. Soon the world will dance with them. The dance macabre of creation."

"The end." Elias said hopefully.

"Yes, the end." The Imperator considered it wistfully for a moment before snapping back to the present. "But that is still a time away for now. We have work to do. Those children need to be watched, closely. We need to out-step them at every turn."

"But surely sir, children cannot stop our destiny for the world?"

The Imperator wagged a finger at Elias. "These children possess a dangerous weapon which could prove to make them a threat to us."

Elias looked aghast at the possibility. "What weapon Imperator?"

The Imperator smiled softly, only his eyes betraying his maliciousness. "Love."

Chapter Eight

The night of terror that Isaac had experienced five years ago had been horrifying beyond description. When he dreamt of that night, when he thought of that night, he often felt like there wasn't enough anguish in him to really feel what he wanted to feel. He felt worse than his body allowed him to feel. What was in many ways just as bad as the actual night was the time that immediately followed it.

After an hour of sitting alone on the front step of his house, the bodies of his friends still laying cold, silent and alone inside, Isaac had summoned up the courage to stand, turn and go back in the house. He'd only looked briefly at his friends bodies, lying crumpled and lifeless like they'd never even been living, breathing things. It was too hard to look at them for any longer than a few seconds, he was terrified by not only the gory sight of it but also by the guilt he felt, crashing through him in such a forceful way that he'd never felt before. It pounded him instantly, he could hear them screaming at him through their lifeless mouths. "Why did you leave us to die? Why did you leave us to die?"

He couldn't bear it, so instead he'd gone straight through to the study where the actual ritual had taken place. There he performed a frantic clean up, getting rid of any evidence that something supernatural had happened. His eyes were full of tears for most of the time that he worked but he didn't stop to cry, he just let the tears hang there in his eyes, making them heavy. He didn't stop to cry either when he phoned the police and told them that someone had broken into his house and killed his friends. Nor did he stop to cry when the police arrived and asked him what had happened and he told them any number of lies - the main one of which was that Tom hadn't even been there that night. It was his peace offering to Tom, that he wouldn't have to be bothered by the investigation that would follow. After all, there was nothing to prove that he'd been there and Isaac knew Tom well enough to know that he wouldn't say anything about it to his father - who for many years had been a disheveled alcoholic.

When Isaac's parents were phoned they drove home immediately. They were concerned of course, worried and upset, but Isaac could tell once they got home that they were also annoyed that their trip had to be cut short. They were home by the early hours of the morning and it must have been almost six before Isaac finally collapsed into bed - the sheets still ruffled from where he'd had his life-changing moment with Tom. Only then did he cry. He cried louder and harder than he ever had before and ever thought he would again. It had felt as though the world had just been flipped inside out, as if everything that had been good had been turned bad.

The following weeks weren't any better. There was a huge interest from the press initially of course, photographers at the end of the garden and on the walk to school. And there were the funerals to get through and the hunt for the killer that no-one would ever find. And all the time Isaac felt like he just wanted to take himself to the police and hand himself in. He didn't kill anyone physically, but he still blamed himself entirely for their deaths. How could he do otherwise? If he hadn't have left the house when he did, if he hadn't have been so stupid just because of his falling out with Tom, then maybe they would still be alive. He'd gone over and over it again in his head - he would have gone downstairs, apologised to Tom - begged for forgiveness even and then he would have stopped them from summoning Verk'an-gorek. It wouldn't have been difficult - the ritual used a specific kind of crystal, if he'd have just smashed that then they would have had no choice but to stop. He'd have used force if he had to - it wouldn't have mattered. Better to have a black eye then be dead. But he didn't do any of that, no - he'd just skulked off with his dented pride and sat in his childhood tree, sat there like a worthless person whilst his friends were having the life ripped from them. For a long time he couldn't even look at himself in the mirror, he hated the person he saw.

He'd gone round to Tom's house a couple of months later, once everything had died down. All he found was sold sign in the front garden and a new family moving in. Tom had gone without a trace. He went back to his house that day and stood in the hall where his friends had died. His parents were out shopping and he'd looked around the empty space. Silence, all except for the ticking of a clock in the background. He was alone. Completely and utterly alone. He closed his eyes to hold back the tears and made a vow there and then that the same thing wouldn't happen twice, to him, or to anyone. What had happened had sickened him, it dwelt in his soul with a weight he knew he would never be able to remove. He also knew he couldn't possibly bear that same weight again for a second time. It would kill him.

From that day onwards he didn't stop. He investigated and sought out every supernatural problem he could find. It wasn't always easy and it was rarely safe but he knew that it was right. Always alone, never allowing anyone to get close for the fear of killing them like he'd killed his friends. He saw so much in those times, in those years between the death of his friends and his move to Monks-Lantern. Demons, ghosts, monsters from under the bed, he encountered all of them. He read and researched, learning as much as he possibly could. And of course along the way he met people and people became interested in him and in what he did. But he always turned them away, not because he enjoyed being alone but because he saw it as his penance.

It had stayed like that for a long time, until of course that fateful first night in Monks-Lantern when he'd met Gabbi at the library. She'd saved him that night, in more ways than one. He'd tried to turn her away instinctively, but something inside him felt different that night. She was so kind, so funny, so loving - he could tell straight away. And he suddenly realised how much he missed that, how he missed people, missed being friends with people, having people to talk to about all the mad, crazy things he did. He realised how very much he'd hated being alone, and after that terrifying night he realised that he needed people. It was strange really, that one terrifying night convinced him that he should be without people but then another terrifying night convinced him of exactly the opposite.

He knew that he'd never entirely forgive himself for what had happened to his old friends but he also knew that it didn't mean he had to be alone for the rest of his life. He could have friends, he could have people he loved and still carry on fighting for those he'd lost. His friends didn't make him weaker. They made him stronger because together it meant they had a powerful weapon on their side. Love.

Chapter Nine

A purpose beyond what they could see. That was the part of the conversation that had worried Isaac and the words played on repeat in his mind. A purpose beyond what they could see. A purpose beyond what they could see. He knew they needed help, he knew they did. Flicking through newspapers and staking out police stations was easy enough but if they were heading into deeper water then they'd more than that.

He'd spent the weekend researching cults and sects with the others, trying to pinpoint a particular group that was involved with Monks-Lantern at one point or another but it was a fruitless search. The only group that they could find a record of was a sixteenth century fraternity of nudists from a time when nudity was apparently illegal in the city. Isaac was sure that as interesting as that sounded, it wasn't the people they were after.

They researched all the most famous secret groups too - just to see if there were any obvious links. They read about the Freemasons, the Illuminati and the Order of Thelema along with many others but they just didn't seem to fit with what little information they had about what was going on there and then in the city.

It was like they were dealing with a whole new group, some heretofore undiscovered secret band of evil. But if the robed guy was right and they did have people everywhere then it was surely a huge group on a massive scale - someone would have noticed them before at some point - there would have to be some kind of record. Unless of course this group really took the "secret" part of a secret society seriously. Maybe they'd been around forever, erasing themselves from history when needed so that they could carry out their goals, whatever they might be. It was a chilling thought.

By the following Monday it seemed that they were no closer than they were before their spying session and if anything they were more confused. With their stack of questions piling much higher than their stack of answers, Isaac decided that it was time for a last resort. They needed help and he had an uneasy feeling he knew exactly where they might find it.

"We're going to go and visit Pete. After the lecture is over." They were sitting in their Monday afternoon lecture with Professor Archington again. It was *Studies of the Reformation Church* this time, much duller than their Friday lectures with him. Isaac had whispered his decision to the others as quietly as he could, but evidently it wasn't quiet enough.

"Mr Jacobs!" Archington called out cheerily. "I know that Luther may not be top of your Christmas card list but please refrain from organising your social calendar whilst I'm talking about him." Isaac sank back down into his seat, not being able to answer the puzzled faces that his friends had presented to him. They had no clue who Pete was, Isaac had never actually spoken to them about him.

"Sorry Professor." he said quietly whilst mentally forcing his face to not turn a violent shade of red.

"That's quite okay. Now if we can carry on, I must impress upon you all the massive change that the reformation brought to the world of religion. A complete change. A complete new order." Archington's voice droned on and on, and whilst Isaac did find him engaging it wasn't enough to liven up topics as dull as the reformation. He saw that some of the class members were sitting with rapped attention, so obviously some people found it interesting.

He doodled for the next half an hour until the lecture finished, occasionally looking intently at Archington and then scribbling pretend notes to make it look like he was actually enthralled. At the end of the lecture Archington hummed a merry tune as he packed up his briefcase, and he waved to them all as they left the room. "Isaac?" he called as Isaac slid towards the door. "A word?"

"Yeah sure." Oh great. More trouble. He mouthed to Gabbi that he would meet them by the fountain outside the Students Union and then walked over to where Archington was.

"You're an intelligent guy Isaac."

"Thank you sir, I didn't mean to-"

"No I know Luther can be a bit dry sometimes. But I do notice that quite often you seem to not be altogether here in the lecture. Your friends are sometimes similar but you more than the others."

"I know." Isaac was shocked. Archington was more perceptive than he'd thought. He had hoped that his impression of a keen worker had been a convincing one. "It's just, well, there's a lot of stuff, outside of uni I mean. But it shouldn't get in the way, I know. I really enjoy your lectures, the eschatology one particularly." A bit of shameless flattery didn't seem like such a bad idea.

"I'm glad. Just stay sharp eh? Read the reading when you can, and just try and give me a few hours of attention in lectures each week. It's all I ask."

"Yes professor. Thank you." Isaac sounded uncertain as he said that last word. Was that something you should thank someone for? Had Professor Archington just given him his version of a pep talk?

"Very good. Right well I won't detain you, planning visits weren't you?" Archington said, smiling.

"Yes," Isaac forced a small laugh, "yes I was." He turned and headed for the door.

"See you Friday then Isaac?"

"Yes, see you then." With that he smiled, and then left the room, hurrying towards the fountain. When he got there he found everyone except Laura, who had gone home as she had felt a headache come on in the lecture and so wanted to rest up in bed. Isaac wished he was going home to do the same - if this visit was going to be as weird as the last one then bed would definitely be preferable.

Chapter Ten

Isaac was sure that Pete wasn't Pete's real name, but he got the impression that asking him for a more accurate name would be a futile task. Pete was, to say the least, mysterious.

"So who is this Pete guy then? Does he go to uni?" Billie asked as they hurried through the city.

"Well I know he doesn't go to uni. As for who he is exactly, your guess is as good as mine." Isaac replied, thinking that he really did know next to nothing about the person they were going to visit.

"But you've met him before right?" Billie continued.

"Just the once, my first week here." Isaac looked up from the pavement and made eye contact with Gabbi. "He was the one who told me to go to the old children's library where I met you."

"You were told to go there?" Gabbi asked, sounding surprised.

"Yeah didn't I tell you?"

"No - you just said that you were investigating. I figured that you just felt like going in like me."

Now it was Isaac's turn to be surprised. "You felt like going in that place?"

"Maybe felt is the wrong word - I don't know, that's what it was like. I just felt like I should go in."

Isaac looked at Gabbi for a moment as they walked. Whenever he had read about people feeling called to a place before it had been in articles about destiny and pre-destination. If Gabbi had felt called to the library then maybe there was some real purpose behind them all being together. He swept the deeper thoughts aside for the time being and focused on the immediate situation.

Ben obviously wanted to get back to the situation at hand too, as he now spoke up in a rather cynical tone. "So he's a guy who sent you to a haunted building once. Is there any reason to think that he can be of any actual help to us now? I mean we're not looking to seek out ghosts."

"Pete's odd, when I saw him before it felt like he knew things - other-worldly things. It definitely felt like he was capable of more than pointing me to the nearest haunted house. And besides - that library was far from just haunted."

Isaac stopped the others outside the building in front of them. Pete lived in a street called Kettle Lane in a flat above what was once a fish and chip shop called Captains Pride. It must have been out of business for some years now - the window was almost opaque with filth and dust, and what could be seen of the inside looked just as filthy. The dirty poster advertising psychic abilities which had drawn Isaac in the first time still hung there, tatty as ever. Many of the old looking houses in the street were boarded up and looked to be in a very sorry condition. The pavements of Kettle Lane fared no better – they were all cracked with weeds growing up through the crevices. The city council had certainly forgotten about this little corner of Monks-Lantern. The teal coloured paint of the door to the flat was peeling badly, and there was a rusty knocker hanging in the centre of the door. However, if Isaac remembered correctly from his last visit, they wouldn't be needing to use it. He pushed the door and it swung open, surprisingly without a creak for a door that looked so decrepit.

Billie looked unimpressed. "This is it?"

"Aren't you going to knock?" asked Gabbi.

"Didn't last time and it worked out fine." Isaac stood on the doorstep for a moment and breathed in a deep breath. He felt uneasy. "Right then. Lets go in."

Elias was pleased that none of the group had looked round as they had entered the door next to the Captains Pride. Being spotted would have been most disruptive to the mission the Imperator had given him. He crept out from his place of seclusion around the corner and advanced to the position he had been instructed to take. The crossbow felt large and obtrusive beneath his robe. It would be a blessing to have it out in the open air.

Inside the building a filthy looking carpet in the same colour as the door led the way along a short narrow corridor to the staircase which twisted sharply up, round and out of sight. There were tattered posters like the one out front hanging half-heartedly from the magnolia walls – these ones advertising old rock concerts that took place in the city as well as some promoting mystical gatherings of one sort or another. Isaac proceeded up the stairs which climbed steeply up to Pete's flat. At the top there was a heap of what looked like dirty underwear which made Isaac's face involuntarily wrinkle up in disgust. He heard a quiet moan of distaste from Billie behind him after he had passed them, so he figured she had seen them as well. The door that immediately faced them didn't look like the door to someone's home, it looked more like a door one might find on the entrance to a public toilet or utility cupboard.

Isaac raised a hand and knocked three times in quick succession. "Pete?" he called out, pushing the door open at the same time, which like the door downstairs was unlocked. In fact it didn't even look as if it had a lock. "Pete are you home?" Isaac stepped into the flat with Billie, Gabbi and Ben coming in close behind him. His eyes adjusted slowly to the relative gloom of the interior. The day had turned to dusk outside and the thin light barely penetrated the room they now stood in. The air was thick with incense, causing him to cough involuntarily as he entered. Heavy metal music played quietly from somewhere in the flat, which he found ironic - usually in his experience heavy metal was played as loud as the volume control would allow. A beaded curtain which hung in the kitchen doorway off to the left of the flat rattled as a reasonably tall and incredibly skinny figure emerged from behind it.

"Ahhh - library boy! Back again!" Pete's voice was cheerful and welcoming, but a hint of amusement was also detectable. His piercing blue eyes were most visible before the rest of him came into clear view - and when he did come into full view he was much as Isaac remembered him. He had shoulder length jet black hair which didn't look particularly styled but neither did it look particularly unkempt. Isaac knew that hygiene and appearance couldn't have been top of Pete's list of priorities - one look at his flat would tell anyone that - but nonetheless his chiselled features, stubbly facial hair and pale, clear skin made him attractive in a rough, rock'n'roll kind of way.

Isaac smiled in acknowledgement as Pete threw himself down into a large, red bean-bag.

"So!" Pete began, throwing his hands dramatically into his lap as if awaiting an exciting story, "You're back and you brought friends! Bloody lovely!"

"Yes, these are my good friends Ben, Billie and Gabbi. I met Gabbi at the library, the one you sent me to." He felt like he was introducing his friends to some insane old relative.

Petes eyes widened, their blue colour intensifying. "Piss off! Really? Well then that has to mean something. You lot, all five of you brought together - it's all so exciting isn't it?" Pete's voice seemed to hint that he was thinking something he wasn't saying.

Gabbi spoke up. "Four, there're four of us." she corrected.

"No, there're five, another one at home isn't there? Shame she got that headache, would have loved to have met her."

The hairs on the back of Isaac's neck tingled. Billie reached out and grabbed his jacket sleeve, showing that she was just as un-nerved. "How did you -"

"There'll be a few more to come as yet too." Pete beamed happily, interrupting Isaac's question. Then his smile faded. "And er, maybe a few to lose as well." His expression turned very grave. He stared at Isaac - a deep, cold stare with deep, cold eyes. "I'm sorry."

"How do we know we can trust him?" Ben asked, turning his head to look at Isaac. He asked the question as if Pete wasn't there, but he was very clearly within earshot.

"Oi bastard I can hear you know!" Pete said with a great big grin on his face, the cold stare gone.

Isaac looked at Ben uncertainly.

Ben continued, whispering slightly although Pete was still within earshot. "I mean he seems friendly enough, but have you looked at this place? It's hardly the décor of one of the good guys."

Isaac could see Ben's point. Pete's flat looked like a classical bad guy lair. The whole of the main room was painted black, there were posters of hellish pictures on the walls and various skulls and other occult style ornaments were placed here and there. Yet whilst this was stereotypically rather concerning, Isaac knew better than to judge a book by its cover, and Pete himself gave an air of strange trustworthiness.

"The truth is," Pete began, leaning forward in his bean-bag and resting his elbows on his knees, "That you don't know for certain if you can trust me. You never can with any person. One bloke could seem perfectly nice and then the next minute he could tear your neck out. You have to choose, because I could never prove it to you enough either way." There was a long silence.

Billie surprised everyone by speaking suddenly. "How did you know about there being a fifth person?"

"Good question! Shame there ain't an easy answer to go with it. Good and easy, that's always a winning combination." Pete said, winking at no-one in particular. He got up from his bean-bag, stretched his arms high above his head and then walked over to the window, cracking it open slightly. From the back pocket of his black skinny jeans he pulled out a pack of cigarettes and a lighter. He lit one and inhaled deeply, blowing the smoke out of the window.

Isaac found it strange that a guy who was so messy otherwise should worry about the smell of smoke. The incense in the flat was so overbearing that Isaac would have welcomed cigarette smoke as an alternative.

Pete leaned casually against the window and paused briefly before attempting to answer Billie's question. "It's like a radio I guess. See now you turn on your radio and you can tune into any number of stations - I'm guessing from looking at you that it would be one with nothing but pop - in other words, nothing but shite,"

Billie looked like she might have protested but Pete didn't give her time.

"My mind is a bit like that. I can tune into other frequencies, other than the one we're all listening to and all watching now. Spiritual frequencies if you like. Higher frequencies."

Isaac was encouraged by what Pete had just told them. "Well then maybe you can help us." If Pete really was connected to some higher frequencies then he may well be able to see what was going on in the bigger picture. "We think there's something bad going on, possibly something big. There have been people going missing for years now and nobody seems to be making a fuss about it. It's completely played down by the papers and the police."

Gabbi added more information, "When we went to the Police we saw a very dodgy meeting, Inspector Ackley was talking to some robed guy - they were talking about quotas being filled and a purpose beyond what we can see." she said.

Isaac picked up the narrative flow again from Gabbi, "And any demons we have come across have mentioned something going on in a bigger picture. Something bad. Please Pete, if you know anything we really need -"

"Yes, yes, calm down for crap's sake." Pete interrupted, stubbing out his cigarette in an overflowing ash tray on the window ledge. Obviously a few drags had been enough. "I know what you're going on about. Just because I live in a dim lit old shack doesn't mean I'm left in the dark." Pete suddenly stopped speaking. His eyes went wide with fear and horror.

Everyone noticed his change in countenance.

"What is it?" Isaac asked eagerly.

"A higher frequency." Pete swallowed and licked his lips as if they were suddenly dry and chapped. "Being left in the dark is one thing," he swallowed again, heavier this time, "but you lot are about to be dragged right into it kicking and screaming." Any warmth that had been in the room was suddenly sucked out by Pete's words. There was a certainty in his voice which was terrifying.

"What do you mean?" Ben asked.

"Something bigger is happening alright, not just the disappearances, something more - something big and messy and it's going to get a whole lot bigger and much, much messier before it's over." Pete's face looked suddenly drained of all its blood. He was pale and sweaty. He looked panicked.

Isaac glanced at the rest of the group - their expressions didn't look much better than Pete's did. Even Gabbi, who was usually firm and confident in scary situations, looked uneasy.

"What can you tell us?" asked Isaac, becoming desperate for a real answer rather than cryptic clues.

"Not much." Pete's breathing was becoming heavier. "But the answer is closer than you think. Much closer."

"What is it?" demanded Isaac.

"Pete please!" begged Billie.

Pete shut his eyes for a long moment and then opened them again. The terror had gone, now replaced with a determined look that was ready and able to help. "I'm sorry," he said, genuine sympathy in his voice, "but it's yo-"

It all seemed to happen at once - the shattering glass and the sickening crunch as the bolt landed firmly in Pete's skull. He crumpled instantly to the floor, blood seeping eagerly from the fatal wound in the back of his head.

Billie screamed.

Gabbi clasped a hand to her mouth in shock before running forward and dropping to the floor beside Pete's body.

Isaac did a double-take - trying to take in what the hell had just happened. "Get down!" he shouted, realising through the shock that they could all still be in danger. He dodged straight to his right, pulling Billie with him as he went. Gabbi was safe below the window line where she knelt next to Pete's body, and Ben crouched down on the opposite side of the window to Billie and Isaac. Isaac had an arm around Billie as he looked over at Gabbi, who was checking for vital signs. The somber expression on her delicately featured face told him all he needed to know. It wasn't long before the obvious questions were asked.

"How could that have just happened?" It was Ben who spoke. "I mean unless -"

"Unless we were followed," Gabbi cut in. "And whoever was following us knew that Pete lived here and what he was capable of doing."

"And someone with crazy bat hearing." Billie added, wiping her damp eyes with her sleeve.

Isaac nodded in agreement. It was a good point. For someone to know just when to shoot they would have had to be able to hear the conversation. Unless they were just plain lucky. Then an even bigger question came into his mind.

"Hearing our conversation is one thing," he began, "but how did they even know to follow us in the first place?"

Elias was rushing quickly along the cobbled streets to tell the Imperator the good news. That psychic idiot had played right into his hands by standing in front of the window. It had made his job nice and simple - especially with the powers of hearing that the Imperator had given him. What power he possessed! Those measly, pathetic students didn't have any idea what was just around the corner. Elias chuckled quietly to himself. It wouldn't be too long now before it all started happening.

"Maybe we're being followed everywhere." Ben suggested.

"But this guy came prepared," Gabbi argued, looking down grimly at the crossbow bolt. "It seems unlikely that whoever's doing this would have guys following us around with crossbows twenty-four seven."

There was a pause in the conversation and everyone seemed to either look down at themselves or look around the room. The fading light shone meekly through the window, softly illuminating Pete's corpse and the figure of Gabbi knelt beside him.

Isaac thought for a moment that she looked like a guardian angel hovering over a mortal charge. They'd all been so rattled by the attack that they hadn't stopped to think what had really just happened. Pete lay dead on the floor because of their visit - because he had been trying to help them. Another dead body. Another dead friend - even if Pete had refused to be labelled as such.

Billie broke the silence. "What are we going to do now?" she asked.

Isaac answered her quietly. "We're going to figure out who did this, and who's taking those people. Then we're going to stop them." He couldn't take his eyes off Pete's body as he spoke. He found himself mentally willing Pete to get up. Get back up, please. Get back up. Don't be dead, please don't be dead. Get up.

"No." Billie spoke again. "I mean what are we going to do about him?" she asked, nodding towards Pete.

He lay there still - he wasn't going to get up again. What had happened had really just happened - and what Isaac knew must happen next broke his heart. He knew it would break Billie's too, but it was unavoidable. Billie looked up at Isaac and then across to Gabbi. She didn't like what she saw in their eyes. Isaac looked back at her. He wished he could give her a different look but he knew he couldn't. Ben looked as bewildered as Billie did.

"No!" Billie choked as she realised what they were intending, tears coming anew in her eyes, "No!"

"Billie -" Isaac started.

"No! We can't just leave him!" she insisted.

"It's not that simple."

"We never just leave people. When people have died before we've always called the police or the ambulance or someone! We always make sure they'll be taken care of!" Billie's voice was distressed but fierce at the same time.

"Billie darling he's right," Gabbi said. "We can't trust the police at the moment, not after what we found out about Ackley. If the police come and they're a part of this then the chances are that they'll try and make us look like the suspects."

"But he was helping us!" Billie moaned, her voice crackled through the tears.

Inside Isaac was screaming out that he agreed with her, but he knew that they had to leave Pete alone. They had to. He didn't want to but they just had to.

"I know." Gabbi's voice was the definition of empathy.

Ben made a suggestion. "We could anonymously call the police, we've done that before."

Isaac shook his head sadly. "I'm not even sure if we can do that this time," he began. "It's like Gabbi says - the less we have to do with this, officially, the better."

Gabbi added another point to the case. "If the discussion we overheard the other night is anything to go by then the chances are that someone from the police knew that this would happen anyway."

Isaac nodded in agreement with Gabbi. "In which case someone could be on their way here now and we're standing around looking very, very suspicious. We need to leave." He tried to keep his tone sympathetic but firm. As sad and shocked as he felt about Pete, he knew that they had to leave as quickly as possible.

Ben nodded in agreement.

Billie still looked utterly distraught, but she too looked up at Isaac and nodded mournfully.

"Okay then," Isaac said, helping Billie to her feet. "Let's go."

Gabbi closed Pete's eyes and kissed him on the forehead. "I'm sorry." she said, and then got up to leave with the others.

Most of the walk home from Kettle Lane was in silence. The sun had now well and truly set and the combination of darkness and shadows meant that each of them was checking over their shoulders now and again to see if they were being followed or stalked by the assailant with the crossbow, but no-one was visible. They heard sirens when they were about half way home but in a busy city like Monks-Lantern that could be for any number of crimes or accidents - there was no way to know if it had been about Pete. Once they were nearly home at the corner of Elsbridge Hill Road, Isaac dropped behind slightly to walk alone with Billie. He put an arm around her and pulled her in for a hug as they walked.

"Are you okay?" he asked. As much as he knew they had to leave like they did, he knew exactly what Billie had meant.

"Yeah. I know why we did what we did." Her voice sounded more cheerful than earlier, but it was possible it was just a front. "Are you?"

"I'm fine," Isaac said, lying through his teeth.

"Are you sure?"

"Well I mean I'm sad, of course I am. But we'll make it right. I promise you, we'll make it so that he didn't die for nothing." He tried to sound reassuring. Evidently it worked, as Billie pulled Isaac in tightly for another hug.

She looked up at him and gave a warm smile. "You're right. We'll figure it all out."

Indoors a few minutes later and everyone drifted off to separate activities. Billie went to speak to Laura who was up in bed, to let her know about everything that had just happened. Gabbi had gone to the kitchen and Ben had gone to his own room - everyone seemed to need some time to reflect.

Isaac called out something about having some dinner in an hour or so before stepping into his own bedroom and shutting the door fast behind him. The door had barely clicked shut before he burst into tears - the uncontrollable sobbing kind that made your whole body shake. He lifted his hands to his face to try and stop them somehow, but it didn't work - the tears kept coming. He fell back against the door and then allowed himself to slide down until he was sat on the floor with his legs hunched up under his chin. He'd barely known Pete, he knew that - but he'd felt strangely close nonetheless. Pete had helped him when Isaac had first come to the city and he'd helped them just now. And now he was dead, just like Isaac's old friends. Was history repeating itself? Who was next? Billie, Laura? Ben? Gabbi? That couldn't happen, it couldn't - he wouldn't let it! He tried to rein in some control and stop his mind from running away with itself. Then his heart almost leapt out of his mouth as there was a sudden knock on the door behind him.

"Hey mate it's me, open up." It was Ben.

Isaac didn't really want to be seen like this. He got up and stepped away from the door, desperately trying to control his breathing so his voice didn't sound like he'd been crying. "Okay, hold on I'm just getting changed." Isaac hoped his lie would buy him a moment to prepare himself for a visitor but his hope was in vain - without further warning the door handle twisted and the door was pushed open.

Ben walked in unabashed.

Isaac looked on in shock.

"Thought you were getting changed?" Ben said after plonking himself down on the side of the bed and casting a suspicious eye at Isaac.

"I could have been naked!" Isaac retorted, happily surprised to find himself laughing at the same time. "Why did you just walk in?"

Ben shrugged. "Meh. Nothing I haven't seen before."

Isaac looked at Ben in shock once more. "When did you -"

Ben was looking at him with a broad grin.

Isaac cottoned on to what he'd meant. "Oh you mean nothing you haven't seen before in general, you've seen naked men in general before. Not naked me." Isaac laughed again.

Ben laughed too and fell sideways onto the bed. "Ahh had you worried there!" he sat back up again. "You silly gay."

"Shut-up!" Isaac said smiling. "Stupid straight man." He went and sat next to Ben on the edge of the bed.

"Ooh good comeback." Ben chucked sarcastically.

Isaac smiled - he enjoyed their banter, it was nice. Comfortable.

"So anyway, are you okay?"

"Of course, yeah I'm fine." Isaac nodded over-enthusiastically.

"Look, mate, you're talking to another guy here alright? I know all the little tricks about how to pretend you don't get upset about things. The over the top nod is right at the top of the list."

"Okay. No, I'm not fine. Two minutes ago I was bawling like a baby on the floor."

"Pete?"

"Yeah."

"We couldn't have saved him you know."

"We could have not gone there in the first place."

"You knew he could have helped us. If we're going to stop whatever this thing is which is happening then we have to get as much help as possible. We had to go, you were right to take us there."

"Was I? I mean -"

"Nah look don't start trying to tell me that we should never have gone. We would have gone eventually, if not this evening then next week or next month. You were right to take us there. The only wrong thing in the whole situation is what was done to him by the monster outside the window. And that has nothing at all to do with you." Ben's logic was very straightforward and man-like, very practical and objective. And it did make sense.

"You're right." Isaac nodded at Ben and tried to smile. "I do feel bad just leaving him though, but I know it was the right thing to do. The right thing for us to do anyway. I'd try contacting his family but I'm not even sure he's got any. I don't even know his full name, god I don't even know if he was really human." Isaac chuckled softly at the thought that Pete could have actually been some kind of supernatural being.

"Then there's nothing you can do, so don't beat yourself up about it."

"No, I know. And I meant what I said to Billie earlier."

"What was that?"

"To not let his death be for nothing. I feel like we're getting close to something, and I'm going to make sure that we get there. For him, and for anyone else this evil plot has already killed or is planning to kill."

"That's more like it, a bit of positivity man. We've got to be positive!" Ben punched the air over-enthusiastically. "Ooh yeah we can do this!"

Isaac laughed. "Wow that's, that's positive!"

"Too positive?"

"No, I like it. I might get you to do it as a morale booster from time to time." Isaac chuckled. "Everyone loves a good air punch to get them going when the chips are down."

"Yeah and speaking of chips I'm hungry mate, let's go get some food."

Isaac agreed. "Good idea." Ben gave Isaac a manly and encouraging slap on the back and then got up to leave the room. Isaac breathed in and out heavily once and then got up to go with him. He still felt sad about Pete, but he felt better for having a cry and then speaking to Ben. And he did feel like they were close to something. His instincts told him that their next clue to the disappearances and the bigger picture would be right around the corner.

Chapter Eleven

Isaac's instincts were wrong. Two full weeks passed after the events at Pete's flat and nothing really happened. University work had kept them all busy, with Isaac having essays due for both Religious Studies and Ancient History. His professor for Hellenistic Studies had given them a fairly wide essay topic of an investigation into any social aspect of ancient Greece, and Isaac had chosen to look at how homosexuality was treated in their society. Some would say it was a predictable choice of subject matter, but Isaac didn't care, he found it interesting - and it was comforting in a way to think of an ancient culture that in some ways was more understanding and tolerant than many were now. The rest of the group were busy working too - Ben even had an exam to take for the Sports Science course that he was on, so he was nose deep in revision. With the fervour of work the two weeks passed quickly, and whilst the more supernatural aspects of life were ever present on everyone's minds, they didn't have the time to dwell on them for too long.

Another disappearance occurred, the second one for February - and as usual it went past without much of a mention at all in the media, just the same small article in the local paper - no doubt written by one of the many that the hooded figure had mentioned at the police station. Inspector Ackley was actually quoted in this article as saying there was nothing suspicious about the disappearance. Isaac figured that after his threat from the hooded man he was taking extra precautions in making sure no-one looked into the missing people in any real depth. Isaac also found it ridiculous that a disappearance was actually being described as not suspicious - surely a disappearance was always suspicious? He couldn't believe that people were just reading the paper and accepting it, but then he figured that by and large that's what people did - they believed what the media told them. If the paper, quoting the police no less, tells you that something isn't suspicious then you believe it because you've been brought up to trust that the police know what they're talking about and that the paper tells you true news. It's only when you question either of those principles that you'd start getting worried, and he supposed that most people didn't question either of them at all. Why would they?

Isaac gave in his essays that Friday afternoon and breathed a sigh of relief that he didn't have anything to give in now for some time. His mind was his own again, and almost immediately his thoughts drifted to where they had been attempting to drift to since their visit to Pete's flat. He knew that only Gabbi would be at home when he got in from delivering his essays, everyone else was either at lectures, or in Ben's case, sitting an exam. He didn't mind though - it was actually just what he wanted, because it was Gabbi that he specifically needed to speak to. Once he got in he quickly took off his coat and shoes and then after a quick scout round downstairs he proceeded upstairs to see where Gabbi was. He found her sitting up on her bed, slouched against the wall, gazing intently at one of the photocopies they were given in class that day. Isaac stood in the doorway, un-noticed by Gabbi. He could see the concentration on her face, the look in her eyes that was desperately trying to understand what was in front of her. Like himself, it was clear that Gabbi too felt that early Christian writers were a little too thorough in their work. He knocked sharply on the door and she looked up, startled.

"Hey," he started, "trying to get to grips with the reading?"

"Trying," she said, smiling and clipping the lid back onto her highlighter. "Trying's the word! I'm not getting very far. What can I do for you?"

"Don't just assume that I'm up here for something serious! You know I might just be wanting to say hi!"

"Are you?"

"No." Isaac sighed. He wished that he could just be starting a casual conversation. "I've been thinking."

"Oh no! Are you okay?" The sarcasm was obvious.

Isaac smiled. Gabbi always knew how to make him do that, every time without fail. "I've been thinking about how we met. In the library."

Gabbi brushed the papers from her lap and sat more upright on the bed. Isaac's choice of subject had obviously caught her attention. "And what have you been thinking about it?"

"It's been bugging me for a while, well since we visited Pete. Things have been a bit busy since then so I haven't been able to talk to you about it," he came in and sat on the bed next to her. "But I've still been thinking about it."

"I think we've all been thinking about that day. What he said, and then what happened," she paused and swallowed heavily. "Isaac what do you think it all means? Things getting big and messy, and the answer being closer than we think?" Genuine worry was etched clearly on her face.

"I know," he said, feeling a twinge of panic himself. "It's all quite worrying. But that wasn't what I've been thinking about specifically. Like I said, I've been thinking about how we met."

"Creepy children's library in a creepy children's hospital." Gabbi shuddered for dramatic effect, "How could I forget. So what have you been specifically thinking about it?"

"Well, on the way to Pete's you said about just feeling like going there that night, to the library, at the exact same time that I was going there. And then what Pete said about all five of us being drawn together, it just seems -"

Gabbi interrupted him and completed his train of thought. "Like there might be some kind of purpose behind us all coming together?"

"Exactly."

"Seems possible. So if we have all been drawn together, starting with me and you at the library, then there's two questions I've got - why and how?"

"They'd be my questions too. And I think I know where we might get some answers." Gabbi looked excited when Isaac told her this, but he knew her hopeful expression would drop when he revealed where he hoped to go for information. "The library." he said, his voice solemn.

Sure enough all hope and excitement drained from Gabbi's face. "The library?" She sounded utterly disappointed.

"The library."

The sky was darkening quickly as the two of them headed out the door to make their way across town to the abandoned children's hospital. They'd wrapped up warm as it was bitterly cold outside, yet despite his scarf and woolly hat the freezing air still bit at Isaac's nose and lips.

"So what are we going to do when we get there?" Gabbi asked, "The ghost children went didn't they? They moved on. There'll be no-one to talk to."

She wasn't wrong. The last time they'd been at the library the spirits of two children who had died at the hospital were being trapped there by a dark entity, a shadow of some kind that had made them its prisoners and was then feeding off their fear. After all, the fear of a child is the strongest and most powerful kind of fear. After a terrifying battle, Isaac and Gabbi defeated the monstrous creature that had haunted the place and the children were free to move on to the afterlife. But Isaac couldn't help but feel that those children knew something, as one of them had exclaimed "you came!" when he saw Isaac and Gabbi for the first time, as if they had been expected. At the time Isaac was happy to brush it off as the confused mind of a poor child who was bound by fear and horror, but now he wasn't so sure.

"We can try and call them back."

"Is that very fair though? I mean they've been through a lot, shouldn't we just let them rest?"

"Yes I know." Isaac's tone was harsh. He was well aware of the moral ambiguity of what they were about to do. He took a deep breath. "I'm sorry.

It's just they could have some information and right now we need every bit of information we can gather." He pulled Gabbi in for a quick hug as they walked and she squeezed back. "Besides we'll only need them for a minute, and they did say they were forever in our debt. Although that could just be one of those things you say but never really mean. Well, we'll see." He crossed his fingers inside his coat pocket. They needed this to work.

Although some of the old hospital had been demolished in the six months they'd been away, the library building remained standing - with what Isaac suspected was local legend keeping it haunted now rather than actual ghosts or demons. Isaac forced the front door open with his shoulder and they slipped inside. The air was damp and stale. Despite the knowledge that the building no longer harboured anything dark or evil the place still gave him the creeps. He looked across at Gabbi who had just switched on a torch. By the light it gave out he could see her face was full of fear too.

Isaac switched on his own torch. "Come on," he said, motioning towards the wrought iron staircase. "Up we go." The main library was up on the first floor, the ground floor being offices and a small examination room. It was a vast, long room that ran the entire length of the building and as Isaac followed the beam of torchlight from the top of the stairs out into the library he could see it hadn't changed at all. The room was made up of different sections - reading corners and play areas, places which should have felt safe and happy but instead looked sad, empty and unnerving. One play area was filled with old dolls, mostly the porcelain kind, which lay tattered and broken all over the floor. Isaac remembered what had happened in that section the last time they were here and shuddered.

"What is it?" Gabbi asked, noticing his movement.

"Oh, nothing, just remembering, you know."

She nodded. "Well let's make this quick then. How do we get in touch with them?"

"I brought this. Ordered it off the internet last week, thought it might come in handy." Isaac announced, pulling an electro-magnetic field meter from his bag.

"Isn't that one of those ghost detector things?"

"Not quite ghost detector, I think a 'something that is possibly supernatural but maybe not detector' might be more accurate," he said with a smile. "But it's better than nothing."

"So how does it work?"

"Everything on earth has an electro-magnetic field around it. Usually it's really weak, with only actual electrical stuff giving off any major readings. Stand under an electricity pylon and this thing would go bananas. Supernatural stuff also seems to give off some kind of electro-magnetic field, like it's disturbing the atmosphere. So the reading on the meter should stay fairly constant most of the time unless it gets close to something electrical or something hopefully supernatural. It's all a bit of pseudo-science but it's better than a poke in the eye with a sharp stick."

"Most things are." Gabbi said in agreement. "Unless you had two sharp sticks, then I suppose a poke in one eye with a sharp stick would be better than a poke in both eyes with two sharp sticks."

Isaac looked at her and smiled. "You know I've used that expression countless times and you're the first person to actually try and think of something that isn't better than a poke in the eye with a sharp stick."

"That's me!" Gabbi said proudly, "Thinking outside the box." She made large box shape with her arms as she spoke. "So anyway, using the possible ghost detector we just have to find the bit of the room with nothing electrical around and which causes it to fluctuate and then hope that we can call the children from there right?"

"Got it in one." Isaac smiled again and she smiled back. Gabbi was smart, she picked up on things quickly. They headed off down the middle of the room, passing stacks of books and piles of old paper. There was a table off to the right with wax crayons and sheets of old drawing paper on it. Some of the sheets had the remains of wax drawings scribbled on them. Isaac's curiosity got the better of him and he went over to look - the last visit had been so hair-raising he hadn't had time to be inquisitive. Most of the sheets were of cats or stick people, but one of them had a dark shape coloured in black with red eyes drawn violently in the centre of it. Isaac held the paper up to the torch. There was child-like writing at the bottom of the page. "Monster in the dark." Isaac read it out aloud and felt a shiver run down his spine. He glanced across at Gabbi who also looked perturbed. They stared at each other for a long moment, communicating fear with their eyes.

CRASH

They both physically jumped and Gabbi screamed a little. She swung the torch over in the direction of the noise, which had come from back down near the stairs. A large rat ran across through the beam of light, its shadow magnified horrifically on the wall behind. Isaac breathed an audible sigh of relief and they both continued deeper into the library. About halfway down the room, the electro-magnetic field meter suddenly started fluctuating wildly. The needle was flickering at the very end of the scale.

"I'd say we've found our spot." Isaac said.

Gabbi came and looked at the meter for herself. "Oh do you think so?" she said, sarcastically, eyebrows raised. Isaac laughed a little before getting three large candles out of his bag. "Blimey!" cried Gabbi, "How much stuff can you fit in that bag?"

"I'll fit you in it in a minute if you don't stop being cheeky!" he shot back at her, grinning briefly. He placed the candles out so they formed a triangle around the spot which caused the fluctuations and then proceeded to fish a lighter out from his coat pocket. Gabbi shone the torch around the room as he lit the candles.

"You know it will be a shame when they demolish this place. It'd be so nice if they converted it and made it into flats, this ceiling is really rather impressive you know."

"Well I'll let you buy one before I do if it's all the same to you. After what I've seen here I don't really fancy hanging around permanently." Isaac said as he shuffled on his knees to the last candle.

"I'm not saying I'd live here, obviously," Gabbi replied. "But it'd be nice for other people."

"I'm sure it would. But I think this whole area has the destiny of being a swimming pool and leisure centre." Isaac got up off his knees and dusted his trousers down with his hands. The candlelight flickered and danced, illuminating the space with a soft warm glow.

"Ooh a swimming pool, sounds great! I'm glad they're knocking this spooky place down now." Isaac gave a little laugh at Gabbi's ability to change her opinion so quickly, and she laughed for a moment too. It was a comfort to find something funny in such a dark and dismal place.

"Right," Isaac said, when the grim atmosphere had once more sucked all the humour from the air. "Let's see if we can make contact." He stood at the edge of the triangle with his arms outstretched into it. Gabbi stood a few steps behind him. Although he couldn't see her, he could still feel that she was there with him, which was of great help - conjuring spirits alone was not something he enjoyed doing. "We ask a favour of the Lord and of the guardian of the gate," Isaac began, his words cutting the deathly silence of the place like a knife. "We ask that two children once passed might return once more. That if they are willing they might come and speak to us once more as we speak to one another. We mean them no harm and we have no ill intent. Our purpose is the truth. Please, please let them pass!"

There was no flash or crash or any disturbance of the air. It seemed that nothing had happened. Isaac sighed. He had really hoped that it would have worked. He turned away and was surprised when he felt something tugging on his trousers. He gasped in shock and turned back round to see that it was indeed the two children - they were standing there in the triangle, looking exactly as they had when he had last seen them. It had worked! They both stood there, frozen in time at five years of age. The little boy had his arm outstretched, his little hand clinging to the denim around Isaac's knee. He had scruffy blond hair and was wearing a shirt, tie and shorts with long socks that went up to his knees. The little girl stood beside him with her long curly blonde hair, wearing a plain grey dress. She stared up at Isaac with her wide eyes. Isaac beckoned Gabbi forwards. It was strange, he knew they were dead but he felt absolutely no fear whatsoever. They were, after all, still children and they were probably more scared themselves. He crouched down in front of them.

"Please sir," begged the little boy, "we were told you wished to speak with us."

"Yes John that's right," said Isaac, smiling. "Thank you so much for coming. Hello Jessica!" The little girl waved with one hand and sucked her thumb with the other.

Gabbi crouched down beside Isaac. "Do you remember us?" she asked.

"Yes miss we remember you!" cried Jessica after she removed her thumb from her mouth. "You saved us!"

"You saved us from the nightmare man!" exclaimed John.

"That's right." Isaac said, keeping his voice calm and soft. "I'm so sorry we had to call you here, but we need your help."

"We'd like to help you sir," said John bravely, "very much we would. But please, please hurry, we're afraid in this place." He reached out and held Jessica's hand, who was starting to look scared and had put her thumb back in her mouth.

"What are you afraid of?" asked Gabbi, "The nightmare man has gone away."

"Yes but we're still afraid." John looked visibly frightened.

"Of what John?"

"The dark. Please be quick we're afraid of the dark."

Isaac smiled warmly. "But it's okay," he began, "we're here and we won't let anything happen to you. The dark can't hurt you. I promise."

"It can." John stared deep into Isaac's eyes and for the first time Isaac felt a twinge of fear in his stomach. "It can. Isaac Jacobs. And it can get so dark it will never ever be light again."

The fear in Isaac's stomach swelled. "What do you mean?"

"Tell us how we can help you!" squeaked Jessica. Both children ignored Isaac's question. "Tell us quickly, we have to go soon!"

"It's about me and Isaac, and our other friends." Gabbi started. "Are we meant to all be together like we are? Were Isaac and I meant to meet the night we saved you?"

"We've already helped you with this!" cried John, as if it were an obvious fact.

"How?" Isaac asked, growing thin on patience. He was getting the impression that these dead children knew much more than they were saying. "What do you mean?"

"We've helped you already by bringing you together."

"So we are meant to be together, all of us? And it was you who brought us together?"

"You all need to be together. Something is coming. You'll want to run and hide, and if you were alone it would be ever so scary!"

"And it was you who brought us together?"

"We were told to. We do as we're told. Good children who do as they're told get pudding."

- 63 -

"Who told you to?"

"Was it God?" asked Gabbi

"Higher frequencies." The words seemed alien coming from a five-year-old's mouth.

"Yes but what does that mean?" Isaac asked. He needed to know more. "And what's coming? What will we need to run and hide from?"

"You all need to be together. Both of you. All of you."

"Can't you tell us more?" Isaac pleaded. "I mean thanks and everything but you're being a bit enigmatic."

"I'm sorry Isaac Jacobs, we can't." John looked towards the ceiling for a moment. "And we have to go. We don't belong here anymore."

Jessica let go of John's hand and tottered over to Gabbi. "You will always be our guardian angel Gabbi Gurtpasha." she said, smiling.

"Thank you," replied Gabbi, smiling back. "Safe journey."

With that the two children vanished, disappearing as quickly as they had appeared, blowing out the candles in their wake.

"Bugger." cursed Isaac, fumbling on the floor for the torch which had been switched off. Once he had found it they headed for the exit.

"So what does that all mean then?" Gabbi asked as they stepped slowly down the spiral staircase. "We are supposed to all be together? There is some purpose around it all?"

"Seems like it," Isaac replied. "I mean they were a bit sketchy with the details but then spirit types always are. From what they said though it certainly seems that we're meant to be together."

"Which is good right?"

"Yeah," Isaac said in an optimistic tone as the reached the bottom of the stairs. "If we're meant to be together then that gives me confidence that if something bad turns up we have half a shot at defeating it." He considered his words for a moment. "All the same though, we probably shouldn't lie back on our laurels and get too cocky about it. Better to underestimate and be happily surprised than overestimate and be crushingly disappointed, or, you know, dead."

Chapter Twelve

When they got home that night everyone was sitting in silence on the sofa. There was a sudden flurry of questions and comments from everyone as they entered.

"Where have you been?"

"Are you okay?"

"We were worried!"

"Did you get attacked?"

Everybody stared at them, eyes moving from Gabbi to Isaac and then back to Gabbi again.

"I need a cup of tea." remarked Gabbi, proceeding to make her way into the kitchen.

"Can you make me one too?" asked Isaac, collapsing on the sofa next to Billie.

"Yeah sure darling."

"So?" asked Billie, eyebrows raised in anticipation.

Isaac looked across the room to see Laura and Ben both keenly staring at him, awaiting a response. Isaac began the story of the night, trying not to miss anything out. Gabbi brought the tea in just as he got the bit about summoning the children, which meant that she then took over and told the majority of the rest herself. Isaac didn't mind this in the least, it gave him some alone time with his tea.

"So we're all meant to be together? As we are now?" asked Ben, his face lit up with a big grin. Apparently he liked the idea. "That's awesome!"

Isaac could see in Laura's eyes that she felt much like he did - that although it was good news they shouldn't rely on it to get them through whatever might be coming.

When she opened her mouth to speak she confirmed that thought. "Yeah it's good, I mean it's great if we know that this is where we're meant to be, but I don't think we should take this as a sign of victory or something. I mean I'm sure everyone has some destiny in their lives, it doesn't necessarily single us out as being really special."

"No I know," agreed Ben. "But it's still good news I think. Makes you feel like a part of the universe or something."

Laura pulled a funny face and Isaac laughed.

"I'm surprised you're so into this Ben," he began, "usually you're the most sceptical about everything!"

Ben laughed too. "Yeah I know. I dunno, I guess destiny is something I believe in a bit. I actually believe in quite a lot, you'd be surprised!" he said with a chuckle.

"Loch Ness Monster?" probed Isaac.

"Nah that's just a log or a seal or something mate." Ben answered, still laughing.

"I think it's good news too," said Billie, who hadn't said anything on the subject yet. "But I agree with Laura and Isaac, we shouldn't let it get to our heads or anything. Pride comes before a fall!" she warned with a smile and a wag of a finger.

"Agreed." confirmed Isaac. "So we move on as best we can, straight forward into whatever badness is coming with just a slight bit of optimism that we're all meant to be here together." He drained what was left of his tea. "Right, I'm exhausted, time for a bath."

Isaac spent over an hour in the bath. It was one of those corner baths with Jacuzzi jets in it - incredibly rare in an old terraced house such as the house was. But then having an architect as a dad certainly meant that he got the nicest house available, and also of course it added weight to his theory of the house being a guilt payment for years of semi-absent parenting.

They'd probably be enjoying a glass of wine by the fire now in their Tuscany villa. It was just outside of Florence in the hilltop town of Fiesole. A beautiful setting. His mum had included several photos in her Christmas letter to Isaac, although that had read more like a generic news update than a personal letter a parent would send to a child. Isaac sighed audibly. Those dead children had been orphans. He felt like he might as well call himself one too and be done with it. He shook his head, determined not to let these depressing thoughts infect him. If he was being brutally honest with himself, his parents absence didn't really bother him most of the time, but he knew it played somewhere in his subconscious.

He closed his eyes and sank down deeper into the water, shifting his thoughts on towards happier places. He found himself thinking about the

Christmas that had just passed. It had been wonderful. Everyone stayed in Monks-Lantern in the house, either because their parents were away or in Billie's case because a visit to the parents house wasn't exactly an enjoyable thought. So they all stayed together and had a really nice Christmas of their own with Christmas dinner, crackers, presents, Christmas movies and a real tree that had been far too big for the living room but Billie and Gabbi insisted on having it anyway. Gabbi did go and visit her dad on Boxing Day as he didn't live far away, but they were all there together on the twenty fifth. It had been so special. Isaac thought hopefully for a moment about the Christmas to come, but then his hope turned sour. With all the predictions of bad things on the way he couldn't help but worry what state they would be in to celebrate Christmas, and even who would be around to celebrate it. A few to lose - that's what Pete said.

Isaac opened his eyes and the world of the here and now came flooding back in. The water in the bath seemed to have suddenly turned very cold and was no longer relaxing to sit in, so Isaac pulled the plug, got up, grabbed a towel and started drying himself furiously, the water on his body seemed to turn to ice as soon as it hit the cold air of the bathroom.

Once he was dry enough not to leave puddles of water on the carpet on the way back to his room he wrapped the towel around his waist and headed out and down the stairs, flicking on the central heating on the way. When he got to his room he closed the door behind him and was preparing to drop his towel when he saw that Ben was lying on the bed, staring absent-mindedly at the ceiling. Isaac was glad he had the sense to properly look round his room before dropping his towel on instinct as he entered the room. He coughed loudly.

Ben looked across at him. "Alright?" he asked nonchalantly.

"Yes I'm fine thanks. Naked under a towel but fine."

"Do you think I'm stupid for believing in destiny?"

"No." Isaac came and sat down next to Ben on the bed, even though he was still slightly damp. "No. No I don't."

"It's just people laughed when I said about it earlier."

"But they weren't being serious or trying to be mean. It's like I said, you are so sceptical about a lot of things a lot of the time that it was just so out of character what you said about destiny. It was just a bit unexpected I guess, I suppose people were a little shocked."

"I guess." Ben still sounded glum.

"We weren't laughing at you, honestly, I promise you. Everyone here respects everyone's beliefs. We're your friends, why would we want to intentionally hurt your feelings?"

"Yeah I know mate. I know. I know it was all just a bit of nonsense banter type stuff. It's just -"

"Just what?"

"My sister. She believed in destiny. In a big way. She was one of those new-age types you know? Scented candles and crystals all round her room. Purple dream-catcher in the window."

"Oh Ben I'm sorry -"

"And when she was in the hospice, in the last days before the tumour - I mean, before she died, she said that she was sure I was destined for great things. So when you and Gabbi came back with news that something else had actually said we are all meant to be here together, well, it was nice. It was like Susie was right."

"I'm sure she is right. Okay? I'm sure she is." Isaac put a hand on Ben's shoulder. "You don't talk about this much."

"None of us talk about anything much. Not really. When was the last time you spoke in depth about your friends from before? Or when did Billie last speak about her parents being horrible to her?"

Isaac couldn't think of anything to say. Ben was right.

"No-one wants to talk about the bad stuff. We all just want to keep going with our lives, not forgetting about it but just keeping it quiet at the back of our minds, to keep it there as a reminder to carry on trying to make a difference. That's what you said to me when we first spoke. That we can all make a difference."

"I really believe that we can."

"Then that's what we'll do then dude. My sister thinks that we can, and now two dead kids think that we can." They both smiled and laughed slightly. Ben took Isaac's hand off of his shoulder and held it for a moment, squeezing it ever so slightly. Then he stood up abruptly. "Right," he said in a much more upbeat tone. "So nothing even remotely soppy or gay happened here. It was all very straight and manly."

Isaac laughed. "Yes, definitely. Do you want to talk about football or boobs to make yourself feel even better? You know I won't have a clue but I can nod in the right places."

Ben laughed too. "Nah you're alright mate. And please don't ever say boobs again. Sorry about the interruption by the way." he said, gesturing towards Isaac's towel.

"It's fine, really. Nothing you haven't seen before right? Loads of wet naked men in the football team!" Isaac said with a laugh.

"Ergh don't make it sound all disgusting and sexy like that you big homo!" Ben said, trying to sound serious but unable to hide his own laughter. "Bloody gays."

"Homophobe!" Isaac laughed before trying to turn serious. "But really, it's fine. Please, please come and talk to me whenever you need to. You know you can right?"

"I do. And likewise man, whatever you need, whenever." Ben smiled warmly.

"Thanks. Oh and I meant to ask, how was the exam?"

"Don't ask."

"That bad?"

"I completely and utterly screwed it up."

"Well you never know -"

"Yeah, I do. Anyway, I think there's probably some dodgy show about lap dancers on TV this time of night, so I'm going to go and be a pervert. Night mate."

"Goodnight Ben, sleep -"

It was too late. He'd gone.

Chapter Thirteen

Several more quiet weeks passed and the mid-march weather brought some spring sunshine with it which was a pleasing change to the bleak weather that January and February had presented.

Although Isaac and indeed the entire group were intensely interested and worried by everything that had happened and everything they had heard and found out, they were finding it difficult to get a lead that would take them somewhere further. Every couple of days they all sat down together and went over what they knew, what Pete had told them, what the children had told Gabbi and Isaac and what they had overheard at the police station. But there was never anything new.

Then finally after nearly three weeks there was some excitement when Billie rushed into the kitchen one Thursday morning. Isaac and Gabbi were sitting against the worktop eating breakfast and they both nearly choked on their cereal when Billie thundered in with the local paper in her hand, waving it about furiously.

"Another disappearance!" she shouted.

"That's the second one this month right?" Isaac asked after swallowing a mouthful of cereal and milk. There had been one earlier in March, about a week after the events at the library.

"Yep," Gabbi confirmed. "So if it's still two a month then that's it until April now."

Isaac read the brief report in the newspaper. It was like all the others, completely lacking in concern and alarm. This time it was a Chinese girl who had come over for a visit before coming to study at the university the following year. The article didn't mention anything about her parents. They never did.

Isaac groaned. "Crap." he cursed. "I feel so useless and stupid!"

"Isaac darling you can't blame yourself." said Gabbi.

"She's right," Billie agreed. "We all feel bad about it, but we can't do anything."

"But that's the annoying thing!" Isaac said, "We know about these disappearances and we know that something bad is meant to be happening. But we can't seem to do anything with that information. The police are crooked for all we know and we don't have enough leads to get us anywhere helpful!" He threw his spoon back in the bowl. Some of the milk splashed out and made small puddle on the worktop.

"I know." Gabbi said. "I know."

Billie stroked his back. "We'll figure it all out Isaac," she said. "Remember after Pete was killed I was upset and you told me that we'd make it right. And we will."

Isaac didn't tell her that he cried his eyes out that night too. "Yeah. Yeah you're right. It's just frustrating I guess. I just wish there was some way we could -" An idea hit him mid-sentence. "That's it!"

"What's it?" Gabbi sounded confused.

"Pete was the only one who seems to have known something about what's going on so far right?"

"Yes but -"

"Then we go and ask him!"

"But he's dead Isaac." Billie said nervously.

"I know that. But those children were dead and we spoke to them."

Gabbi shook her head. "That was different though, they had been ghosts for so long in that place that there was a shot we could contact them," she said. "And even that was a long shot, to be honest with you I'm surprised it worked."

"Pete was never a ghost, he died and moved on." Billie said.

"We don't know that. Maybe he didn't move on. And even if he did we could call him back."

"Isaac-"

Gabbi sounded sympathetic but Isaac didn't want to know."This could work Gabbi!"

"I think you're just getting excited because you feel bad about being helpless."

"But we have to try. We have to. Otherwise we'll just keep sitting here, the disappearances will continue and this horribly bad thing will come and we'll have no way to fight it." Isaac stood up from sitting on one of the stools and began pacing around the kitchen. "Please guys. Please we have to try."

Gabbi and Billie exchanged uncertain looks.

"Okay." Gabbi said with a smile. "Okay we'll try."

That evening they all headed out for Pete's flat except for Laura who argued that since she didn't go before it might be more profitable if she didn't go this time either. Some ghosts only appear before those who they have seen before or have known in life. Isaac felt determined as he strode through town with the others, heading towards Kettle Lane. This would work. He was sure of it. It was the only possible way that he could see they would be able to move forward with anything. Pete had known something and he had been about to tell them when he was killed. They had to find out what that something was!

Nothing much had changed in Kettle Lane since they were there a month ago. The door to Pete's flat was unlocked as it always used to be, and it was with slight trepidation that Isaac stepped over the threshold. As certain as he was that this could get them the information they needed, he was still nervous, just as he had been at the library. He had asked Gabbi to do the actual summoning this time but she refused on the grounds that if Isaac felt so strongly about this working then maybe he is supposed to do it, that maybe it needs to be him in order for it to work. Isaac flicked on the lights for the stairs and landing before proceeding to head up and into the flat itself. They found Pete's flat empty and the body, thankfully, had been removed, although by whom they couldn't be certain. Isaac guessed that it hadn't been by anyone friendly.

He didn't waste any time in getting started. "He died over by the window so I guess that's a good place to set up." he surmised as soon as they were all inside the flat. Nobody really replied, but Isaac took the candles out of his bag and started setting them out regardless.

Ben coughed uncertainly.

"What?" Isaac asked. "What's wrong?"

Ben looked reluctant to speak, but he did anyway. "What if this goes wrong?"

"Wrong how?"

"I don't know, like what if he isn't the same?"

"He will be." Isaac looked at Gabbi and Billie and saw they looked a little worried too. "It'll be fine, I promise. Better than a poke in the eye with a sharp stick and all that." He bent over and lit the three candles with a lighter from his pocket and before anyone else could protest he outstretched his arms and started the incantation. "We ask a favour of the Lord and of the guardian of the gate. We ask that a man once passed might return once more. That if he is willing he might come and speak to us once more as we speak to one another. We mean them no harm and we have no ill intent. Our purpose is the truth. Please let him pass!"

Just like in the library with the children, there was no immediate sign or signal to say that anything had happened. But then there was something, a kind of atmosphere, like a sense in the air. A feeling. A bad feeling.

"What's gone wrong?" Billie chirped, obviously picking up on what Isaac had just felt. He felt the first pang of why didn't I listen to them go through his head.

Ben furrowed his brow. "It didn't work?"

"These things are never a hundred per cent sure to work." Gabbi said, sounding as though she too was worried by something but didn't want to admit it. "Maybe it's a sign that we weren't meant to speak to him."

"But it feels like something's wrong here." Billie insisted. "I'm getting the same feeling I got back in my parents house when the bad thing was there. Isaac I'm right aren't I? Something's wrong here."

Isaac hadn't spoken so far because he wasn't sure of what to say, and because he was ridden with shame about having been so sure that this would work and ignoring the pleas of his friends. Now he had to say something though. "I think it worked," he said, licking his dry lips in anxiousness. "I think something's here with us."

"I can't see anything." Ben said, looking about the room.

Just at that moment, Isaac's eyes fell upon something that sent an immediate cold chill down his spine and caused his stomach to tighten and twist into a knot.

"Look a bit closer." Isaac muttered, indicating with his eyes to the spot behind Ben and the others.

They all immediately looked as though they really didn't want to turn round and it was with great cautiousness that they slowly turned their heads - as though they were expecting some terrifying monster to be standing right behind them.

"I can't see anything." Gabbi said in a whisper.

Isaac offered some clarification. "The door." he said. "Look at the door."

The door was facing Isaac but behind the others, and you couldn't see much of it in detail as it was so gloomy in the flat. The most obvious thing about it really was the thin strip of light that shone underneath it from the landing on the other side.

Billie physically jumped back in terror. "Oh god!" She must have seen it.

"Isaac mate, much as I'm enjoying the world's scariest game of eye-spy, do you think you could give me a clue?" Ben was still looking at the door along with Gabbi.

"Look underneath," Billie said, standing back by Isaac, "Look in the gap underneath!"

"Oh!" Gabbi said quickly, her voice edged with fear.

A split second later and Ben must have seen it too as he let out a small yell of surprise. "Shit!"

"What's the scariest thing you can see underneath a door when you know you're alone in the building?" Isaac asked rhetorically as he stepped forwards and stood next to Ben. "A pair of shoes."

Clear and distinct in the tiny gap underneath the closed door were two dark shapes - two dark shoe shapes.

"Is it Pete?" Billie asked. "Is that him on the other side of the door?"

"Why doesn't he just come in?" Ben whispered. "Should we call out?"

"No." Gabbi said. "I don't know. Isaac?"

Isaac's mind was racing, heart thumping. What if it was Pete? What if he needed their help? But was still that feeling inside all the time - something had gone wrong. "We should stay quiet for a minute I think."

"Is it Pete though?" Billie asked.

"I don't know." Isaac said. "I'm sorry, I shouldn't have done this. We should blow out the candles and send him or it back."

"Wait!" Billie cried quietly, "What if that is him? What if he needs our help?"

"You were sure something had gone wrong a minute ago." Isaac said, feeling just as confused himself as Billie clearly was.

"Yeah, but what if the thing that went wrong is in here with us, and that's Pete stuck out on the landing? What if something nasty came through with him and it's trapped him out there? It could be torturing him!"

Ben cut in before Billie could continue. "I agree with Isaac, I think we should blow out the candles and leave. This is all getting very Monkey's Paw now and I don't like it." Ben looked at Isaac for him to agree.

Isaac was lost in his thoughts, he'd only half heard Ben. Who was on the other side of that door?

"Isaac?"

Ben's voice called him back to reality. "Sorry. Yes, yes we should blow the candles out now I think." Isaac couldn't take his eyes off of the door, he felt transfixed by it. "Definitely, now." He still didn't move to blow out the candles. "Gabbi? What do you think?"

"I don't know. If that is Pete and he needs our help like Billie said then I hate the thought of sending him back. He might be depending on us. But I can feel that uncertain feeling in the air, like there's something not quite right." Gabbi too looked transfixed by the door. "Sorry, I wasn't much help there really was I?"

Isaac found himself stepping forwards, towards the door. "We need to know for sure." He edged closer and closer, hearing his heart beating loudly in his chest and hearing too the audible nervous breathing of his friends behind him. He kept on inching forwards, not taking his eyes off of the shoe shapes in the gap underneath. They stayed unmoving. Within moments he was right up against the door so that it almost touched his nose. Nobody spoke, nobody seemed to even dare breathe now. All was silent. Slowly, as though any sudden movement might trigger some kind of alarm, he turned his head to one side and gingerly leant forwards and placed an ear against the cool white surface of the door.

Then he listened. He focused every bit of mental energy had into listening, straining to hear anything from the figure standing just a couple of inches away behind the door. He shut his eyes, blocking out sight in case it interfered with hearing. He listened, listened, listened, staying quiet for what seemed like ages but was probably only a few seconds. Then he heard it. He jumped inside, but he didn't make any movement physically. He felt his blood chill and goose pimples pop up all over his arms and legs. Three words being whispered so softly and quietly it was impossible to tell who was saying them, but also so intently and purposefully that Isaac knew that whoever they were they meant every syllable.

"Let me in."

"Pete?" Isaac whispered in a voice as tiny as the one from the other side. "Pete is that you?"

"Let me in."

"I can't - I don't know, I need to know if that's you Pete!"

"Let me in."

"If you need help, we'll help I promise. But I need to know if that's you or not!"

"Let me in."

"Is that all you can say? Maybe it is you, maybe Billie's right and something's trapping you or affecting you somehow. Is that right? Just say yes, just say yes and I'll help you I promise. Please."

"Let me in."

"Please Pete, help me here. I'm stuck okay? You were the only one who knew anything, we need you. So please, please tell me it's you because if it's not and you're someone or something else then you shouldn't be here - and if I take a risk and open the door and let you in then what then? You could be some murderous demon who corrupted the ritual I used or the spirit of a mad axe murderer from years ago. If I let you in you could hurt people, you could hurt us." Isaac paused and sighed quietly. "I want it to be you, I really want it to be you. I need it to be you because I need help." Isaac stopped whispering, opened his eyes and turned his head from the door. He found the others all looking at him anxiously. He looked back at them and shook his head and shrugged a little before walking back towards them from the door.

"Anything?" Gabbi asked.

"It wants to be let in, whatever or whoever it is."

"It spoke?"

"Yes, but it was so quiet and indistinctive. It could have been Pete, could have been a demon, could have been Doris from the canteen at uni for all I could tell." Isaac sighed. "All it kept saying was let me in. Over and over."

Billie spoke up. "So do we let him in or not? Maybe we should."

Ben frowned. "Should?" He didn't sound impressed. "Don't you mean shouldn't? This couldn't have trap written on it more if I'd taken a pen myself and written trap a million times on all the walls. Isaac, you can't open that door mate. None of us can. It's too risky."

Isaac felt conflicted inside. He wanted it to be Pete so badly, he wanted Pete's help. But then there was that strange feeling of something having gone wrong - but then maybe that was just because of the whole shoes under the door thing which was quite un-nerving whether it was Pete or not. He had a feeling inside, a feeling of trapped hope ready to be set free at the prospect of it really being Pete and him being able to help them. They needed to know what he was going to tell them just before he was killed! But of course if it wasn't Pete then maybe that's what the thing was counting on - them wanting it to be him. Counting on them being desperate, on them coming to the conclusion that the only way to know for sure would be to open the door - and then of course it could all be too late. On the other hand though, it could be him. The answers they needed could be but the pull of a door handle away. It was cyclical confusion going round and round. He was still torn in two as he found himself starting to move forwards towards the door again.

"What are you doing?" Billie asked nervously.

"I think I'm going to open the door." He didn't fully believe his own words, there was still an internal battle going on inside him as to what to do but his body seemed to have sided with the part of him that wanted to open the door.

"You can't!" Ben said quietly but hotly. "Please, think about this!"

"We have to be sure Ben!" Isaac shot back. "If that's Pete then he has information that we need. It's as simple as that, we need that info."

Ben looked a little exasperated. "Gabbi, Billie? Tell him, please."

Gabbi looked at Isaac when she spoke. "I trust him. He'll make the right choice, and whatever choice that is we'll deal with the consequences together."

"This isn't about trust, I trust him! This is about what's on the other side of that door and I don't think it's Pete."

"I think it might be." Isaac said, still not sure if he believed himself. He was very close to the door once more. "I can just open it a crack and if it isn't Pete I'll give you the nod and you can blow out the candles."

"Isaac -"

Isaac held a hand up the silence Ben and reached for the handle. He gripped it with his left hand, it felt cool and a little clammy to the touch. Again there was the tense silence from behind, and again he heard the faint whispered plea from the other side of the door. Isaac took a deep breath and braced himself to push down on the handle - it was now or never. He felt his friends' eyes burning into the back of him. Don't do it. Do it. Maybe do it.

"Let me in."

Isaac bit his bottom lip and went to push down on the handle. His arm didn't move. He stood there tensed, ready to push in an instant but he didn't. He couldn't. Ben was right. Whatever or whoever it was on the other side of the door, it felt wrong. Even if it was Pete it felt wrong. He released his grip on the handle and turned back to his friends.

Ben looked like he was about to collapse with relief, Billie smiled even though she too had thought it might have been Pete, and Gabbi smiled and nodded in support, displaying very subtle signs of relief herself.

Isaac walked in silence to the candles, knelt down and blew them out in three quick puffs. He looked over his shoulder to the door - the feet were gone.

A few minutes later they left the flat, finding nothing but empty air on the other side of the door as the exited. On the walk home the girls went off in front a little bit, leaving Isaac walking side by side with Ben.

"You should be proud of yourself mate." Ben said casually.

"I should be?" Isaac chuckled a little. It had all been a bit of a mess really, not one of his proudest moments. "We're no better off than we were before and I did something which, looking back on it, was pretty reckless. And if I'd opened the door it would have been even more reckless."

"But you chose not to. I know I was yelling and squawking at you but I bet that was a bloody hard decision to make, to not open the door. You put aside what you wanted to do and you realised what you needed to do, or, more accurately, needed to not do. That's what good leaders do."

Isaac wafted a hand at Ben dismissively. "I'm not a leader."

"Yes you are! You brought us all together, you inspired us to help. You're a leader because we follow you." Ben's words were unexpectedly touching. "I follow you."

"I nearly messed up tonight though."

"Which is why you have amazing people like me to call you out when you're making a mistake. And the girls of course, but you know I'm better." Ben laughed.

"Thanks Ben." Isaac said, smiling. He felt a little better about the evening now.

"And one more thing - we need to stop having these touching conversations man."

"Yeah I know." Isaac smiled at Ben. They didn't always see eye to eye but he was always there for him. "Permission to hug?"

Ben considered the request for a moment. "Meh. Granted." He grinned and they embraced for a moment.

"Hey gays!" called Billie from up ahead of them, "Stop making out and get a move on! I'm cold and neither me nor Gabbi have house keys on us!"

Isaac and Ben sighed and ran to catch up with the girls. Within ten minutes they were home. Once through the front door they all stood in the hallway to take off their coats and shoes, and whilst they were doing that Laura came rushing out of the living room to meet them. Isaac saw immediately that her face looked serious. Something had happened.

Chapter Fourteen

"Isaac," she began, her voice serious and a little shakey.

Isaac's stomach turned over yet again that night. Please, please, he couldn't handle any more bad news today.

"I didn't know whether to call you or not, but something-"

"Hello Isaac." A light, husky yet manly voice.

Isaac's stomach tightened. He knew the voice even before he'd looked up. It had changed slightly but he still knew it regardless. Isaac looked up from Laura's face and towards the living room door where the figure stood. "Tom." he muttered in disbelief. His exterior must have looked calm enough but inside every organ was churning, his brain felt like it was on fire and his heart was beating faster and louder than he could ever remember it beating. He felt worse now than he had done in a long time.

Tom's face was rigid and stern looking, no sign of friendship. "It's been a long time. Four years? Five?"

Isaac ignored his question and just about managed to ask one of his own. "What are you doing here?" It was the only thing he could think of to say.

"I'm here to help, believe it or not. You're in trouble and I've come to save you. Isn't that what I do?" Tom gave a small smile, barely detectable and then walked back into the living room. All other eyes turned to Isaac. This was going to be a long night.

A few minutes later and everyone had rather awkwardly introduced themselves. Isaac had then immediately asked Tom for a few moments alone outside before they started talking as a group. He had questions and he was sure Tom would have questions too. The garden was dark but the glow from the house afforded them enough light to see by. Isaac sat down gingerly in a plastic garden chair that appeared to be growing out of the tangled mess of weeds and grass. He sat as if the chair might break, but in reality he was more worried that he would break. Tom appearing out of the blue was a complete shock, in fact to call it a shock was a colossal understatement. He felt more than a bit queasy inside, in fact he felt as though he would be able to be physically sick without too much encouragement. Tom sat down on another chair next to him. They both stared up at the dark night sky for a moment. It was a starless night.

Despite his nerves Isaac spoke first. "You haven't changed much." He looked across at Tom. He still had a healthily tanned face, but his short hair had grown a little longer, and was brushed across into a scruffy side parting. It did suit him however. He also had some light stubble visible on his jaw and chin. Again, like the hair, it suited him.

"Haven't I?"

"I'm sorry." Isaac verbalised the apology that had been living in his mind for the last five years. It felt good to say it, but it didn't give him peace. He knew he'd never have complete peace from that night.

"About what?"

Isaac cringed at the thought of having to spell it out. "About what happened that night."

"You mean the night when you completely insulted me, rejected me and then left me and our friends to die?"

Isaac grimaced at the bluntness of Tom's words. "I'm sorry." It was all he could say.

"I know you are."

Isaac thought it would be a good idea to steer the conversation away from their last encounter. "So," he began, attempting to sound a little lighter. "What have you been doing?"

"I moved to Ireland, got some way off distant family over there. I met some other people like me, like us. Like our group used to be. Like you seem to have here now." Tom looked back round towards the house.

"Do you work?"

"Ahh, nice of you to just assume I didn't make it to university."

"I wasn't - its just you were never very keen at school, I never had you pegged for a student life."

"Well I guess you were right because I never did go to university. You were always the brain box." Tom looked across and they shared a smile for the first time in years. "I got myself a job in a book store, second hand books, really interesting. That's where I met Hope."

"Girlfriend?!" Isaac was stunned.

"No you daft twat, you do remember what our last argument was about don't you?"

"Yeah that's why I was shocked. Just a friend then?"

"A very good friend. She's the reason I'm here." Tom leant forwards in his chair. "It seems, Isaac, that something bad is happening. And you're right in the thick of it."

"When did he turn up?" Billie asked Laura as they stood in the kitchen and tried to spy on Isaac and Tom.

"About twenty minutes before you got back. The most awkward twenty minutes of my life." Laura said, stirring the milk into her tea.

"Old love interest?"

"He wouldn't say, wouldn't say much of anything. Only that he'd come to help and that he knows Isaac from way back. Come to think of it, we've never spoken much in detail about Isaac's past. Only that his friends got killed by that demon."

"Well whoever he is he'd better come in soon and tell us whatever he knows. I'm a nervous wreck after today. Tea will make me feel a bit better though." Billie said, smiling and picking up the mug of tea that Laura had just made.

"Yeah what happened?"

"We did the ritual thing, but we don't know what we summoned. It could have been Pete, could have been some crazy ghost. All we could see were shoes under the door." Billie said spookily.

Laura's eyes opened wide. "Sounds scary!"

"Yeah it was. Isaac was about to open the door at let it in but he didn't which was probably the right thing to do. I felt bad for him, I think he was just feeling so crappy about not doing anything that he was ready to do whatever it took even if it was a bit dangerous. Not that our lives aren't dangerous anyway, but you know, we avoid unnecessary danger when possible."

"Well we were all starting to feel a bit frustrated I think. And frustration can push you to do dangerous things."

"Definitely." Billie peered out into the garden. "With any luck this new guy might be just what we've been waiting for."

Laura also peered out the window and then quickly stepped back. "Act natural, they're coming in!" A few moments later Isaac and Tom entered the kitchen and walked through into the living room.

"Nice spying girls, very covert!" Isaac remarked as he walked past.

Everyone then gathered in the living room. Ben had to sit on a cushion on the floor because all the chairs were taken. Isaac was sitting next to Tom on the sofa, a little too close - his stomach was still reeling and churning about him even just being there, never mind being squashed up next to each other.

Tom started talking straight away. "I was told to come here by my friend back in Ireland. She sensed that something bad was about to happen here and that all of you, to a greater or lesser extent, were involved somehow. Now-"

Ben cut him off. "Sorry to interrupt, but you said she sensed something bad? How exactly? I mean was it like a prophetic vision or is she some kind of medium or what?"

"It's hard to explain. Some people in the world are just able to tap into these kinds of things. It is a gift they're born with. How they choose to use it, or whether they choose to use it at all is really up to them."

"Tapping into higher frequencies." Gabbi said solemnly. "Like Pete."

"Yes," agreed Isaac, "and our helpful dead children."

"She said she couldn't tell me much specific, she said a lot of it was more a feeling than an actual crystal clear vision."

"What did she tell you?" asked Ben.

"That something impossibly bad was going to happen in Monks-Lantern, something that had implications for the whole of the world." Tom appeared remarkably calm for someone delivering such bad news.

"But she couldn't tell you what exactly?"

"No, unfortunately not." Tom paused for a second and inhaled an audible breath. "Although, saying that, she did tell me one more thing."

"What was it?" asked Isaac quickly.

"Alright give me a second I'm getting there! She said it was the only definite thing she could see. All the rest was just a feeling but this, this she could see clearly."

"Tom, stop building suspense - what was it?!"

"Professor Robert Archington." Tom stated the name clearly and calmly, it obviously meaning nothing to him. Everyone else in the room looked shocked to the very core.

Chapter Fifteen

Tom clearly hadn't expected the reaction that he saw before him. Everyone was looking completely stunned. Isaac's eyes were full of worry and confusion and his brow was furrowed. His expression was mirrored in the others.

"What's wrong? Who is he?" Tom asked, obviously eager to figure out why everyone was looking so astounded.

"He's one of our professors at uni." Gabbi explained, sounding as if she was still taking it in.

"My favourite one too!" Billie exclaimed.

"Well, maybe it doesn't mean that he has something to do with it in a bad way." Laura suggested. Tom opened his mouth to contest that idea, but Laura continued speaking. "I mean your friend, she didn't say if the name was good or bad right?"

Tom again opened his mouth to start speaking, but was frustratingly stopped again, this time by Isaac. "It's bad." he said, his voice shaking a little. "Remember the day we went to Pete's, we were in Archington's lecture right before we went. We were sitting in the front row, he must have been within earshot. I said that we should go there after the lecture - he heard me, we know he did. He told me to stop organising my social calendar."

Billie looked like she still didn't want to believe it. "But how did he know what Pete we were talking about? And how can you remember that that quickly? My memory's rubbish!" she cried.

"I would imagine that our Pete had a reputation in supernatural circles. If Professor Archington really is in on this then the chances are he knew exactly which Pete we were talking about," Isaac answered. "And what can I say, I must be an elephant."

Tom saw his moment to speak and seized it. "If I can interrupt for a moment?" he began, although the question was entirely rhetorical. "Hope did imply that he was involved in a bad way. I think we can rule out any hypothesis which has him as an innocent victim. The question is now, how do we move on from here?"

"Well I don't think we can do anything else tonight." Isaac said with a sigh. "We might as well just all try and relax. I imagine Tom is quite exhausted and to be honest I am too. Mentally and physically."

Everyone murmured in agreement but all remained sitting still in silence for a further few minutes, still taking in the news that their favourite professor was involved in whatever was happening. Laura broke the stillness of the moment by picking up her and Billie's now empty mugs and taking them into the kitchen. Billie quickly followed her. Ben got up and went upstairs and a few moments later Isaac heard the shower start.

"Oh crap," he muttered. "I really wanted a bath!"

"Yeah I wouldn't mind one too." Tom said, gazing at Isaac.

Isaac looked away awkwardly and found Gabbi's gaze instead. She came over and plopped herself down on the sofa next to Isaac and Tom. She casually rested her head on Isaac's shoulder and put an arm across him.

"One last disturbing thought?" she asked as though she were offering him a sweet.

"Oh go on then."

"The disappearances, the coming badness and now Archington being a bad guy - they're all going to be linked aren't they? All part of the same thing."

"Knowing our luck Gabbi my love, I'm more than certain that they are." Isaac said with a smile, despite the lack of cause for one. "The question now is how are they all linked? What does our professor have to do with a coming badness and what does that coming badness have to do with people disappearing? And what do those people disappearing have to do with our professor?"

Gabbi looked up at Isaac's face from her position on his shoulder. She smiled and laughed a bit. "Well done," she said. "You've just made an impossibly confusing situation even more confusing."

Isaac laughed too. "I'm glad I'm good for something."

Tom however seemed unimpressed. "I don't know how you can be so jokey about something like this."

"Because," Isaac replied, "If we didn't find time to laugh then all we'd do is cry."

Tom still didn't look impressed. "I see."

"Don't worry, we take it all very seriously, believe me. But we can take things seriously without walking around with a permanent grimace on our faces."

"Fine. If you say so. If you think death's funny then fine."

Isaac was beginning to feel cross. He still felt bad about what happened that night all those years ago, but he certainly didn't appreciate Tom just appearing in his life and criticising the way he went about it. "How dare you. How dare you say that. After everything that happened -"

"How dare I? After what you did how can you accuse me of being in the wrong?!"

Gabbi got up and joined Billie and Laura in the kitchen.

"I know I did wrong Tom, there's not a day that goes by when I don't think about that."

"And yet what's happening now is hilarious is it? Were you having a good laugh sitting out in your tree? Hahaha, how funny, I just broke Tom's heart and left them all to get killed -"

"Who said it was hilarious? Who said that? And you told me to go, you told me to leave! Remember? I sat in that tree and I cried Tom, I cried. I was fifteen-"

"No excuse!"

"I'm not trying to make excuses."

There was a stony, awkward silence. Then suddenly Tom burst out laughing. Wild laughter.

Isaac was stunned for a moment and leapt back a bit on the sofa. But soon he found himself laughing uncontrollably too.

"You're a right stupid idiot, do you know that?" Tom said after a minute of non-stop laughter, wiping tears from his eyes.

"Yeah I know," said Isaac, still chuckling himself.

"Are you guys alright?" Laura had appeared nervously at the door from the kitchen. Behind her Isaac could see Gabbi and Billie both staring in with confused expressions.

"Yeah, yeah we're fine," said Isaac, clearing his throat. "I think sometimes you just have to laugh."

After the explosion in the living room, Isaac and Tom retreated into Isaac's room. They spoke some more about what happened and they came to the conclusion that it was inevitable that they had one big row, as they must have both been harbouring some pent up anger over that night at Isaac's house. Tom conceded that he could see that Isaac did take his life seriously and Isaac apologised for calling Tom heartless. After all, it was just heat of the moment stuff really. As confused as he was about Tom being back, he was in truth happy that he was there - and so happy to see him after all that time. And he was grateful for the news that he brought, as unpleasant as it was to know that Professor Archington was involved somehow it was good to finally have some kind of lead. The conversation was just starting to turn away from the supernatural and towards more personal issues when Isaac heard the bathroom door open and Ben's quick footsteps hurry along to his room.

"Ah, the bathroom's free!" he announced, relieved. "Do you want to go first or shall I?" Isaac prayed that Tom wouldn't come out with some cringe-worthy suggestion about them just sharing the bath and thankfully no such suggestion came.

"Well I am pretty shattered. I don't suppose I could be cheeky and go first?"

"Of course, of course you can. There are some clean towels in the airing cupboard, just help yourself. And here-" he reached down into a pile of clothes on the floor and fished out a pair of pyjama shorts. "They are clean I swear, I just don't really iron much."

"Thanks." Tom smiled. "Where am I sleeping Issy?"

Isaac was shocked by him using his teenage nickname. No-one had called him that since, well, since that night. "Well, there's the sofa, or the floor in here if you like -"

"Sofa will be good. Thankyou."

Isaac had half expected Tom to jump at the chance of sleeping in his room. Maybe he was being too assumptive. Or maybe he was being too conceited. "Night night then." Isaac said as they stood facing each other, Tom having one hand on the door handle.

"Yes," Tom said, almost as if he was waiting for something, "night night." And with that he walked out of the room and up the stairs.

Isaac collapsed on his bed, face down in his pillow. He moaned quietly and then flipped over. He felt truly exhausted, physically and emotionally. He was so happy to see Tom, but at the same time the memories and feelings that were coming back were ones he wished he could push aside. He fell asleep right there and then, completely missing his chance for a bath, and didn't wake up until five in the morning.

His sleep had been still and dreamless, he imagined his life seemed too much like a dream at the moment for his brain to come up with anything more imaginative. Remembering that he never did get a bath he trudged upstairs, feeling just as exhausted as he had before his nine hours sleep. The bath made him feel slightly better and by the time he had got out and then got dressed he was feeling better still. By that time it was almost seven and Ben was up, so Isaac had breakfast with him in the kitchen.

"So this Tom guy," Ben started.

Isaac suddenly realised that the gang didn't exactly know who Tom was.

"Who is he exactly? Was he involved in that night, you know, the night your friends -"

"Yeah. He was the only one who survived."

"But, and correct me if I'm wrong man, I get the feeling he was more than just a friend?"

"He was, and he wasn't." Isaac looked through at Tom who was still snoring on the sofa. "It's complicated."

"So tell me."

"He loved me. He might still love me for all I know, but that might just be me being big-headed."

"And you didn't love him back?"

"No. I mean I did care for him. But it wasn't right." Isaac paused. "I lead him on a bit," he admitted shamefully, taking a gulp of his tea.

"I've lead plenty of girls on."

"Did your leading them on coincide with a life or death supernatural situation?"

Ben laughed uncertainly. "No. No it didn't. It coincided with a too much alcohol situation."

"Yeah see mine did. Hence the awkwardness." They both sat on the kitchen stools, uncertain of what to say. Isaac thought he had best try and lift the mood. "Still, touch wood things aren't as bad as they could be just yet," he said, tapping the nearby mug tree. "So we live in hope." Isaac smiled, and Ben smiled back. "Besides, I think the whole our professor being a bad guy thing is slightly more important than my interesting personal life."

"Nah it's all important Isaac. But yeah, Archington being a bad guy is worrying. Very worrying."

"Indeed."

"What do you think we should do?"

Ben's question was a very good one. Unfortunately Isaac didn't have an equally good answer.

Chapter Sixteen

Everyone was up and dressed by ten and although both Billie and Laura had to go in for a lecture at eleven and Gabbi had some errands to run in town Isaac decided it would still be a good idea if they had a quick meeting before everyone went off. He wasn't exactly sure what he was going to say in the meeting but he felt that one should be had anyway. After Tom's revelation last night it would seem strange not to talk about what had been revealed. He was hoping that they would get a brainstorm going and someone would come up with a good idea - although through no conscious choice of his own the majority of the time everyone looked to him for the answers and the ideas.

Isaac had noticed that he had become the leader of their little group, something which Ben had confirmed after Isaac's mistake of trying to summon Pete the day before. It wasn't that he entirely hated being placed in that position, in a way he was flattered, in a way he supposed he enjoyed it in a vain kind of way - but he really didn't feel like he had much more of a clue than anyone else most of the time.

He had talked to Gabbi about it once, a couple of months after they all became friends. She had said that it was because he had been the main driving force behind them all coming together - he had inspired everyone to help. When they all discussed their experiences it had been him who suggested they do something with the knowledge they had. She had used the metaphor of him being the one who had enlisted everyone into their little army, which was a metaphor he didn't particularly like as it made it sound far too violent. However, the way things were headed now it was getting very violent. Maybe they were an army, he'd certainly been in more than a few fights. But if they were he wasn't so sure that he wanted to be the leader - with the role of leader came great responsibility and he wasn't at all sure that he had done a very good job of leading the night his friends were murdered. Nonetheless, most of the time he was looked on as the one in charge, so he had decided just to do the best he could and hope that he was strong enough to cope. He didn't want to let anyone down.

"Right," Isaac began. "I just thought we should all throw some ideas around about Archington. Now that we've got this lead I think it would be good to follow it up the best we can."

Everyone nodded in agreement. They were all sitting in the living room, with Isaac himself standing at the door into the hallway, so that everyone else could have a seat and Ben wouldn't have to be sitting on a cushion like the dog in the corner again.

"Maybe we should do some background research on him?" suggested Billie. "Try and find out where he came from, that kind of stuff. There might even be police records if he's been involved in bad stuff before."

"Yeah good idea." agreed Isaac.

"Police records though Isaac?" Gabbi asked. "I mean we saw that dodgy policeman Ackley - if it is all connected then Archington would be involved with that." she argued

"And then if they are all allies then they would make sure there wasn't any incriminating evidence lying around. Yes, good point. But still I think some background research into his past would be helpful."

"I'll make a start now," Billie said, "and then I can carry on when I get back from lectures."

"I'll help." Laura offered.

"Great. Thanks guys that'd be great." Isaac said with a smile.

"What about something more to do with now though?" asked Tom.

"How do you mean?"

"Well it's all very good looking at where he comes from, but shouldn't we try and find out where he's going now? I mean that's the key right?"

"He's right," agreed Ben. "We need to know what he's up to now. Otherwise the disappearances will just keep happening."

They were right, Isaac knew they were. Biographies would only get them so far. But he had no clue how to go about finding out anything else. He didn't even know where to start. It wasn't like there was a website where evil genius's posted their master plans for everyone to see. It had been hard enough getting the little information they had now. However, just as things didn't look too hopeful he remembered something - something tiny and possibly entirely useless but it was something. He kicked himself mentally for not remembering it sooner, much sooner - he should have thought of it as soon as they had seen Ackley with his hooded accomplice.

"Ah-ha!" he cried uncontrollably.

"What?" asked Tom.

"It might not be anything, but I just remembered, ages ago, ages - before

Christmas even, I was on my way back home from Bubble-Gum when -"

"Sorry, what? Bubble-gum?" Tom sounded confused.

"It's the gay nightclub." Gabbi filled him in. "Isaac goes there to hunt for men. We go there to drink." she smiled.

"Yes, thank you Gabbi for that predatory description of me. Anyway, I was walking back home and when I passed the guildhall I saw this robed man go inside. I just figured, well, I don't know what, it was before all of this stuff going on at the moment began, I just thought it might have been a monk I guess."

Billie looked excited. "But now we know that there are robed guys involved somehow, like that one we saw talking to Ackley!" she cried.

"Exactly," Isaac said. "I know it's not much to go on, but it's a start. Maybe if tonight Tom and I go down to the guildhall, see what we can find out. There might be some information on Archington there."

Tom nodded in agreement with Isaac's proposal and everyone else seemed satisfied too. Isaac could have chosen any of the others to go with him and part of him wished that he had. But he decided that Tom was probably the best choice - after all he had come all the way from Ireland to help despite everything that Isaac had done to him. It wouldn't exactly be fair to leave him at home to do the washing up.

"Well we should head into uni if we're all done here." said Laura.

"Yes, yes of course," said Isaac. "Just be careful though, if you see Archington then it's probably best to stay out of his way."

"Yeah definitely. We'll run as fast as our little legs will carry us if we see him." Billie said.

"Speak for yourself about little legs!" Laura laughed. "I'll go and get my shoes on."

Soon enough everyone who was going out had gone, leaving Isaac, Ben and Tom in the house. Ben started watching football on TV and was therefore counted out in terms of any type of communication, which left Isaac alone with Tom. There was still an awkwardness between them and it got so confusing and strange that by one in the afternoon Isaac invented a lecture and darted into uni. By rights he should have had a lecture with Professor Archington later that afternoon, but given the circumstances he thought it would be best to avoid it entirely.

As he walked towards uni he met Billie, Laura and Gabbi, who were all just returning home. He filled them in on the situation with Tom, much in the same way he had filled Ben in that morning. They were all very understanding, which Isaac was most grateful for. He was about to remind them not to go to the lecture later on that afternoon with Archington when Gabbi herself said that they shouldn't go, which everyone agreed with. Once they had parted ways he continued into uni and sat in the library all afternoon - staying there until half five when a rather grumpy old librarian told him he had to leave because the library was shutting.

When he got home ten minutes later he found everyone sitting in the living room talking and laughing, with Tom appearing to be the centre of attention.

"Here he is!" Billie cried happily.

"Sounds like you guys are having fun." Isaac said, happy that they were all getting along but also hoping that Tom hadn't been talking in too much detail about what happened between them.

"Yeah Tom was just telling us about what you were like when you were younger!" Billie grinned. A part of Isaac died inside at this news.

"How was your lecture?" asked Tom.

"Huh? Oh yeah, it was fine. Boring but fine." he muttered uncomfortably. He felt bad lying to Tom, he had felt bad avoiding him all afternoon. But it was just so weird seeing him, it was like five years ago had suddenly jumped up from its grave and punched him in the face. Isaac sat down on the arm of the sofa. "So what have you been telling them?" He kept his tone light but at the same time was very keen to find out exactly what had been said.

"Oh you know, just about how we were at school - you remember that time in PE? Mr Roberts?"

"Oh!" Isaac chuckled awkwardly. "How could I forget?" He felt a wave of relief wash over him, happy that Tom had just been telling innocent schoolboy stories.

"When are we headed out then?"

"Later I think. About ten?"

"Sounds fine to me. Gives me time to have something to eat."

"Yes I was just feeling a bit peckish myself. I'll put a couple of pizzas in the oven, will that be okay?"

"Mmm great." Tom's eyes lingered on Isaac for a long moment.

"Okay, cool." Isaac moved through into the kitchen to get dinner ready.

Gabbi followed him after a few moments. "You okay?" she asked.

"Yeah I'm fine. How's he been?" Isaac asked, glancing through to look at Tom who was busy checking something in his pockets.

"He's been fine. He seems nice, just a little - well, I don't know."

"A little what Gabbi?"

"A little obsessed, maybe. With you. It's all Isaac this, Isaac that - he hasn't said one thing about anyone from Ireland. I think maybe you need to talk to him." She paused, as if wondering whether to brave what she was going to say next. "I think he still likes you."

Isaac wasn't surprised to hear that. He wondered again if that made him conceited. "Maybe. I'll try talking to him, when we go investigate the guildhall perhaps." Isaac groaned. "I hate having that sort of conversation."

"Well nobody enjoys it. But I mean if he is going to be around here for a while you can't keep running into uni can you?"

Gabbi was right, of course she was right. Isaac and Tom hadn't discussed their feelings for each other properly since he'd turned up and it was obvious that something needed to be said. Billie came and joined them as Tom went upstairs to use the toilet.

"Me and Laura found out some information on Archington!" she announced proudly.

"And what do we know?" Isaac asked, unwrapping the pizzas and turning the oven on - happy of the change of topic away from subjective emotions and towards objective information.

"Born in England but moved to Scotland when he was still quite young in his early twenties. And there it seems that he joined some kind of religious group, not sure what though - no website or resource we could find was very specific."

"Religious group? Sounds like it could be our friends the hooded guys." Gabbi suggested.

"Could be. They do have that crazy cult look about them." Isaac said. "What else did you find out?"

"Well then there isn't anything, it's like there is a whole big gap missing. Some of the resources we found mentioned a marriage, but others didn't. And then there's really nothing until he became the professor we know and used to love five years ago."

"And since then?"

"Nothing strange or weird. Just normal professor type stuff. Sorry it's not much more help."

"Don't be ridiculous!" said Isaac, pushing the pizzas into the oven. "It's very helpful - more than helpful. That religious group bit in particular. And the marriage, I've never seen him with a wedding ring on."

"We should look into that then." Gabbi said.

"Yes we should." Isaac agreed. "However, if we're very, very lucky then hopefully tonight me and Tom will turn something up at the guildhall that may well give us the answers we need."

Ten o'clock came round quicker than Isaac had expected it to, and he and Tom were soon out of the door and on their way to the guildhall. It was a little chilly that night so Isaac had worn his long scarf and he breathed into it as they walked. He knew that if he was going to talk to Tom about his feelings then it would be best to do it before they got there as once inside they would need to focus more on getting the information they needed rather than talking about who still cared for who. Still, the question was how to bring up the conversation in the first place.

"So," he began, swallowing heavily. "I think if we just keep an eye out for any people in robes as we head towards the guildhall and then hopefully if they go there themselves then that should prove that-"

"So have you found someone?" Tom asked as though it were a casual enough question.

Isaac hadn't expected it at all. It seemed that Tom wanted to talk about exactly the same thing as Isaac wanted to. Although now that Tom had broached the conversation Isaac was losing courage. The awkwardness seeped into the atmosphere.

"Oh - erm - no, no I haven't. Not yet anyway." Isaac coughed and tried to avoid making eye contact. "Have you?" he asked, attempting to sound casual like Tom had but instead sounding very awkward.

"No." Tom looked across to Isaac as they walked, forcing eye contact, "There was never anyone else."

Isaac cringed and felt torn inside at Tom's words. Part of him felt like thumping Tom for saying something like that and part of him felt like hugging him because he was being honest and really rather sweet. But Isaac didn't love him. Not properly, not like that. So he refrained from doing either and instead just offered an apologetic smile.

Tom obviously sensed Isaac's confusion. "It's okay, I know you don't - I know you don't feel the same as me."

"Tom, it's been five years. I'm not that person I was anymore. I stopped being that person that night and I've grown even more since then. You don't know me anymore. How can you love someone you don't know?" Isaac tried not to sound harsh but he thought some actual honesty might help the situation.

"I could get to know you again."

"Tom -" The guildhall suddenly appeared in front of them as they rounded a corner. "We're here."

Tom let out an exasperated sigh, obviously annoyed that Isaac had cut him off mid flow.

Isaac was aware of Tom's annoyance but was now much more focused on getting inside and getting some information. Confusing emotional talk would have to wait until later.

"So what now? We just sit and wait? Wait for a hooded guy to turn up and then just ask him for the tour?" Tom's sarcasm was obvious.

"Nope."

"What then?"

"I've seen them go in here before -"

Tom interrupted. "Yes I know you said, but do we know if they're -"

"And," Isaac started, regaining control of his sentence. "There's one going in right now. Look." He motioned towards the hooded figure moving towards the arched wooden door of the building and then going inside.

Tom rolled his eyes and looked at Isaac. "That was luck, sheer luck that's all."

"Yes it was. Lucky us." Isaac stared seriously over at the guildhall. They could be on the verge of finally discovering what was going on. Or they could be on the verge of a massive disaster. "Only one way to find out," he muttered, finishing his train of thought aloud.

"What?"

"Let's go. It'll probably still be better than a poke in the eye with a sharp stick." They headed off across the street to the guildhall. It was a medieval looking grey stone structure, if it had a bell tower then it would have looked very much like a church. There was scaffolding around most of the building and a smattering of builder's tools lay about the place.

"Is this place still in use? Only it looks like it's on its last legs." asked Tom.

"Well that's what makes all this so interesting. The council are building a new guildhall up the other end of the city closer to the council offices. This one hasn't been used in quite a while now." They paused at the entrance from the footpath. There was a stone courtyard in front of them, with a fountain in the middle that no longer worked. Beyond that was the main door.

"So if this isn't in use then what are they doing with it? The scaffolding and everything I mean."

"Well that's just it. This scaffolding has been up since it stopped functioning and nothing has been done. No builders, nothing. It's like they want the city to believe this place is under construction or something so no-one comes in."

"Like a massive disguise." Tom said, with some admiration in his voice.

Isaac had to agree, it was a good way to keep prying eyes out.

"But who's they? Archington?"

"Let's find out."

They crossed the courtyard and silently slid open one side of the heavy, wooden double doors. Inside there was a corridor which went out in either direction and another large set of double doors much like the main doors straight ahead of them. Both directions were dark and Isaac was going to suggest the doors in front when he saw the faintest glimmer of light coming from the corridor on the left.

Isaac snuck in quietly, turning to Tom and putting a finger to his lips before beckoning him forward with the same hand. They crept down the flagstone corridor. Isaac could see that there were numerous paintings on the walls but in the poor light he couldn't tell what they were of.

They turned the corner at the end which went round to the right. It was all clear, but one of the doors at the far end of that corridor was slightly ajar and light flooded out. Voices were just about audible but completely indistinguishable. They hadn't moved forward very much before the voices cleared up a little. Isaac felt his stomach sink when he realised that one of them was definitely Professor Archington. There also appeared to be two other voices which he didn't recognise at all.

Isaac and Tom stopped in an alcove containing a statue, several feet from the door. Isaac was too intrigued with what was being said in the room to look and see what the statue was of, all he knew was it was large and white. It took a few seconds of strained hearing before the voices became clearly audible. Both Isaac and Tom listened intently.

"The last sacrifice is complete?" It was Archington.

"Yes Imperator. Ninety nine souls have now bled upon the box. Drip, drip, drip, drip, drip!" This voice was hissing and childlike.

"I'm sorry I had to miss it. Unfortunately I was setting essays today and my absence would have been noticed. Still, it doesn't matter. Everything is as we need it to be."

"But Imperator," another voice spoke, this one rather ordinary compared to the hissing of the first. "What about the children? The ones who were with that psychic when I killed him?" Isaac's heart rate quickened. This was the man who'd killed Pete! And Imperator? Archington is the Imperator?

"Yes they are a nuisance. But they have their part to play." There was a gap as if the three of them were exchanging glances. "Don't worry. They'll be dealt with in time."

"Master shall be very cross if they were to interfere!" the hissing voice exclaimed, sounding excited. Isaac was now in little doubt that this particular character was either a demon or possessed. Creepy with just a touch of insane.

"Yes, very true," said Archington sternly. The thought of Archington becoming very cross would have been a thought to scare Isaac even before he'd found out that Archington was a bad guy. "There is little to do for a while. Be patient and prepare - our time is coming."

There was insane giggling for the hissing voice.

"Yes Imperator." said the other voice, a radical contrast to his hissing partner.

"Right, I should go. I have a ton of marking to do before the morning." There was no reply to this from the two minions, only the sound of a chair scraping and then a door opening and shutting loudly.

Isaac panicked for a moment that Archington would walk past them, but he must have gone out of a back door as no-one came. Isaac and Tom stared at each other from either side of the statue. Isaac's worried expression was mirrored in Tom's own face. Isaac glanced up at the statue. He now saw that it was a replica of Michelangelo's David. He smiled through the worry. He'd always liked that statue.

They let a few minutes pass before leaving the alcove and heading towards the room where Archington had been. They inched closer and closer to it, straining to see if they could hear any sound. The room was completely silent. Isaac shrugged and reached out for the door handle to push it all the way open. Just then the door was ripped open from inside. Both Isaac and Tom screamed - a menacing face glared and snarled at them with pitch black eyes.

"Tasty young ones have come to me!" the hissing voiced figure squealed with delight. He was bald with incredibly pointed features and his entire head and much of his face was covered in tattoos.

Isaac couldn't even begin to decipher the tattoos, he was far too busy being terrified to decipher anything. Instinctively he grabbed Tom's arm.

"Look Elias!" called the demon to his partner, "Tasty treats have been brought to us. Tiny little lambs who are so, so afraid of the slaughter!" he licked his lips revealing horribly rotten teeth.

The other man, Elias, appeared in full view.

"Who the hell are you?!" Elias bellowed – he was definitely human, fairly tall, well built with a thick looking neck and hard, square facial features with a deep brow. He wasn't bald like the mad demonic one but his dark hair was shaved very short all over. A flash of recognition flew across his face when he saw Isaac more clearly. He laughed "The friends of the psychic! Come on Skarl, let's deal with these now."

Skarl nodded slowly and happily. "May I pretty please feast on their insides?" Skarl asked politely.

Every muscle in Isaac's body tightened. He was terrified but the adrenaline was doing its job. Thank-you adrenaline.

"Of course my friend. Take them now!" With that the human strode powerfully forward and Skarl advanced slowly, laughing and beckoning with a thin, bony finger for the two of them to go to him. Isaac and Tom looked and each other and nodded before throwing themselves forward at their attackers. Isaac collided with the human in a tackle round his waist, pushing him back up the corridor towards the statue until they both tumbled to the ground. He could hear a fight behind him but daren't look round. Sitting astride his attacker he managed a good punch to the face before he was flung off. Elias was on his feet quickly and advanced on Isaac who was still on the floor. Isaac managed to kick Elias in the stomach from his position on the floor which subsequently gave him enough time to get up. Elias swung for him and Isaac blocked his punch before smacking him neatly in the chin with his free fist. Elias swung again and was more successful - a straight blow to Isaac's right eye sent him staggering backwards. This was quickly followed by a punch to his stomach which made him bend double in pain.

"You're nothing." Elias mocked. Spurred on by a thought of Pete and knowing that this was the man that had killed him, Isaac summoned enough strength to plant a knee squarely in the Elias's groin, causing him to bend double himself.

"You're not much yourself." Isaac noticed a bust of some kind of philosopher on a pedestal behind him and seizing his moment he grabbed it and swung it for Elias's head. It was a heavy object but he just about managed to connect it with the back of the Elias's skull. Elias fell instantly to the floor. For the first time since the fight began Isaac was able to look over at Tom and was relieved to see him worn out but victorious, standing over the body of Skarl. "Is he dead?" Isaac called out to Tom.

Tom jumped. "Hard to tell," he said, recovering from the fright Isaac had just given him. "Demons like this guy don't have a pulse."

"Oh yeah." In the heat of the battle Isaac had forgotten that Skarl was a demon. "Quite right."

"How about yours?"

Isaac bent down and checked the pulse. "No, just unconscious. Just as well, he might be evil but he's still a person. Not sure I like the idea of actually killing someone. Having said that I don't know what to do with him though." He stood up and walked back down towards Tom. "I guess we could just tie him up and leave, although what will we do when -" Isaac was cut off as he felt someone pounce on his back. A strong arm tightened round his throat. Elias! He wasn't unconscious at all!

"Isaac!" Tom cried, running towards him. Elias sent Tom flying with a punch from his free hand.

"You think you could just defeat us like that?" The man's voice was full of hate and he spat as he spoke. He forced Isaac to the floor, still holding him tightly from behind. Isaac could feel Elias's grip getting stronger. He struggled for breath. "Our power is immense and you know not where it lies! We are capable of things you daren't imagine, and when our day comes you -"

There was suddenly a great thud sound from behind, and Elias's grip suddenly released before Isaac heard him collapse on the floor. What on earth was going on? Tom was still getting to his feet - it couldn't have been him! Isaac rolled over onto his back and looked up at his rescuer. He couldn't believe his eyes.

Chapter Seventeen

Isaac's first thought was that the statue of David had somehow come to life. The man standing before him was the most handsome man he'd ever seen. He knew that was a cliché to think that, but it was true. This man, whoever he was, he was gorgeous. He had a swathe of wavy, tousled blond hair which framed his features perfectly. He looked about the same age as Isaac, his face clean shaven and well defined with very statuesque features. In fact Isaac did look again at the statue of David just to make sure it hadn't come to life. It stood still in its alcove. This man was real. Isaac quickly glanced at Elias who was laying still on the ground, the bust of the philosopher laying next to him. The man standing over him offered a hand down to Isaac and he took it, feeling a tingle rush through him as he did. Tom was also getting to his feet, and he appeared to be eyeing the stranger a lot more warily than Isaac was.

Isaac couldn't think of what to say to the man, but he thought he'd better say something. "Thank you," he said, stuttering slightly. He then realised what a crushingly obvious thing that was to say. He put a hand to his forehead and wiped the sweat off of it. Oh great, now he'll think I'm sweaty.

The man just smiled. "No problem." His voice was warm and comfortable. Isaac smiled back at him and they just stood there smiling inanely at each other for what seemed like minutes but probably wasn't that long. He had a nice smile. A really nice smile. Isaac felt something happy in his stomach that he hadn't felt in a long time.

"Who the hell are you?" Tom asked brashly, breaking the silence. Isaac shot him a frowning look.

"I'm Jack," the newcomer said, extending a hand to Isaac. "Jack Tooley."

Isaac shook his hand. It was firm. Manly. "I'm Isaac," he smiled at Jack. "Isaac Jacobs."

"Yeah never mind your name Jack Bond." Tom said sarcastically, "Who the hell are you? What are you doing here?"

Jack's warm smile vanished somewhat. "I'm from London," he said flatly. "Something strange happened up there last week and I traced a lead back here."

"So you're what, a P.I?" Tom asked, sounding unimpressed.

"I guess that's what you'd call me if you had to call me something. Also professional baked bean can stacker at the supermarket." Jack gazed at Tom for a moment, "And how about you? Professional punch bag?"

"Excuse me? How dare -"

Isaac cut in and interrupted Tom. "You said something strange had happened?" He had been gazing dreamily at Jack until that point but when he felt the friction between Tom and Jack rising the thought it would be best to intervene and steer the conversation somewhere else. "How did you know to come here?"

"My friend, she came down to visit one of her friends who goes to uni here. Just as she was about to get on the train to go back to London some guy tried to grab her." Jack explained as he picked up the bust of the philosopher and walked it a few feet back to the pedestal. "There you go Plato. Or whichever one you are. Anyway, my friend got away but she said the guy who attacked her was robed like a monk and covered in tattoos." Both Isaac and Tom looked round at the still body of Skarl, which thankfully hadn't moved.

"Our friend the insane cannibal over there." Tom said, still eyeing Jack with suspicion.

"I tend to like looking into things with a bit of a paranormal twist, have done ever since I saw my first ghost when I was a kid. And well, this seemed to have paranormal written all over it - especially when she said his eyes were completely black. Demonic possession I figured, so I came down to have a look."

"Yes but how did you know to come here?" Tom asked. Isaac didn't take his eyes off of Jack.

"Followed you two of course. I think it was the just keep an eye out for any people in robes part that tipped me off." He shot Isaac a smile. "I wasn't going to make my presence known but when I saw you getting strangled I thought I'd better step in."

"Well I'm very glad that you did." Isaac said with a smile. It was a smile that was about more than just really fancying this new guy, it was also about genuine appreciation. He had, after all, nearly died. He owed Jack a lot of gratitude. "Thank you."

All three of them set about tying up the two assailants using some industrial tape Jack had spotted amongst the builders tools outside before heaving the bodies into a broom cupboard. Isaac knew it would only be a matter of time before they were found and the truth of that night would get back to

Archington. However, he hoped that considering Archington's patient approach to their destruction and his interest in their purpose in all of this that he wouldn't then just order their deaths immediately. He hoped so anyway.

"What about Skarl though?" Tom asked. "Do we exorcise him or banish him or destroy him or something?"

"No, we don't do anything. Not yet." Isaac was firm. His thoughts about their future had made him think seriously about the situation. They needed to move carefully from now on. "We need to get our heads round everything. And something tells me that Skarl is more than just a common or garden demon that has infested the already dead body of some poor homeless man." Tom nodded in agreement and Isaac was glad to get some support from him - he felt like they were on the same page for the first time that night. "I suspect that he's probably a soul dweller."

"Ahhh," Jack said with an air or recognition, scratching the back of his neck thoughtfully.

"You've heard of them?" Isaac asked, impressed.

Jack nodded. "It's horrible."

"What is it?" Tom seemed frustrated that he wasn't in the know.

Isaac answered him. "Some demons just fill up a human body, alive or dead, and simply manipulate the body - like a person getting in a car and driving it around," he explained. "It's the most common form of possession around."

"Yes I know all that."

"Soul dwellers," Isaac continued, "burrow further into a person than just their muscles and bones. They burrow into their souls and then slowly destroy them. They tear them and burn them until -"

"Until there's nothing left." Jack completed Isaac's sentence for him.

"They become, in effect, a demon in human form. They're much more difficult to banish or destroy." Isaac stared at the unconscious Skarl as if looking at a rare animal in a zoo.

"So why don't all demons do it then?" asked Tom.

"Most demons prefer to be able to move around and be a spirit from time to time. Like moving house I suppose, if they get bored they can move on - go and ruin someone else's life. Once you burrow into someone's soul however, you're stuck there." Isaac closed the door on the cupboard. They had a quick look in the room that Archington had been in, but nothing helpful or incriminating had been left. Not that Isaac was expecting there to have been anything left - he got the impression that these guys were pretty good at keeping their activities under their hats.

They were just leaving the room when Jack surprised Isaac for the second time in the night. "Right, I should go."

The disappointment on Isaac's face must have been obvious to see. "But it's so late." Isaac's protests were probably just as obvious as the look on his face was. "You'll never get home!"

"Ahh there'll be trains. I'll be okay." Jack assured them. Isaac was at a loss for words now - the happy feeling from earlier was well and truly gone. "Thanks for the help and information - I'll start looking into it all straight away. Ninety nine souls and a box right?"

"Yeah," Isaac said, forcing bravado, trying to act as though he didn't care that Jack was about to leave. He knew he needed to get a grip - he didn't even know if Jack was gay! "That's right. Good luck."

"Right." There was an ominous pause as if someone was waiting for someone else to say something. But nothing was said by anyone. "Bye then." Jack smiled at Isaac and looked quickly at Tom. "I'll see you around." With that he turned on his heel and walked round the corner of the corridor and out of sight. Isaac and Tom were left alone in the guildhall - except for their unconscious attackers of course.

"I'll see you around?!" Tom said, mimicking Jack's last words. "Pfft that is such a cliché."

"Shut-up." Isaac wasn't really cross at Tom, he couldn't be. After everything that had happened between them he couldn't blame Tom for a slight bitterness towards the newcomer. He pulled Tom in for a small hug and then headed for the door himself. "Come on Tom, let's go home."

Chapter Eighteen

The air was freezing outside now and it was a bit of a shock after they had been having some quite warm spring days. Isaac felt glad that he'd decided to wear his long scarf. The pavements and roads glittered with the cold and there didn't seem to be anybody else out on the streets.

"I think tomorrow it would be a good idea to look into this ninety nine souls bleeding on the box thing. It doesn't sound too friendly to me." Isaac said as they walked.

"Yes I think that sounds like a good idea." Tom sounded as though he were elsewhere.

"Are you okay sleeping on the sofa again? Only you could share with me if you like." The offer came out of nowhere. Isaac knew it was the wrong thing to do and he knew he was saying it for all the wrong reasons. He knew he was just feeling bad about Jack leaving as soon as he arrived. He didn't even know if Jack was gay but he was already acting like he was obsessed with the man. Psychopathic demons he could just about handle - dating was a whole different game entirely. He was getting frustrated at his own thoughts.

"I'm leaving, Isaac."

The reply left Isaac stunned. "What! When?!"

"Now." Tom's voice was firm. "I mean come off it, you don't really want to share a bed with me. You're feeling needy and you'd start something like last time and then suddenly realise it was wrong. We'd be five years ago all over again."

Isaac knew it was true. "Yeah, okay, I shouldn't have just offered that. This is all so confusing for me, I know - and I know things are a bit awkward between us. But why does that mean you have to go? You only just turned up!"

"I've done what I came here to do. If I stay much longer then I'll find it harder to leave at all."

"Then stay!" Isaac proclaimed, knowing he was talking any kind of nonsense now. "Stay for good!"

"Isaac. For someone so good when it comes to supernatural stuff, you really are thick as two short planks on this real world stuff aren't you?" Tom said with a smile. "You know I can't stay forever. There's no room at your place, I don't have a job - not to mention the whole thing with us." They had stopped walking completely now and just stood in the deserted street facing each other.

"But -"

"But nothing."

Isaac could feel his eyes welling up. He was so confused! Tom was right, he'd become strangely accustomed to demons and ghosts and everything weird, but these kind of things that every human on the planet had to deal with, these kind of things were still a complete minefield. He knew Tom was making sense though. He wasn't sure how he knew, but he knew that he was. "Well at least let me walk you to the train station."

"Thank you." Tom smiled again and Isaac forced one back.

They headed off together away from the direction of home and towards the train station. When they got there there was a train already waiting on the platform. The platform was deserted – not a soul to be seen.

"It's okay, I've got a few minutes until it leaves." Tom said after a quick glance at the timetable. "Time enough for a big emotional goodbye."

Isaac nodded, forcing a smile and a small laugh. He felt the prickle of tears sting the corners of his eyes. "Yeah."

Then there followed a silence. Isaac stared at Tom and Tom stared straight back. Isaac felt like he might be sick, he still cared about Tom after all. He didn't want to say goodbye so soon.

"Where does the train go?" he asked at length.

"Portsmouth."

"Portsmouth is in Ireland now?"

"No, but my aunty lives there. I can stay with her for a day or two before heading back home."

"Oh." Isaac cursed himself as he felt his voice cracking as he spoke. "Well that will be nice."

"Should be."

Isaac struggled to think of any more pointless small talk so he just blurted out the truth. "I wish you'd stay."

"I wish I could too. But I can't – you know I can't. And you know I shouldn't, not really. We're not fifteen anymore. You were right earlier, we're different people now." Tom said sadly. "And that's good Issy. That's good."

Isaac wiped tears messily from his eyes. All these emotions and things he wanted to suddenly say were erupting to the surface, pressurised and speeded by the waiting train. "I never thought I'd see you again," he garbled hastily. "I hoped, I mean you know sometimes I dreamt. But I never thought I would, not really. I thought you hated me."

Tom shook his head fervently. "Never." He paused for a moment and then grinned. "Well, maybe a little, once upon a time. But not properly Isaac, not you. Not ever."

Isaac nodded through his tears and exhaled heavily. "What will you do back in Ireland?"

"Back to work, not all of us are student layabouts. Some of us have got jobs you know!"

Isaac laughed heartily, happy for the moment of levity amid the sadness. Then he remembered there was a question he'd wanted to ask Tom – something he'd wondered about for five years. "I wanted to ask you something - something about that night."

Tom nodded, he knew what night Isaac meant. "Go on."

"You knew Verk'an-gorek's name, you spoke it to banish him. But he said that no one on earth knew it."

"That's right, he did say that."

"Then how did you know it?"

"I would have thought the answer was obvious." Tom leant in close and lowered his voice to a whisper. "I'm not from earth."

Isaac's mouth dropped open. "What?! What do you -"

Tom burst out laughing. "You idiot, of course I'm from earth!"

"Oh. Right, yes of course you are."

"The name was just in a book in your room with a description."

"Really?" Isaac furrowed his brow. He didn't remember that name being in any of his books.

"Yeah. You had a pretty freaky book collection, I'm not surprised to be honest." Just then an automated voice came out loud and nasally through the tannoy system, telling them that it was the final call for Tom's train. "Right." Tom said with a sigh. "Time to go."

Isaac's tears were in freefall mode now. He blinked heavily, trying to stem the flow but it didn't help much. "I hate goodbyes."

"Oh I know you do." Tom gave a bittersweet smile. "But we didn't get to say it last time. I want to say it now." Without further warning Tom reached out and grabbed Isaac, holding him in a tight hug.

Isaac hugged back just as tightly, nuzzling his face into Tom's shoulder, making the most of every second.

"Goodbye Isaac." Tom whispered.

"Goodbye." Isaac choked back.

They parted and Tom backed up towards the open doors of the train.

"Tom, wait!" Isaac called out urgently. There was something else he had to say. "You know, about what happened that night. I am so, so -"

Tom interrupted. "Issy." He shook his head and held a finger to his lips whilst wearing a sad smile. "Shhh."

Isaac did as he was told and held his tongue, held the apology that he'd already made but felt he needed to make again and again eternally.

Tom got on the train and stood in the open doorway. "Take care of yourself? And be careful with Archington."

Isaac nodded. "I will. Take care too." Isaac brushed his fringe from out of his eye. "I'll see you again though right?"

Tom nodded and smiled at him through tears of his own. "Count on it."

Isaac was about to speak again when the train doors shut with a loud clunk and Tom was sealed from him. The train started pulling away from the platform almost immediately. Isaac thought he saw Tom say something, thought he saw his lips move – but he couldn't be sure. He put a hand up to wave and just caught a glimpse of his old friend wave back before the train sped up and left the platform.

Isaac walked home slowly with a slumping step, folding his arms around himself in a kind of self-hug. The last couple of days had been intense, a lot of old thoughts and memories had been stirred up and it had left his brain more scrambled than usual. When he reached the house the put the key in the lock and turned it with a sigh before leaning forwards and letting his body weight push the door open. When he'd shut the door behind him again he saw Gabbi come out into the hallway from the living room.

"Hi darling, where's Tom?" she asked with a worried, caring look.

Isaac said nothing, he simply walked forwards with his arms outstretched.

Gabbi, being the person she was, knew exactly what he meant and knew exactly what was needed. She opened her arms wide. "Come here."

Chapter Nineteen

Isaac filled everyone in on what he'd learnt at the guildhall the very next morning. The story created a sombre mood in the living room as Isaac told it. The only news that raised a few smiles was Isaac mentioning his handsome life saver, Jack – although that small piece of joy seemed very small indeed compared to all the gloom.

Laura asked the obvious question once Isaac had finished speaking. "So what do we think this ninety nine souls bleeding on a box is about then?"

"Sounds like it could be some kind of ritual to me." Gabbi said.

Isaac nodded in agreement. "Yes that's what I thought. But whatever it is it's not done yet - Archington made that clear. It looks like we have a bit of time before anything else happens, so that's a blessing. Sort of."

"And Archington - he's not only involved with the bad guys, he's in charge of them?" Ben asked.

"Seems like it yes - they addressed him as the Imperator. Mind you, we know what he's like in lectures. He's the voice of authority. It makes perfect sense he's the leader."

Billie raised a hand as though in a lecture herself. "And what was that whole thing about us being dealt with in time? That's frightening." she said.

"Well I'm hoping that the time when we'll be dealt with is a little way off as yet, which will give us time to stop Archington before this plan of his comes to fruition." Isaac said. Just then a thought struck him. A really rather obvious thought that should have struck him much sooner. "The disappearances!" he cried, "How many have there been? How many in total?"

Laura leaned forward and grabbed the big red folder from the coffee table which contained all of their findings so far. "Well," she said, leafing through the papers inside, "we counted two a month, every month. There's been two this month and we followed them all the way back to February four years ago when there was just one, so that's -" She made muttering noises as she worked out the equation in her head.

"Ninety nine." Gabbi got there first.

The clear truth hit Isaac instantly. "Ninety nine disappearances, ninety nine souls bled onto the box." It seemed stupid now but he'd never actually thought about counting up the number of missing people before.

"And nobody causing a fuss about it. Nobody caring." Billie said mournfully.

"Bled means more than just people going missing though doesn't it? This isn't just ninety nine disappearances. This is ninety nine murders." Gabbi said, her voice just a whisper.

"I think it would be best if we stay away from Archington's lectures completely now." Isaac said, looking out at the day which had, like his spirits, become grey and dull, "We're not safe anymore."

"Isaac." Gabbi said softly. "We never were."

Two days of research later and Isaac spotted a welcome distraction from his emotional turmoil – and from the wider problem with Professor Archington - in the local paper.

Three girls had been attacked outside a building site whilst walking home after a night out, and rather disgustingly they'd all had two of their fingers bitten off by their assailant who they described as being a thin, raggedy man with a terrifying face. The whole thing screamed demon to Isaac – either a fully physical one or a spirit demon possessing a man, possibly even another soul dweller like Skarl.

Keen to take his mind off things he decided to head out that evening and investigate. Everyone else seemed busy with actual work for their courses so he settled it in his mind that he'd go by himself. However as he pulled on his jacket and headed for the front door he bumped into Laura as she came down the stairs with an empty glass in her hand.

"Oh are you off out?" she asked, nodding to Isaac's jacket.

"No, no – well yes, I am. But it's nothing important, just a walk."

Laura raised an eyebrow. "You know you're really bad at lying."

Isaac smirked. "Okay, it's not just a walk." He pulled the newspaper clipping of the article from his pocket and handed it to Laura. "Here."

Laura scanned the text and wrinkled her face up in distaste after a few moments. "Fingers? Are you going after this thing now?"

"Well I was just going to have a look. You know it's been all Tom and Archington and mysterious boxes the last few days, I just fancied something a bit different."

"Like a finger eating monster?"

Isaac shrugged. "A change is as good as a rest."

Laura chuckled. "Well let me get the others, we'll all go -"

"No! No they're working, you're working. It's fine."

Laura shook her head. "You shouldn't go alone, you could come back all fingerless." She paused for a moment. "Just let me come with you, hmm? I could do with some air, ancient Judaic law is starting to give me a headache."

Isaac smiled – he was glad to have the company really. And Laura was good company to have when you were feeling contemplative and reflective due to her quiet, unassuming but supportive nature. "Okay."

"Great. I'll grab me coat."

The building site in question was about a fifteen minute walk from the house, away from the direction of the city centre. They stuck to mainly quiet residential roads - it was only eight o'clock but it felt more like midnight because of how silent it was. It was a cloudy but mild night and it had rained for most of the day so the walk involved a lot of puddle hopping.

"What's this building site going to be?" Laura asked as they approached the hoarding that surrounded the site.

"Houses I think." Isaac said, keeping his eyes peeled for any thin figures loitering in the shadows. "A shame really, I wouldn't mind having an Asda here."

"Oh yeah I love Asda." Laura agreed longingly. There was a comfortable pause. "You've been quiet these last few days."

"Have I?" Isaac asked, feeling his face prickle with awkward heat. He knew he'd been quiet.

"Yeah. I expect Tom coming back like that was a bit of a shock to the system."

Isaac looked at Laura and gave her a wry smile. "That would be putting it mildly."

"Are you okay though?"

Isaac waved Laura's question away with an exaggerated waft of his hand. "Oh yeah, I'm fine!"

"Isaac."

Isaac let his bravado drop. "It's been a bit of a rollercoaster recently - Tom coming back and then going again so soon wasn't exactly easy." Isaac thought of his mad mix of emotions he'd felt over the last week – it made his brain ache just thinking about it all so he decided to now put it all to the back of his mind and ignore it the best he could. "But I'm okay, really I am."

Laura looked at him with those deep, intuitive eyes. "Sure?"

Isaac nodded happily. "Sure as sugar."

She seemed happy enough with that reply. "Goodo."

They walked on a few steps more. "Thanks." Isaac said casually.

"For what?"

"For asking."

Just then they reached the main gates to the building site. Isaac scanned the area and then peered through the metal gates. It was dark but he could make out piles of bricks and a couple of diggers.

Laura peered through alongside him. "Any sign of a raggedy finger eater?"

"No." Isaac narrowed his eyes. Suddenly he thought he saw something move quickly in the shadows next to one of the diggers. "Wait!"

"What?!"

"I don't know, could have been something. Could have been a fox."

Laura sighed. "We're going in for a closer look aren't we?"

Isaac looked at her and smiled. "You know me too well." There was a large loop of metal chain-link that held the gate shut, but it was sufficiently loose that if you pushed one side of the gate you could make a gap in the middle big enough to squeeze through if you breathed in. "Come on!"

Moments later and they were both through and in the midst of the building site. Isaac grabbed a couple of spades and handed one to Laura. She took it silently and they advanced on the mud splattered digger that Isaac had seen movement near.

Laura raised the spade a little in readiness. "Come on," she whispered. "Come on."

Isaac caught something moving in the corner of his left eye. "Over there!" he cried, shifting direction and heading across the soft muddy ground towards a pile of bricks.

Laura followed, still holding the spade up. "If this is where this thing lives then it knows the layout better than us. It could be running circles round us, leading us into a trap even -"

"Look out!" Isaac yelled as a thin streak of a figure dressed in rags landed with a high pitched growl and a thud in front of them – it must have climbed on top of the digger and leapt at them from there. Isaac saw the terrifying face the article had mentioned – thin and elongated with wrinkled skin, a puckered nose and a nasty looking little mouth surrounded by thick black lips.

The figure stood there, arms outstretched as though it were ready to catch Isaac and Laura should they try and run. "Behold, humans!" the figure cackled in a surprisingly unimpressive voice. "I am Krahn, a beast from beyond your nightmares! A monster from the darkest, foulest -"

KLONG! Isaac brought the flat of the spade down on the demon's head.

"Ow!" The demon yelped, staggering back and clutching his disfigured temple with stubby paw-like hands. "What did you do that for?!"

Isaac exchanged a dubious look with Laura. A demon playing the victim? This was new.

Krahn pointed angrily at them with one hand whilst keeping the other on his injury. "This has got hate crime written all over it!"

"Hate crime?" Isaac was flabbergasted.

Krahn nodded and bared his pointy little teeth at them. "You heard me!

Bloody humans – you think you can just barge in here and start whacking me with a dirty great spade just because I'm a demon. These wrinkles offend you do they?" he asked angrily, rubbing his cheeks furiously and pulling at the deep set wrinkles in his skin.

Laura raised a hand. "You've been eating people's fingers!"

Isaac jabbed his spade threateningly in Krahn's direction. "Yeah! And we didn't barge anywhere. Our entrance was very sneaky and unassuming."

Krahn raised a wrinkly eyebrow. "If you say so. And so what if I have been eating people's fingers?"

Isaac couldn't believe he was even arguing this. "It's wrong."

Krahn cocked his head to one side. "Why?"

"Because!" Isaac yelled.

"Because isn't an answer. In the wild animals eat each other all the time. I don't even eat the whole person, just a few fingers." Krahn said plainly. "Just because you're a human you think you're above the food chain? I suppose you'd have me starve!"

"You just can't go around eating people's fingers!"

"Why not?!"

"Oh for crap's sake this is ridiculous!" Isaac shouted. "I'm not standing here arguing morality with a, with a -"

"Go on, say it!" Krahn goaded viciously. "With a demon? I knew it, a demophobe through and through. Too good to talk or have a debate with me are you Mr High and Mighty? Would you like to just hit me with your big spade again?"

Laura interrupted. "Just out of interest," she asked, keeping a firm grip on her spade, "why just the fingers?"

"If you must know I like the crunchiness." Krahn explained matter-of-factly. "And the nice little bit of meat on the underside – beautifully tender. Especially on students, all that writing they do really softens up the -" He caught himself mid-sentence. "Wait why am I explaining all this to you?"

Isaac and Laura looked at each other and shrugged.

Krahn pointed at them again. "Back off and leave me alone!"

Isaac raised a finger of his own in warning. "Only if you promise not to eat any more fingers. Go to the butchers, buy a pork knuckle or something."

Krahn stared at them for a long moment with his dark, glistening eyes. "Do you know, talking to the two of you has had quite an effect on me." He sounded quite remorseful now, his tone was suddenly humble – stripped of its irritating fieriness. "Listening to you speak, listening to your words – it's made me realise I am something which I honestly didn't think I was before you came in here."

Isaac wondered if they had actually just performed a miracle and made a demon realise it was in the wrong. He looked at Laura – she looked baffled. They both looked at Krahn and gave him small, uneasy smiles.

Then the demon's regretful expression turned to one of sudden malice. "I'm hungry!" he snarled, advancing on them suddenly with arms outstretched.

Isaac knew it was too good to be true. He swung his spade sideways as Krahn approached, striking the creature in the torso.

Krahn groaned and staggered but didn't fall.

Isaac went to strike again but Krahn grabbed the full length of his arm with surprising strength before spinning him round and sending him rolling to the ground a few feet away.

Krahn sneered and started advancing on Laura.

"Back off!" she warned, holding her spade out in front of her.

"Come on, just let me have a nibble!" Krahn garbled eagerly. "I'll just take two, maybe three!"

Laura jabbed at him with the end of the spade. "Over my dead body!"

"Hmm, not as tasty off a corpse. But if you insist!" He grabbed the shovel end of Laura's spade and twisted it sharply, wrenching it from her grasp and chucking it aside.

Isaac was uninjured and back up on his feet. He ran at Krahn and swung his spade as hard as he could, hitting the demon flat on the back of the head as he moved closer to Laura. For a moment Isaac panicked that the blow hadn't even hurt the creature but a split-second later Krahn collapsed silently to the ground.

Laura came and stood next to Isaac. They both looked down at the body. "He was…weird."

"Yeah." Isaac nodded. Krahn had been quite possibly the weirdest demon he'd ever encountered. Certainly the only one to call him a demophobe. "Weird's the word. Weird and dead though, that's the main thing. No more finger food."

They both smirked and then a second later they both screamed as Krahn seemed to resurrect from the ground and launch himself into the air like a rocket, knocking them both flying as he did so.

Isaac felt cold mud greet his face as he landed on the ground for a second time that evening. He went to get back on his feet but was stopped by the feeling of a heavy foot on his back, pinning him down.

"I don't normally kill people," Krahn spat, "but with you two I think I'll make an exception."

"Get off me!" Isaac gargled as best he could despite his face being pressed sideways into the muddy ground. He struggled and pushed against Krahn's foot but he couldn't move an inch.

"Let's have that hand." Krahn said menacingly.

Isaac yelped in pain as he felt his arm being pulled awkwardly upwards from the ground.

"Might as well have a few appetisers before the feast!"

"No!" Isaac yelled, not quite believing he was about to feel his fingers being bitten off.

Suddenly – a voice! "Oi!" It was familiar! Really familiar!

Isaac felt his arm drop to the ground and the weight come off of his back. He heard some rushing footsteps, a few yelps and groans and then a swooshing noise followed quickly by a light thud and then moments later by a heavier thud. He turned over in the mud. First he saw Laura, getting back on her feet unharmed. Then he saw Krahn, headless on the ground. Then he saw the person who'd just saved him, sword in hand. "No way!"

Jack Tooley stepped forwards and held a hand out to Isaac. "This is becoming a bit of a habit, me saving you from certain death. We really must stop meeting like this."

Isaac stared at Jack with his mouth hanging wide open. "Again?" Isaac spluttered, taking Jack's hand and allowing himself to be pulled up to his feet. Jack was every bit as handsome as Isaac remembered him being from a few nights before.

"Who's this?" Laura asked, wiping the mud off her face as best she could.

"This is Jack." Isaac said without taking his eyes off of his saviour.

"Jack? As in that hot guy you mentioned from the other night?"

Jack grinned. "Hot guy?"

Isaac smiled awkwardly. "Yes, yes and err yes."

Jack walked over to Laura and shook her hand. "Nice to meet you."

"And you." Laura smiled and did a strange sort of mini curtsey. "I'm muddy."

Jack raised his eyebrows. "Funny name."

Laura laughed. "No, sorry – I mean I'm Laura and I am muddy. Muddy Laura, or Laura the muddy even perhaps. I'm babbling now, I'll stop." she chuckled.

Isaac wasn't chuckling. He didn't understand this at all. Jack being at the Guildhall was strange enough, but now him being here too just didn't add up. His happiness and relief at seeing jack again was quickly being replaced by a nasty shadow of a thought. He had a horrid sinking feeling that Jack might actually be an incredibly good looking snake in the grass. A spy sent by Archington. "How are you here? Why are you here?"

"Now, I know this looks suspect." Jack held his hands up in surrender. "But honestly, there's an innocent explanation. I was looking online earlier today, I was trying to find out more about that box from the other night. I went on the website for your local paper and whilst researching on there I saw this piece about girls getting their fingers bitten off." Jack shrugged innocently. "I thought I'd come and check it out."

Isaac shook his head. "But you live in London! You haven't just popped down the road like us, you've got tubes and trains and possibly even buses! Did you, did you get a bus?"

"Only from my flat to the tube station."

"See!" Isaac backed away from Jack. "Who are you working for, really? Are you working for Archington?"

"No you idiot!" Jack laughed, waving Isaac's accusation away with a waft of his hand. "Look, alright – you caught me." He sighed heavily. "I also came because I wanted to see you again."

Isaac put a hand to his ear in case he'd misheard. "Come again?"

Jack walked up close to Isaac. "I wanted to see you again." he said in a hushed, manly tone. "I figured you'd be investigating this too."

Isaac could smell Jack's aftershave. It was good. Good god it was good. "So you're -"

"Yes. And you're -"

Isaac smiled. "Yes."

"I wanted to give you this." Jack quickly brushed his loosely curled mop of blonde hair to one side before procuring a folded piece of paper from his pocket and passing it to Isaac. "I wanted to give it to you before, I don't know – I felt like we clicked. But your friend made it a bit awkward."

"Tom, yeah." Isaac opened the piece of paper – it was a phone number. He smiled. "Your number."

"I mean, you know – if you don't want it, that's fine. It's just it's not every day you meet another man who's that way inclined and also spends his spare time hunting monsters."

Isaac gulped. Jack did smell really good. "I also like shopping."

Jack nodded and smiled. "Shopping is good."

Laura coughed loudly and deliberately. She had unwillingly just become the third wheel.

"Sorry Laura." Isaac called.

"No, it's fine!" Laura said. "Just still muddy and cold that's all."

Isaac had quite forgotten that he too was covered in mud – he must have looked a right state.

"Why don't you invite Jack back to the house for a cuppa?" Laura suggested.

Jack looked uncertain. "Oh I wouldn't like to intrude -"

Isaac shook his head forcefully. "You wouldn't be! Honestly, you wouldn't be."

"Okay then, cup of tea would be nice."

"Good."

"Good."

Chapter Twenty

Jack stayed with them for a couple of hours that night before having to dash off and catch his train. Isaac was sad to see him go, as with everyone there at the house they hadn't had much time to talk privately. When Isaac said goodbye to him on the doorstep he wondered whether to go in for a kiss or whether that was too much too soon – the last time he'd kissed someone in that way it had ended up being the worst night of his life so he was apprehensive to say the least. In the end it was just a hug, but it was a good hug.

Every evening after that night they spoke on the phone without fail, never once running out of things to talk about as they got to know each other. Mostly they spoke about beautifully useless and trivial things - like what their favourite cuddly toy was when they were little, or what kind of donuts they liked best. Isaac loved jam and Jack loved custard. They both loved pepperoni pizza. Jack had a fear of sock puppets which matched Isaac's own ludicrous fear of cotton wool. This man was a complete escape for Isaac, but a comfortable escape in the fact that whilst they spoke about so much else other than the supernatural, that part of life was never a secret. Jack knew, he knew everything, so it felt okay. It was a comfortable escape because Isaac knew that if he needed to he could talk to Jack about the supernatural stuff. And they did talk about that sometimes, although Isaac spoke about it so much with his friends that by the time he spoke to Jack in the evening he had very often run out of steam and just wanted a few hours of random and innocent conversation.

Then on the following weekend Jack came down and stayed at the house. It had been wonderful – if also terrifyingly nerve-wracking to begin with. After his kiss related fears before, Isaac was relieved that they had their first kiss with absolutely no problems whatsoever. They spent a lot of time just snuggling in Isaac's room which was so ordinary to so many people but to Isaac it was extraordinary and absolutely amazing. They also went for a proper date into the city centre, to the cinema and for a meal. The others seemed to love Jack too – he was certainly a hit with the girls as he had a great sense of humour, he had Billie in stitches a lot of the time.

Sadly, the happiness that Jack was bringing came hand in hand with the growing danger that Professor Archington was bringing. Isaac felt very much that his brain was running on two tracks – on one side he had normal life which he loved, with Jack and his friends. Then on the other side running parallel he had supernatural life, with people being murdered by his university professor. That side he didn't love as much. For the first time in a long time he resented it, he resented the supernatural for being in his life, for stopping him from just being a normal person. The more he felt what it was like to live a normal life, the more he wanted it.

They had to be realistic though of course – Archington couldn't be ignored. In the following weeks everybody did their best to avoid him whilst they attempted to figure out exactly what he was planning. Avoiding the lectures that they had with him on a Friday and Monday were easy enough - they had all missed some of those lectures anyway over the course of the year due to various distractions, so now it was just a case of not going at all. Their other lectures during the week posed more of a problem however, as whilst everyone was keen to not have any direct contact with Archington there was the worry of falling behind on work and completely failing the year if they avoided all of their lectures entirely. Therefore anytime someone had to go into uni for a lecture they left a good half hour early, allowing enough time to adequately sneak unnoticed through campus and get to the right room. Although being rather time consuming it seemed to work and no-one had any direct encounters with Archington, although Billie came close one day when she was entering her lecture room just as Archington turned the corner at the end of the corridor - but it didn't seem like he saw her so no real damage was done.

Isaac was sure that hiding was their best option until they knew more about what Archington was up to - but the now cloak and dagger aspect of what had been one of the few normal aspects of their lives was draining. University had been a safe place, a place where they were like any other group of students – it belonged on the normal track, not on the supernatural one! Now it wasn't safe anymore things were definitely getting more stressful, although Isaac was determined not to let it affect him too much. He still had to try and live a life, still had to try and travel the normal track - they all did.

"There's nothing here," Ben said in a defeatist tone.
It was a Friday night in early April and Isaac and Ben were busy

researching in the living room. It was a beautiful clear night outside, and Isaac stood at the window looking out at the stars.

Ben sighed loudly. "There's never anything here." He was sitting on the sofa, staring at the laptop screen looking completely frustrated.

Isaac came away from the window and sat in one of the armchairs. "I know." The research had, so far, been fruitless. "But we have to keep looking."

"Yeah I know we do. All I'm saying is that it's been two weeks, two full weeks since we found out about this box thing and we've found nothing on it."

"Something will come up. We have to believe it will. Have the girls phoned yet?"

Billie, Laura and Gabbi had taken to going for walks around the city on nights they had free to see if they could spy any robed guys or demons doing anything that might give them a clue as to what exactly was going on.

"No, not yet." Ben sighed and picked up a large book on mythology and folklore. He leafed through it for a moment. "This is shit man."

"Ben -"

"No I mean it, it is. We know nothing. Pandora's Box is all that keeps coming up, and you know it turns out that wasn't even a box."

"Really?"

"It was a jar. It just got screwed up in translation I think."

"Wow, I never knew that. I still think Pandora's Box has more of a ring to it then Pandora's Jar though." Isaac smiled and Ben smiled back, despite the frustrating situation.

"Maybe it's not even a famous box, I mean it could just be a random cardboard box for all we know."

"Maybe. But I should think it's got some mystical qualities about it, whatever it is. I've read articles before about some ancient rituals using blood as a way to open things, portals for example. Maybe if people have been bled onto this thing then that's what opens it."

"And then what's inside? I can't imagine it'll be anything friendly."

"No, I think that's something we can be certain of." Isaac looked at the time. The girls should be back soon. "Right," he said, changing the topic. "Close that book for a minute. We need to discuss Sunday."

"Sunday?"

"Gabbi's twenty first."

"Yeah, right, okay. I got a card upstairs." Ben pointed upwards with his finger. "It's got a dog on the front."

"No I mean what are we going to do for it? I was thinking we all go to Bubble-Gum Saturday night and then a nice meal somewhere on Sunday."

"Ahh I don't know mate, do you think it's a good idea to do anything right now?"

"Of course it is. Look I know our situation is bad, I am very well aware of that believe me. I mean who is it that's been metaphorically whipping everyone into researching this thing whenever we can?"

"Yeah I know you've been very keen, we all have - but I'm just not sure that going out and partying is the right thing to do." Ben looked confused. "Not when there are ninety nine dead people and something bad on the way."

Isaac felt a twinge of shame. Ninety nine people were dead - more than likely anyway. "Ben I can't help thinking that if we cut ourselves off from everything happy and normal then we'll just end up being useless in this. Death is horrible, okay, I hate it. I lost three friends -"

"And I lost my sister."

"Exactly. So I know it's awful. We both do. But we won't fix anything or make the world better by just being miserable ourselves. Besides if something seriously bad is coming then we should try and enjoy happy moments whilst we can."

Ben considered Isaac's words for a moment and then nodded in agreement. "You're right. Bubble-Gum it is."

Five minutes later after more party planning Isaac heard his mobile phone ring. He rushed to pick it up - it was about the time that Jack usually phoned.

"Hello?" Isaac said expectantly, not even bothering to see who was calling before he spoke.

"Hey!" It was Jack.

"Well this is a nice surprise!"

"Surprise? I phone you at this time everyday!"

Isaac laughed. "Yeah I know but it's still a nice surprise to hear from you."

Just then Ben walked past where Isaac was standing in the hallway and stuck two fingers down his throat in an exaggerated gagging motion. "Disgusting gays!" he mouthed with a smirk.

Isaac shooed him away with a swift wave of his free hand. "How are you anyway?"

"Pretty good thanks. Know why?"

"Why?"

"Because I have a return ticket to Monks-Lantern booked for tomorrow!"

"Hooray!" Isaac's heart lifted immediately. He hadn't expected to see Jack again so soon. And with things not looking so good regarding the box research it was definitely a lift he needed. Even better, it meant that Jack would be able to go to Gabbi's birthday celebrations.

"I swapped some shifts around at work and got the weekend off. I remembered you said it was going to be Gabbi's birthday so I thought it would be a good weekend to come down."

"Yeah I just organised it all with Ben. We're going to go to Bubble-Gum on Saturday night and then a meal on Sunday I think."

"Ooh that's the place with the ball pit right?"

"That's it."

"Sounds good to me sweetheart. I'll have to leave Monday though, but still it's better than nothing."

Isaac felt a pinch of sadness already at the thought of Jack leaving, and he hadn't even arrived yet. He tried to push it out of his thoughts. "Well then I'll make the most of you for the two nights I have you."

"I'm sure you will!" It was obvious from the way Jack spoke that he was smiling.

Isaac was smiling too. Jack had come to mean so much to him in such a short time. It was because of Jack being such a happy, normal part of his life that Isaac felt hope that he and his friends could still do normal things like birthday parties. And hope was definitely a good thing.

Isaac carried on speaking to Jack for another half hour before he heard the front door slam. The girls were home. With the noise of the door he was ripped back out of his comfortable escape in Jack's voice and immediately thought whether they had found anything useful. Luckily Jack had to go anyway as he had a late shift at the supermarket to get to, so they said goodnight and Isaac was able to go and join the others in the kitchen. He came in just as Gabbi was half way through a sentence.

"- for a while but he managed to lose us in the market square."

"I don't think we were being sneaky enough." said Billie sadly.

"Who's this? Archington?" Isaac asked.

"No," Gabbi spoke again. "Just a robed guy we think. Caught sight of him half way up the high street, heading away from the direction of the guildhall. Could have been going anywhere."

"Or," Laura said, "as we thought on the way home, he could have been there deliberately to lead us away from the guildhall. But there's no way to know for sure."

"Either way we know nothing really conclusive." Gabbi said, pulling her large blue woolly hat off of her head. Her long hair spilled down past her shoulders. She smiled at Isaac apologetically. "Sorry darling. Another slow night."

"Don't apologise!" Isaac exclaimed, "We haven't found anything either." He knew they looked on him as being in charge but he didn't like the idea of them apologising to him. They hadn't done anything wrong at all.

Ben raised a hand to interject. "Only that Pandora's Box isn't actually a box. It's a jar." Everyone looked at him curiously. He stared back at them. "What? It's interesting!" He coughed a laugh and the others giggled a bit themselves.

"And you know what else is interesting?" Isaac said, determined to stay on the slight wave of happiness that had just swept through the kitchen. "Birthday celebrations!"

Gabbi faked a shocked expression that people had remembered. "Aww well we don't have to do anything, I mean we are pretty busy -" she started.

"Uh-uh! I've already had this conversation with Ben. We're going to Bubble-Gum tomorrow night - it's been ages since we've been."

"Oh it would be nice to have a night out!" Billie said excitedly.

Laura nodded in agreement. "I don't think we've been anywhere really since the beginning of January for Isaac's birthday."

"Which is why it is an excellent idea to go out Saturday." Isaac said. "Jack's coming down as well, so it's extra exciting!"

"Cor he really likes you!" Billie said. "Two weeks in a row!"

"Yeah this is getting pretty serious with him isn't it?" Gabbi asked.

"I think it is." Isaac beamed.

Everyone stood for a moment in quiet contemplation.

Billie broke the silence by abruptly coughing. "Well," she said, "I think it's time that single people like me who don't have an adorable boyfriend to come and see them should go and have a bath and go to bed." She smiled at Isaac.

"Yeah me too I think." Gabbi said, grabbing her hat from where she had placed it on the worktop. "But I'm so excited about tomorrow night! Hooray Birthday!" she shouted as she walked out of the kitchen and headed for the stairs with Billie.

"That's a really good idea to go out Isaac." Laura said once Billie and Gabbi had gone upstairs. "Gabbi deserves a good birthday. And we all deserve a good night out after the past few months."

"Yeah I agree," Ben added. "I know I was a bit doubtful earlier, but you're right. We'll need to stay together and stay positive to beat whatever's coming. We'll need to stay human."

Professor Robert Archington sat behind his desk in the guildhall, staring thoughtfully into the middle distance. The body on the floor in front of him had finally stopped shaking, the last dregs of life having left it. The blade in his hand felt heavy, and looking down he realised it was dripping blood onto his trousers. He cursed and put the knife up on the desk, attempting to wipe off the blood with his free hand but he only succeeded in making it worse.

"Elias!" he called out.

There was a second's pause before the wooden door opened and the hooded, heavy set figure of Elias entered. "Imperator?"

"Remove this blasted fool from the floor."

Elias looked a little alarmed at the dead body. "Was that Jaspeth?"

"Yes. The idiot led some of Isaac's friends close to the sacred space. Have I not instructed all of you time and time again that those children must not know anything about the sacred space yet? They shouldn't even know of its existence, as far as they are aware this building is our headquarters. That is how it has to be - at least until I am instructed otherwise."

Elias looked fearful. "He truly was a fool then Imperator. I will make sure the others are aware."

"Good. I do not suffer fools Elias, you know that. You're lucky I decided to suffer you after discovering you and that maniac Skarl bound up in a cupboard. Perhaps I am going soft. Anyone else who makes the mistake Jaspeth did will pay with their lives - be they human or demon."

"I understand Imperator." Elias went to drag the body out of the room. "What would you have me do with the corpse?"

"Weight it down and cast it into the river, or give it to Skarl to eat for all I care. Just remove it."

Elias nodded curtly before swiftly dragging the corpse out of the room. "Imperator." he muttered reverently as he pulled the door shut behind him once more.

Professor Archington sighed wearily, despite his anticipation for the time to come. The first triumph was almost at hand, so close now - so very close. He was just about to stand from his desk when he turned ever so slightly and jumped at what he suddenly saw out of the corner of his eye. It was her again! Blurred and just out of focus, there she was. He didn't turn fully because he knew she'd go if he did. "Please." he begged. "Please not now."

"Why are you doing this?" she asked. "This isn't right. You know that. This isn't the man I -"

"This isn't right?" he interrupted angrily. "Is what they did to you right? How can anything be right or for that matter how can anything be wrong? This isn't right and this isn't wrong, this is purely this. This is purely all there is, all there is for me now. And it may not be right or wrong but it will be good, I can promise you that."

"You called that man a fool just now, but Robert - you're the biggest fool of all. You're so lost now, I don't think even I can reach you. Why are you doing this?"

Professor Archington turned angrily to look at her. "I'm doing this for you!" he bellowed, but it was too late. She'd gone.

Chapter Twenty One

Jack stepped off of his train the next day looking cheerful and cheeky as he always did. On the times Isaac had done train journeys he was left feeling exhausted and ready to collapse, but Jack seemed to be unaffected. Amid a flurry of smartly dressed commuters Jack ran along the platform in his basketball trainers, jeans and hoody towards Isaac, enveloping him in a big hug when he reached him. The sexy smell of Jack's aftershave filled his nostrils – it was fast becoming his favourite smell in the world.

From that moment of meeting on the platform onwards the afternoon seemed to rush past. They got home and had a cup of tea and a chat whilst the girls were out shopping for new clothes to go out in and Ben was engrossed in a football match on the television.

Then they spent some more intimate time together in Isaac's room, blissfully ignoring the cavalcade of noise which came from the rest of the house when the girls returned home and forced Ben to sit through a fashion show of their purchases from town. Isaac knew it was a corny thing to think, but when he was alone with Jack on his bed time really did seem to stop. That's why it was a great surprise when Isaac picked his watch up off the side table and saw that it was already gone six. It was still broad daylight outside though, which made Isaac smile - summer was on the way.

Jack had fallen asleep in bed so Isaac pulled on a pair of tracksuit trousers and a vest top and went out to make them some dinner. He joined in a bit of pre-going out dancing in the kitchen with Billie, taking care to completely ignore the stack of books and papers that sat untidily in one of the armchairs in the living room. No work tonight he thought, supernatural or otherwise. Tonight was about having fun and being normal. There would be plenty of time to work on things next week.

Isaac and Jack ate their dinner of chips, baked beans and sausages in bed under the covers as Jack was still feeling a bit sleepy and whilst it was clear that summer was on the way it was by no means hot and bed was a good place to keep warm. By the time they had finished eating it had gone seven and it was time to get ready to go out. They both showered - Jack had suggested that showering together would be quite a fun idea and whilst Isaac was sure that it would be he couldn't risk the chance of getting into something that they didn't really have time to finish. Although they had been intimate together, they hadn't slept together yet and Isaac could only imagine that a hot and steamy shower would lead in that direction. He was ready to sleep with Jack, he was definitely ready, but not a few hours before they were supposed to be going out.

Another hour later saw them both washed, dressed and sitting around talking and laughing with the others over a few bottles of wine. Well, wine for everyone except Ben who preferred cider as he thought that wine was a girl's drink. When Isaac made the point that he and Jack weren't girls Ben just looked confused and shrugged. Everyone was in a really happy mood, and it seemed that Isaac's enthusiasm for a normal night out to really celebrate Gabbi's birthday had infected them all. The girls looked amazing in the dresses they'd bought in town earlier that day – Gabbi looked very much the birthday girl in a mid-length royal blue dress with silver detailing on it, her hair freshly curled and styled, smelling of the expensive perfume she only wore on very special occasions.

"You look beautiful." Isaac said to her when they had a few moments alone in the kitchen.

"Thanks darling." Gabbi smiled broadly. "You do too."

Isaac looked down at Gabbi's shoes – silver stilettos. "Killer heels!"

"I know right." Gabbi said offhandedly, tossing her hair back in a diva-esque fashion.

Isaac himself was wearing a navy coloured smart shirt and Jack was wearing a similar shirt in dark red. Ben wore a smart polo shirt – very manly looking but lovely nonetheless, a bit like Ben himself. They took the obligatory photo of all of them together as now was probably the best they were going to look all night, and then at half past nine they headed out towards Bubble-Gum.

When they got there the line to get in was huge, just as Isaac remembered it being when he used to come a fair bit before Christmas. It was completely dark by now and the chilliness from earlier had turned into really rather freezing temperatures, making the wait even more arduous than usual. Eventually they all filed in past the disgruntled looking bouncer and proceeded down the stairs into the club.

"It's underground?" Jack asked, sounding excited.

"Oh yeah," Isaac said, "and just wait until you see the ball pit, it's like the best thing ever!" He could feel the wine from home had definitely kicked in - this was going to be a good night.

Billie was struggling a bit with the steps - she had drunk the most back at the house and was obviously feeling it. "Why do they put big going down stairs in a club? I'm going to fall and kill myself and be dead before I've even got in! Then I'll look stupid!" she exclaimed, stumbling slightly. Gabbi grabbed her and held her up. Everyone laughed, Billie included. It was a bit daft really, having a load of steps to go down to get into the club, although the particularly funny thing was watching the real drunks try and clamber up the stairs at the end of the night.

Inside, the club was heaving. There was the usual crowd of really, really gay guys who tended to hang out together in groups, and then there was the student crowd which made up the majority of the people. The club itself was one huge room really, with the toilets and a small room for actual conversations off towards the back - although when Isaac had been in there it didn't seem like there was much talking going on. In the very centre of the main room was the ball pit and jungle gym which looked like it had been stolen right from a children's play centre and just dumped in the nightclub. Either side of that were two big dance floors and then all around the edge of the room were several bar areas and sofas and other places to sit. People were swarming over the jungle gym like wasps and the ball pit seemed to be more people than balls.

Isaac indicated towards the nearest bar and the others nodded. They all bought cocktails and then managed to find some sofas which they sat on until they had finished drinking. Nobody said very much, except the odd conversation shouted in each other's ears, but nonetheless everyone seemed to really be enjoying themselves. Isaac certainly was - he kept trying to touch Jack in inappropriate areas in what he thought was a very inconspicuous way, but knowing that he was quite drunk it probably wasn't inconspicuous at all.

"Ball pit time!" Gabbi announced as she slurped the last of her cocktail.

Everyone nodded excitedly and so they pushed through one of the dance floors and came to the edge of the ball pit, which really was rather big - the size of an average sized swimming pool Isaac would have thought. Luckily a few people had got out and so they jumped in with relative ease, and went on to chuck balls at each other and generally fall about and act like the drunken idiots that they were. The girls tried sexy dancing in the balls which was hilarious to watch and just when Isaac was least expecting it Jack came up beside him and instantly locked him in a long, passionate kiss. Isaac didn't resist at all, allowing himself to be completely lost in it. They were waist deep in the brightly coloured plastic balls and Isaac could feel Jack touching him just out of sight under the surface. He reciprocated eagerly and was just starting to wonder whether he and Jack should pay a visit to that back room when he felt Billie grab him and pull him out of the pit, mouthing that they were all going to go and dance and that he and Jack should come too.

They all danced and drank some more and then danced again, and when it came close to midnight they found themselves in the ball pit once more.

"In one minute you'll be twenty one!" Isaac screamed excitedly at Gabbi.

"Oh gosh I know, practically an old lady!" she said laughing.

"Okay here we go!" Isaac shouted, "Ten, nine, eight, seven, six, five, four, three, two, one -"

"Happy Birthday!" Everyone shouted together, all of them wading towards Gabbi before falling on her and hugging her. Soon they were all piled on top of her and Isaac could feel her frantically jumping about and hugging them all as best she could. Then all of a sudden her movements stopped. Then in the next instant she jolted forcefully, knocking them all backwards slightly. Isaac looked straight across and saw her standing there in the ball pit, bent double in pain. And then she screamed.

Chapter Twenty Two

"Gabbi!" Isaac cried, rushing forwards as best he could through the balls. His first thought was that they'd hurt her when they'd jumped on her.

"What's wrong?!" screamed Billie.

They all clustered in around Gabbi as she stood there, bent over, one hand on her stomach and one on her head.

"Too close, too close!" she muttered, her voice twisted with agony. They all backed off immediately, but as Isaac did so Gabbi shot out the hand that had been holding her stomach and grabbed his arm with it. "Isaac." she said. She wasn't shouting, yet somehow Isaac could hear her over the din of the music. All of a sudden his happy drunk feeling had gone completely. "Something's happening." She looked up at him and stared him straight in the eyes. The look was one of pure terror.

"Okay I'm taking you outside." Isaac said, putting an arm around her and motioning her towards the exit of the ball pit.

"Shall we come too?" Laura asked.

"No, I think maybe too many people might make her feel worse. I'll come back in a minute." He nodded to the others and exited the ball pit behind Gabbi. They hurried silently towards the exit, Gabbi still clutching her head and convulsing slightly. Isaac didn't have time to feel bad about his perfect normal night out having just been ruined, although he knew instantly that it had been. Right now he had to take care of Gabbi. As they rushed up the stairs to the exit he noticed that Jack had come with them. "Sweetheart what are you doing?" Isaac asked.

"I'm coming with you. I know too many people might make her worse, but it's just me." He looked at Isaac sincerely. "I want to help you."

"Okay," Isaac nodded. "Thank you." Although if he was being honest he really didn't know if Jack would be able to help at all. Come to think of it, he didn't even know if he himself would be able to help. What could be wrong with her? Had Archington done something? His mind raced with possibilities. Once outside he leant Gabbi against a wall, worried that if he sat her down on the floor he might not get her up again.

A particularly disgusting looking drunk guy came over and attempted to relieve himself against the wall just a few feet away from them.

"Somewhere else eh?" Jack said to the man, putting a hand on the guy's chest and pushing him backwards. The man looked disgruntled but walked away anyway.

Okay, thought Isaac, so Jack has helped. He quickly turned his attention back to Gabbi, who was taking deep breaths. "Gabbi what's wrong? Did we hurt you?" he asked.

"No - no you didn't, it wasn't that. It just suddenly started. In my head." she whispered, sounding quite frail.

"What is it?" Isaac asked. Gabbi was gritting her teeth and moaning now, clasping her head with both hands.

"I don't know," she gasped. "It's like my head is being torn open. Like it's being torn open and stuff is being rammed in." She moaned again in agony.

Isaac looked at Jack and gave him a worried expression, which he in turn gave straight back. "What kind of stuff? I don't understand!"

"I don't know, I'm sorry -"

"Don't apologise! It's -"

"It's like - Isaac it's like there's something bigger, something too big for my brain but it's being forced in." Her voice had suddenly become eerily calm. "I don't know what it is, but it's going in."

"Does it still hurt?"

"Yes. Like hell."

"You seem calmer though."

"Yeah I know, I don't know why. But yes, it still hurts. Blimey yes it does."

"Okay." Isaac looked at Jack. "We're going home."

"What about the others?" Jack asked.

"Just text one of them, you took all of their numbers last week right?"

"Yeah, but shouldn't we -"

"Gabbi needs to get home and that place in there is like a sea of people. It'll be fine, just text them and say to head home as soon as they can."

"Okay, I'll just get my -"

"No! No, no." Gabbi interrupted Jack, forcing a hand up in objection, "This was meant to be a night of fun right?"

"Gabbi you need to go home." Isaac said.

"Yes, but they don't. Tell them to stay and have fun, please. Tell them I want them to."

Isaac sighed. She was probably right - if they all went home right now then there wouldn't be much they could do. No point ruining six nights when you can just ruin three. "Okay," he smiled. "Go ahead Jack, text them and tell them to stay."

They rushed home as quickly as they could, with Gabbi going from grabbing her head and groaning to just being silent and looking shell-shocked. By the time they got in she had mostly stopped crying out loudly and instead just seemed to be quietly dealing with the pain in her head.

"I'll take her upstairs." Isaac said to Jack.

"Okay my love - I'll make some tea yeah?"

"Yes I think that'd be a good idea. Thankyou." He smiled at Jack and kissed him quickly on the cheek before helping Gabbi up the stairs. Once he had got her in her room he helped her get into bed. She seemed to look much calmer as she lay her head down on the pillow, her long hair going out untidily in all directions. "How are you feeling?" he asked tentatively.

"Better. The pain's going away a bit." she afforded him a small smile. "It's just a dull ache now."

"Good." Isaac smiled back. He sat down next to her on the bed.

"Sorry for ruining the night darling."

"Don't you dare. You couldn't help it. Besides the main thing now is making you better and stopping whatever did this to you. It must have been Archington. Bastard."

"It's okay Isaac. It's okay to be cross."

"Why would I be cross at you?"

"Not at me. At the situation."

"No, honestly I'm not cross. Well I'm cross that someone or something has done this to you. Of course I'm cross at that." Isaac smiled, but it must have looked as fake as it felt. "I'm fine."

"I know this night was meant be proof of us still having normal lives somehow."

"Tonight isn't and wasn't about my niggling paranoid insecurities." Isaac said calmingly. "You've just had something power drill its way into your brain, stop being so selfless and insightful and just think about yourself for once. We can talk about the crazy crap in my brain when you're better."

Gabbi smiled weakly. "You know everything will be alright don't you? Normal lives or not, we're all here together and none of us are going anywhere. I'm certainly not."

Isaac nodded and patted Gabbi's hand. "Thank you dearest. I'm glad of that." He stood up from where he'd been sitting. "I'll go and check on that tea. We'll find out what happened to you Gabbi, I promise. We'll sort it out."

Gabbi nodded appreciatively. "My hero. Mr Biscuit-Face."

Isaac smiled. "Mr Biscuit-Face to the rescue." He turned and headed for the door, looking back once more in time to see Gabbi's eyes close. She must have been so tired. "Sleep tight Gabriella. Happy Birthday."

Back downstairs, Isaac found Jack about to carry the cup of tea up to Gabbi.

"Don't worry about the tea for Gabbi, she's gone to sleep."

"Probably for the best." Jack said. "After that madness she'll need plenty of rest." He paused a moment. "Ooh that rhymed."

Isaac laughed. "You're a funny one you are."

Jack smiled and sat down on the sofa. "Sit with me." he instructed.

Isaac did as he was told. He sat down next to Jack, leaning his head back and resting it against the soft fabric of the sofa. "I am whacked." he said emphatically.

"I'm not surprised." Jack said. "Your brain's been quite busy tonight hasn't it?"

"Has it?" Isaac was intrigued by what Jack meant.

"You can't pull the wool over my eyes. You are a very worried young man."

"Young man?" Isaac laughed. "You sound like granddad saying it like that."

"Yeah well I am older than you!"

"Two years! One and a half!"

"Yeah well it still makes me wiser. Sometimes anyway." Jack smiled. "You got worried tonight when Gabbi collapsed."

"Of course I did, she -"

"No I don't mean worried for her, or not just worried for her anyway. I saw it on your face."

"Saw what?"

"You had a plan for tonight, I know you did. You wanted it to be normal, free of spooks and monsters -"

"Jack -"

"No let me finish. You wanted that and then when Gabbi collapsed you saw all of those hopes collapse with her. Normal night, gone. Normal life, gone. If a night out can't work what hope do you have for life in general?"

"Not much hope?"

"Every hope Isaac. Every hope. Mad things don't just happen because of the supernatural you know. We could be the most quote unquote normal people out there and still find ourselves in no end of trouble. God I went out once and ended up being projectile vomited on whilst being told off by the police for relieving myself in public. And my clothes were new, imagine how pissed off I was!"

"That's disgusting." Isaac laughed.

"Yeah it was. But this is my point sweetheart, crazy stuff happens to every kind of person. You could turn a corner tomorrow and get knocked down by a bus or you could get mugged by a completely human attacker – no demons involved at all! But people don't let those possibilities stop them. You don't let fear of things going wrong stop you enjoying your life. You enjoy it, whatever type of life you have you live it and you enjoy living it. And okay your life, all our lives – maybe they're a bit more exciting than the average life out there, but they're still just the same as anyone else's when you break them right down. Friends, family, love, loss – it's all the same."

Isaac found his eyes welling up as Jack spoke. He nodded in agreement with Jack's words. "You're right." he sighed and then groaned loudly. "It's been quite an emotional hour."

Jack smiled warmly. "It's okay. And you know, as bad as it has been tonight, and as worried as I am about Gabbi, I would still much rather have our night ruined by some exciting albeit scary supernatural occurrence than someone vomiting on me. And that's speaking from experience." Jack laughed.

"Yeah, I suppose." Isaac smiled. He did think that maybe he would have preferred vomit to Gabbi's life being in potential danger, but he knew what Jack meant. "Oh dear it's a funny old life this."

"Yes it is." Jack agreed. "But I'll tell you one more thing."

"What?"

"You wouldn't change it. Not really. You like helping. Plus you're a massive supernatural geek."

Isaac laughed. "You're very perceptive." He paused for a moment and looked at Jack. "I love you." It was the first time he'd said those words to Jack. There was a brief moment of panic in his brain as to how they'd be received.

Jack smiled broadly at Isaac. "I love you too."

Panic over. Isaac smiled with relief and happiness.

Jack reached out and took Isaac by the hand, giving it a little squeeze and a rub as he did. "Let's go to bed eh?"

Chapter Twenty Three

Isaac woke up far across the bed from Jack on the morning after their night out. The sun was up but he could just tell it must still have been early, he always woke a little earlier than usual when he'd been drinking the night before. Although the disturbing events of the night had sobered him up quite quickly he still felt a little sting in his head to remind him of the wine he'd put away. He winced a little and groaned to himself before remembering who was in the bed with him and rolling across under the duvet to cuddle Jack's naked form from behind. That warm, lovely smell greeted him. He breathed in deeply and smiled happily despite the sting in his head and the ongoing drama he knew he had to deal with that day. The cuddle received little reaction, just a small but appreciative squeeze of Isaac's arms as Jack was quite obviously still asleep. Isaac didn't mind, he was happy just to lay there and bask in the innocence of the moment. He drifted in and out of sleep again for the next few hours, only properly waking up when Jack started to get more active himself.

"Hello lover!" Jack said in a croaky voice, right before stretching and letting out a loud yawn.

"Good morning!" Isaac leant forward and kissed him quickly. "How did you sleep?"

"Very well thank you. Even though you were Mr. Snorey Snorisson." Jack chuckled.

Isaac chuckled too. "Well I guess we should get up. I can hear movements in the kitchen." He heaved himself up so he was sitting upright in bed and looked at the time - it was quarter past nine.

"What's the time? Research o'clock?"

"Pretty much. Maybe some breakfast first though." He leant across and kissed Jack again before getting out of bed and pulling on tracksuit bottoms and a plain black t-shirt. "I could make pancakes. Or I could attempt to make pancakes at least."

"Sounds good to me baby. You can go and start if you like, I'll be out in a minute."

"Okay." Isaac said, heading out the bedroom door. "Don't be long!"

Sure enough he found Billie and Laura in the kitchen, also making breakfast. He filled them in on everything that happened the night before after they left the club and they all agreed to start researching what it could have been after breakfast. Ben had apparently gone swimming, something that he liked to do after a night out as it made him feel less hung-over. Gabbi was still asleep in bed and they thought it all best to leave her there in case waking her up brought any pain back. Apparently the others hadn't stayed long at all after Isaac, Gabbi and Jack had left as they felt so worried about Gabbi. The thing that held them up was that they had decided to stop for a takeaway from Jimmy's Pizza and the queue there had been huge.

"Have we got pancake stuff?" Isaac asked, opening up cupboards around the kitchen.

"We've got milk and flour but no eggs." Laura said. "Were you going to make some then?"

"Yeah, a little romantic breakfast for me and Jack."

"Aww!" Billie and Laura exclaimed at the same time.

Isaac smiled. "I know. Us gays are just too cute for words." He opened up the cupboard that he kept most of his personal food in and noticed a box of cereal bars on the top shelf. "Ahh I'd forgotten about these, they'll have to do!" He quickly looked towards his room - no sign of Jack. He stepped across the kitchen so he was right beside Billie and Laura. "We had sex last night!" he whispered.

"Oh my god!" Billie gabbled. She put the tea she'd been holding down on the worktop. "Like proper sex?" She lowered her voice for the next part. "In the bum?"

Laura laughed out loud. "Billie what are you like?!"

Isaac laughed too and then quickly put his finger to his lips incase their laughter aroused suspicion. "Yes." He giggled a bit like a naughty schoolgirl. It was childish really but it was funny.

"What was it like?" Billie asked. "I want details!"

Laura looked at her and raised an eyebrow. "Really?"

Billie looked like she was thinking for a second and then shook her head. "Okay I don't want details." she laughed. "But what was it like, you know, in general."

"It was really good." Isaac said. "Like really, really good." He paused for a moment. "I love him."

Billie squawked slightly at this news and giggled. "That's so exciting!"

"Bless you you're so cute the two of you!" Laura said smiling. "Have you said it to one another?"

"Yeah, last night - oh wait, here he comes."

Jack had emerged from Isaac's room and was walking across to the kitchen. He was dressed in the same jeans and hoody he'd been wearing the previous day. "Morning everyone." he called cheerfully.

"Morning!" came the joint reply from Billie and Laura, both of whom were smiling.

"No pancakes baby." Isaac said apologetically. "Cereal bar okay? Not quite the same I know but it's better than a poke in the eye with a sharp stick."

"Sounds perfect." Jack smiled.

By quarter to ten they had all eaten and they were just finishing washing up their plates and mugs. Ben still hadn't returned from swimming and Gabbi was still asleep upstairs.

"So," Laura began as they all walked back into the living room and slumped down onto the sofa and chairs. Jack sat leaning against Isaac on the sofa. "What do we think happened last night?"

"Archington. Must have been." Isaac said.

"That's what I thought," Billie said. "But if it was him what exactly did he do? If Gabbi says that there is something new or something that's been shoved in her brain, what did he put in there?"

Isaac thought for a moment. Suddenly he remembered something. "I read a book once, all about channelling demonic spirits and whatnot. It is possible, if you have enough power, to curse someone with a demon - like force it into that person's body."

"Well if that's the case it could either be hard to fix or incredibly hard to fix if it's a soul dweller." Jack said.

Laura jumped in. "We've done some exorcisms before though. And Isaac you've done some before you came to uni too right?" she asked. "It shouldn't be impossible to fix - if that is what it is."

Isaac bit his lip in uncertainty. Exorcisms nearly always carried a risk to the person who was possessed. He couldn't bear the thought of hurting or possibly even killing Gabbi. If Archington really had sent a demon into her then the chances are it would be a powerful one. And a powerful demon would mean a difficult exorcism. "We'd need to be certain before we did anything. Also Gabbi mentioned that whatever has been shoved in her brain isn't open yet, like she isn't aware of what it is. It's like it's in there in a box."

"A box?" Laura said in an obvious tone.

"Like the box we've been trying to research for the past two weeks?" Billie asked.

Isaac had to admit it did make some sense. They hadn't been able to turn up anything on this box and now Gabbi says there is something in her head which hasn't been opened yet. Opening is exactly what you do to boxes.

"So the box is abstract?" Jack asked.

"Maybe," Isaac pondered. "Like something that only exists in the realities of the mind and the spirit." He looked up at Jack who looked uncertain. He had to admit it did sound a bit like they were clutching at straws. But there was a link there and when they otherwise didn't have any leads at all then they had to take any lead possible. "You don't think it sounds likely?" he asked Jack.

"I'm not sure. It does sound a bit thin to be honest, but then you guys have been here doing this much longer than I have. Trust your judgement. And if it's wrong then you haven't lost anything - it's just back to square one that's all."

Billie sighed. "I hate square one."

Isaac knocked gently on Gabbi's bedroom door a few minutes later. He heard a quiet voice asking him to come in so he entered, carrying a glass of water with him.

"How's the Pakistani patient?" he asked brightly.

"Feeling a bit rough." Gabbi croaked. "No splitting head pains, just some random aching." She seemed happy to see Isaac. "But I'm okay. How did it go last night after we left? Did the others have a nice night?"

"I think they did yes. They didn't stay long after we left but they enjoyed themselves I think." Isaac said.

Gabbi smiled despite looking really quite tired. "Good."

"Here, have some water." Isaac passed the glass of water over to Gabbi, sitting himself down on the side of the bed at the same time.

"Thanks," Gabbi took the glass gratefully. She smiled, took a sip of the water and immediately spat it back out, spraying water all over the bed sheets. "Eugh!" she cried, her face screwed up in disgust. "Salty water?!"

"We thought you might be a demon." Isaac said apologetically.

"A demon?" Gabbi looked horrified and insulted.

"Yeah. Sorry! It's just we weren't sure and you know demons on a very basic level don't really like salt that much so we thought if we gave you salt water we could see your reaction."

"And?" Gabbi still sounded shocked.

"Demon free I think. I mean yeah you screwed your face up, but you didn't sizzle or sprout horns at all."

"The cheek of it, thinking I was a demon." The shocked face remained but there was also a smile now. "What made you think that I even might be?"

"Well I remembered reading about people sending demons into other people's minds - like a curse or a hex, and we wondered if that's what Archington had done to you."

"Well better safe than sorry I guess."

"Do you feel like you know anything new or different about what happened?"

"Nothing. To be honest it seems to have passed. Whatever it was, it's fading. I feel better already since I've woken up this morning."

"That's good though, that you are feeling better."

"Yeah it is, but the closest I was to knowing what's happened to me was when I was in immense pain. Now it's like nothing even happened at all. I can't even feel anything in there any more." Gabbi sighed and pouted deliberately.

"Look don't worry, we'll get answers. In the mean time let's just be glad that one way or another you're feeling better. I'm not about to lose you." He reached out and held Gabbi's arm for a moment. Just then they heard the front door slam - it sounded like Ben coming back from swimming. "We should go and fill him in on the plan."

"Plan? What plan darling?"

"The plan I've just thought up to get answers."

Isaac went downstairs whilst Gabbi got up and got dressed. The others had started getting Ben up to speed with what had happened whilst he'd been swimming. Then once that was all done and Gabbi had come down from her room Isaac told them how he thought they would be able to get some answers.

"Are you serious?" asked Laura, eyes wide open in disbelief.

Billie was wearing a similar shocked expression. "Yeah are you serious? Like serious, serious?"

"Absolutely." Isaac replied. "I think things have gone far enough now. It was fine the past few weeks but after what's happened to Gabbi I don't think we can just hide anymore. We need to confront Archington."

"Sounds like a good plan to me mate." Ben said, nodding supportively.

"Yeah me too." said Jack. "Seems like a very good idea."

Isaac was glad to have their support but he was still worried about how the girls felt. "Gabbi what do you think?" he asked.

"It's very different to how we've been so far." She paused and looked down for a moment. A second later she looked up brightly. "I like it."

"Good." Isaac said. "How about you two?" he said, turning to Billie and Laura.

"I think it's just because it is so different to anything we've done before." Laura said.

"Yeah we've mostly been about the spying or the following or the sneaking so far. But yeah, I think it's a good idea. A bit scary, but a good idea." Billie said, smiling bravely now.

"Me too." Laura agreed. "So when are we going to do this?"

"Tomorrow." Isaac announced. Shocked expressions returned to faces around the room. "I know it's soon." Isaac had predicted their concerns. "But who knows what he's planning next or what further thing he's got planned for Gabbi. We're supposed to have a lecture with him tomorrow evening as it is. If we go in at the end of that lecture he'll be alone in the room."

"What if he gets violent?" Ben asked. "I mean that's fine, but what do we do? Fight back?"

"If we have to. We've all fought before. But I don't think it will come to that. In the uni there will be people close by, he can't do anything too drastic without blowing his cover of being a kindly old professor."

Although Isaac was sure people were still uncertain, everyone still nodded in agreement. Tomorrow night, they confronted Archington.

Chapter Twenty Four

The rest of Sunday was quite relaxing all things considered. There was some slow research done - they didn't find anything out but knowing that they would be confronting the very man who held all the answers the next day it wasn't that much of a worry.

It was still Gabbi's birthday of course and so the atmosphere was quite happy in the house, even though everyone's minds were no doubt elsewhere. After the meeting in the morning they had all given Gabbi presents and cards - Isaac had got her a new top he had seen quite a while ago and had decided to buy in advance, Billie and Laura had clubbed together to buy a really nice handbag and Ben had got her a card with a DVD voucher inside - choosing actual presents was evidently not his strong point. After they had watched Gabbi open her presents they all had a rather crude but enjoyable lunch of bacon and sausage sandwiches and then they spent the afternoon lazing about in the house, either talking or playing on Ben's video games.

Isaac and Jack disappeared off to his room every now and again for some quiet time together, just the two of them. Isaac enjoyed each moment to the full, knowing that Jack would be gone the next day. Given how short they were on time, Isaac had assumed that they would stay in that night and just snuggle and watch a film, so he was surprised when Jack said otherwise.

"Let's go out tonight." Jack suggested casually.

They were in the kitchen and Isaac was washing up a few mugs. Jack had come up behind him and given him a hug. He stayed with his arms wrapped around Isaac as they spoke.

"Go out? Where? Bubble-gum doesn't open on Sundays."

"No I don't mean out like that. Let's just go for a walk."

"Just a random walk through Monks-Lantern?" Isaac chuckled. The idea wasn't entirely unappealing. The sun was just setting now and it did look like it was going to be a clear night. It would be nice to look at the stars.

"Yeah, why not? It'll be like the night we met."

"Okay, a walk it is." Isaac finished washing up the mugs and emptied out the water from the washing up bowl. "But first -" He quickly turned round, twisting out of Jack's arms and began splashing him with water from his wet hands.

"Oi!" Jack shouted, "Pack it in!"

Isaac chased him round the kitchen until Jack found a pint glass half full with water on the worktop. He grabbed it and held it in front of him menacingly as if he were brandishing a gun. "Any closer and I'll throw it!" he said laughing.

Isaac was laughing too. "No you wouldn't!"

"I would!" Jack waved the glass forwards and backwards, sloshing the water about.

Isaac considered his options for a moment before diving towards Jack, head down and arms outstretched. Jack chucked the water. Most of it landed in Isaac's hair, but some flew further and soaked his back. Isaac grabbed hold of Jack and tickled and cuddled him for a moment, both of them screaming and laughing.

"I love you." Isaac said once they had calmed down a bit.

"Good." Jack smiled. "I love you too."

They headed out the front door for their walk at nine in the evening. It was another chilly night, so they were both dressed in coats and gloves. Completely by accident they both had nearly identical coats, both of them black double-breasted pea coats. They weren't quite identical though - and even if they were it wouldn't have mattered, his and his matching coats - it would have been quite funny. Isaac still wasn't exactly sure where they would walk to so he just figured they could head out and see where they naturally drifted towards. It was a beautiful night, the sky was perfectly clear and all the stars were shining brightly.

It was also very nice as the streets were more or less deserted so they felt more than comfortable walking along hand in hand. It wasn't that it would be dangerous to hold hands in the middle of the day in the city centre, Isaac didn't fear an attack and he was certain that Jack didn't. Still, sometimes the stares that were occasionally experienced could be unwelcome.

They were just talking about how they would decorate Isaac's house if they had lots of money when Isaac noticed where they were naturally drifting towards - Saint Andrew's cemetery. They had walked around the outer edge of the city centre, it was mostly residential and if they kept walking on the road they were on they would either end up in the cemetery or they would end up taking a smaller road which Isaac knew led to a very rough housing estate which you certainly wouldn't want to walk through at night time unless you had to. So it seemed like the cemetery was the better option, although that wasn't to say that Isaac was completely happy about it. He knew what could be found in cemeteries from time to time- and he and Jack were unarmed. He had been to St Andrew's before and he was sure that there was another gate on the opposite side which would bring them out to a main road and from there they could get home. They should be okay if they walked through quickly and kept their eyes peeled.

"We're going in the cemetery?" Jack asked as they neared the wooden gate which served as the entrance.

"I'm afraid so baby. It's this or chav-land down that road." Isaac swung the gate open and indicated with a nod of his head to the road in question. Jack looked down the road. A gang of teenagers on bikes could be seen loitering in the distance, drinking what looked like cheap beer.

"I think I'll take the dead guys."

"Good choice."

The cemetery was deserted by the looks of things, which wasn't a surprise at half nine at night on a Sunday. It was fairly well lit, with lamp-posts lighting the main paths which went around the area. It was fairly typical as cemeteries went - lots of ornate grave stones in various states of disrepair, lots of mature trees with low hanging branches which made the already dark spaces away from the paths even darker. The fastest route through was fairly straight forward and it only took about five minutes to walk if that. Three minutes if they ran, maybe two if they ran really fast. Isaac looked across at Jack - he didn't seem worried at all and Isaac didn't want to panic him unnecessarily.

"Why are we rushing?" Jack asked.

Evidently Isaac hadn't hidden his fear that well at all. "We're not rushing."

"Yeah, we're walking at like fifty miles an hour. I don't come to cemeteries often but when I do I quite like looking at the graves."

"Oh sorry," Isaac said, preparing a lie in his head. "I just suddenly need a wee and I know there are some public toilets just the other side on the main road." He said it all too quickly. It was a bad and obvious lie although Jack only gave him a funny look.

"Just go behind a tree here if you need to. Oh!" Jack exclaimed loudly.

Isaac panicked. Had Jack seen something? "What? What is it?"

"Behind a tree! We could do it behind a tree!" Jack was grinning.

"Behind a tree, are you kidding? Have sex, behind a tree, in a graveyard?" Isaac laughed.

"Yeah, why not?" Jack was laughing too.

"Okay, I cannot begin to list the reasons how -" Isaac stopped dead, he stopped walking and he stopped talking. His stomach clenched and turned over.

Jack stopped next to him. "What? Isaac you look terrified, what's wrong?"

Jack asked, fear clearly rising in his voice.

"Dead ahead of us, through those trees, there was a light from somewhere. One of these lamps I think, shining through the trees."

"Right, so -"

"There's no light there now. Something's moved in front of it. Something's there." There was a huge lump forming in Isaac's throat, and his stomach had turned over several more times.

Jack was now starting to look just as worried. "What is it?"

"A ghoul." Isaac said grimly. It was the only thing it could be.

Ghouls were demonic physical beings - not like possessed demoniacs where it was a human possessed by a spirit demon. They were soulless, disgusting creatures with long claws, sharp teeth, sunken black eyes and wrinkled and disfigured pale skin. Monks-Lantern seemed to have more than its fair share of them too and although Isaac hadn't encountered any since Christmas he was sure that didn't mean that they had all just gone away. Ghouls stayed hidden during the day as they were blind in daylight - they could only see in the darkness. In-fact the darker it was, the more pitch black it was, the easier they could see. Just when a person was at their weakest in the darkness - blind, unable to see their hand in front of their face, ghouls could see with perfect clarity.

A ghoul's purpose in life was to devour dead flesh - human flesh if possible, however they could get it. They scavenged a lot in cemeteries and graveyards but they weren't against hunting fresh meat if they could do so without being caught.

Man had spread and grown so much in the past centuries that the ghouls were nowhere near as prolific as they once were, but they were still just as dangerous. They moved silently in the shadows, watching, waiting - just a dark shape in the darkness.

Isaac had known them to like standing in people's back gardens at night, just out of reach of the lights from the house, hoping that someone would wander out into the dark where they were vulnerable and could be snatched away.

Killing them was fortunately relatively simple, they functioned much the same way as a human so anything that would kill a person would likely kill a ghoul - although of course a ghoul was at three times the strength of the average person so it still wasn't easy. Isaac wished he'd thought to bring a dagger or some kind of weapon with him.

"What do we do?" Jack had grabbed a tight hold of Isaac's coat sleeve.

Isaac took Jack's hand and held it tightly, all the time not taking his eyes off of where the light had been in front of them. He thought about an answer to Jack's question. They were in the middle of the cemetery with no weapons - there was only one thing they could do.

"We run."

Suddenly the thing moved and the light was visible again. It was coming.

"Now!" Isaac shouted and they belted off down the path back in the direction they had come from - they were still closer to that gate than to the other one. Isaac felt like he was going to trip over at any moment as he wasn't looking at all where his feet were going, he was just trying to run as fast as he possibly could. Luckily he was quite a fast runner as he had reasonably long legs. Jack kept right along side him and Isaac kept a tight hold of his hand. He didn't dare look round to see where the ghoul was for fear of stumbling and falling but he could hear scrabbling footsteps behind them. They kept running, as fast as they could. Rounding a corner, Isaac saw the gate they had come in through up ahead. "There's the gate, we just have to get out-" Isaac flew face down onto the path. The bricks stung his face and hands. He knew he'd been pushed - the ghoul had caught up with them.

Jack fell with him as they'd been holding hands so tightly and Isaac heard him moan in pain as he too landed sharply on the brick path.

Isaac instinctively rolled over onto his back to see their attacker. What he saw made him feel sick to his stomach.

Chapter Twenty Five

Foul and stinking, the ghoul stood towering over them. It was thin and wild looking, dressed in black rags that covered it from shoulder to knee. Its head was bulbous and shining, the skin of its face a pale grey and horribly rippled, disfigured and deformed. Its eyes were sunken and were glistening black in colour - there was no white to be seen at all. The lips were a deep black too and beyond them inside its disgusting mouth there were rows of jagged, crooked teeth protruding from gums which were just as black as the lips that surrounded them. Blood dribbled and dripped from its mouth and landed in spatters on its festering rag like clothes - it had clearly just been feeding when Isaac and Jack had caught its attention. At the end of its wiry grey arms there were long claws from thin fingers which now clicked together menacingly in anticipation.

Isaac looked from the ghoul to Jack, who was staring up at it in fear mixed with complete and utter disgust. Ghouls didn't speak any language that Isaac knew of, so there was no point wasting time with conversation. Adrenaline coursed through Isaac's body - it was just what he needed. They would get out of this alive. They had to.

Without any further hesitation Isaac thrashed out with his right leg, kicking the ghoul on its shin. The ghoul staggered backwards slightly, snarling like a wild beast, allowing Isaac and Jack time to get up from the ground.

"Find me something I can kill this thing with!" Isaac shouted.

"Like what?"

"I don't know! Something sharp or blunt or heavy or something!"

The ghoul growled at them loudly, baring its rotting teeth.

Jack nodded quickly and ran off. Before the ghoul had time to give chase Isaac kicked with his right leg again and planted his foot in the creature's stomach. It bent slightly and Isaac moved in, punching up on the ghoul's chin, sending it backwards a little bit more. They had been two lucky shots though as the very next moment the ghoul lunged at Isaac and collided hard into him, sending him careering off to the side of the path. The ghoul then grabbed him by the shoulders, its sharp claws digging into his coat but not quite reaching his skin. He was yanked backwards and fell to the ground again - the ghoul was quick to stand over him, panting and snarling. Its breath stank. Isaac blocked a punch from the ghoul which was aimed for his face and then he thrust a knee up into what he presumed was the creature's groin. The ghoul flinched but it didn't recoil. If anything Isaac was sure he could detect a kind of smarmy grin appear on the ghoul's hideous face, as if taunting him for attempting to hurt organs that obviously weren't there. The ghoul opened its mouth wide, screaming down at Isaac - a terrifying kind of wailing scream mixed with a deep, guttural growl. Saliva and blood dribbled down constantly onto Isaac's coat.

With every bit of strength he had, Isaac pulled his knees up to his chest and then kicked out with both feet at the monster. This made it move, and with a deathly howl it staggered backwards. Isaac hopped to his feet and punched it twice across the face before receiving one across his own face in return. He blocked the next punch that came at him and then grabbed the ghoul by the arms and attempted to throw it to the ground. Its skin was dry and scabby to the touch. After a moment locked in each others' arms, Isaac succeeded in unbalancing the ghoul and forcing it to the ground a few feet away from him. He heard footsteps and whipped his head round to see Jack running towards him with a rusty spade in hand. That would do nicely.

"Sweetheart, catch!" Jack tossed the spade to Isaac when he got close enough.

Isaac caught it with both hands. It was nice and heavy - perfect. The ghoul looked up at him from the ground, snarling wildly.

"Snarl all you like," Isaac said, raising the spade high above his head. "It won't make you any prettier." He brought the spade crashing down onto the ghoul's head. There was no remorse, confusion or sadness in the ghoul's black eyes as the spade fell. Isaac didn't feel bad about killing the creature - the crunching noise the spade had made when it met the ghoul's face hadn't been pleasant, but he could live with it.

"That's gross." Jack said looking at the ghoul's face after Isaac lifted the spade back off. "Is it dead?"

"Dead as a dodo." Isaac tossed the spade to one side. "They're horrible creatures but they're still pretty easy to kill. About as easy as killing people."

"I see. That doesn't mean you've actually killed people though right?"

"Oh gosh no." Although upon saying that Isaac's thoughts did instinctively flash to his three dead friends. He sighed, looked at the ghouls body and then looked down at his pea coat, covered in various fluids. It'd be a hard time explaining the stains at the dry cleaners.

"Good. What do we do with the body?"

"We can just leave it in the bushes. Once the sun comes up it will decompose pretty quickly, bones and everything."

"Okey-dokey, a bush burial it is. You take the arms." Jack said, grabbing hold of the legs.

Together they carried the body into the nearest dense bushes they could find and after dumping it they hurried out of the cemetery and headed home - just in case there were any other ghouls around.

Isaac was still pumping with adrenaline as they walked back. "I think we did pretty well back then."

The streets were empty as they walked.

"We did. Only just though - I wouldn't have liked to have faced that alone. And I wouldn't have like you to have faced that alone either."

"You're telling me." Isaac nodded. He wouldn't have liked to have been there alone either. Although he had done the fighting in the end, it was Jack who had found the spade and if he hadn't had done that then Isaac would have more than likely been killed. He was never going to go to a cemetery after dark unarmed again.

"Which is why," Jack continued, "I've decided something."

"What's that then?"

"I'm staying an extra day so that I can go with you when you confront Archington."

"What?!" Isaac didn't know what else to say - his mouth dropped open in shock. He was touched, of course he was, but he couldn't be sure it was for the best. Archington didn't know anything about Jack yet as far as they knew. Exposing him like that would put him in unnecessary danger. Isaac suddenly realised that this was the first time that he hadn't wanted Jack to stay longer.

"I don't want any arguments! I can call in sick to work or something - I don't know. But I want to be here for you, so even though you're leading all this you've got someone to lean on. So I'm staying."

"Thank you," Isaac smiled at Jack. Despite his concerns for his boyfriend's safety it would be great to have Jack by his side tomorrow. "That means a lot."

"Yeah well you mean a lot to me. Besides, I'm thinking come seven o'clock tomorrow, there'll be some drama. And I'd hate to miss it."

Chapter Twenty Six

Monday evening came around all too quickly. Confronting Archington had seemed like such a good idea when Isaac had first suggested it. He'd been feeling so angry about Gabbi getting hurt and also so frustrated at their lack of progress that it had seemed like such a proactive thing to do, taking the fight to the bad guys. However now it seemed like a terrifying idea, the very thought of it put knots in Isaac's stomach.

Interestingly it wasn't the danger that scared him, it was the fact that it was Professor Archington they were confronting. It was their professor, the one who - ironically - was still in charge of whether they passed the year or not. But it was too late to back out now, they were confronting him - knots in stomachs or not.

There was a lot of discussion as to whether to go in armed or unarmed. Armed would no doubt feel safer but they had to remember that they'd be confronting him on campus and if he was underhanded enough he could just call in the police and get them arrested for brandishing weapons at him in a public place. Eventually then they opted for unarmed, Isaac just hoped they wouldn't live to regret that choice.

At five to seven they arrived outside the lecture room where Archington was teaching the class they were supposed to have been a part of. They waited there in the corridor for the class to finish and for the students to leave.

Isaac's stomach twisting nerves were oddly subsiding a little and being replaced with a curious form of confidence. Actually being there in the moment seemed to have given him some mental adrenaline of sorts. The others all looked rather nervous themselves - to any passing students it must have looked like they were waiting to receive a telling off for not turning up to class. As the sound of bags being packed started drifting from the room Isaac looked at his friends and nodded and they all nodded back in a nervous but determined kind of way.

"So what do we do again if he gets violent?" Billie asked in a hurried voice.

"If we think we can handle him, fine. If not, we get out. There's a very nice big crowded lobby full of people just out that door." Isaac said, indicating to the door at the end of the corridor. "He won't hurt us there. That's our safety zone."

"Okay. Cool." Billie nodded several times, as if trying to convince herself it was all okay too. "Have I got time to go to the toilet?"

Isaac smiled at Billie. "In a word - no."

Just then the door to the lecture room opened wide and students came rushing out. Cindy Lackness gave them an odd look as she passed them, obviously noticing that they hadn't been there the past few weeks.

"Here we go then." Isaac muttered grimly once the last student had left and the door had swung shut behind them. He pushed heavily on the door to the lecture theatre and walked in with a firm step, the others right behind him.

Professor Archington was there looking just as he always did, dressed in a tweed suit and a green checked shirt. His white hair was combed neatly, he looked so gentle. How could a man like that be capable of such evil deeds? He was organising sheets of paper on the front desk and didn't look up for a moment. When he did, he did a double take. Isaac was pleased that he was a little shocked to see them - they could use that to their advantage.

"You know I usually advise my students to arrive punctually at the beginning of a lecture, not punctually at the end. What can I do for you?" Archington's voice was calm and wise like it always was. Only now they knew it was all a lie.

"You can spare us the act professor." Isaac said firmly.

Archington looked at them quizzically. "I'm quite sure I don't know what you mean. Is something the matter?"

"You tell us." Isaac threw the only thing he had brought with him at Archington who caught it with both hands. It was a newspaper from a few weeks before, open at the page of the article which mentioned the last disappearance. Isaac had circled the short piece in red pen.

"Oh." Archington said, looking down at the paper. A faint smile warmed his face. "I'm still not entirely sure what you're getting at though. It says here that no foul play is suspected."

"It's lying." Isaac said, becoming tired with Archington's games. "Which means it has a lot in common with you. That girl in the article has been murdered, right here in the city. And we know you were behind it."

Archington smiled further. "What a wicked, wicked thing to happen. Someone must have been very, very bad indeed to do such a deed."

"Ninety nine people have gone missing, ninety nine people have died. Ninety nine souls bled upon the box to use your own words. We know exactly what you've been up to and we know that you know all about us too. So really, spare us your games."

"Oh Mr Jacobs," Archington chuckled. "Spare you? You'll beg me to before I'm finished." Those final words had a cold edge of malice which sent a chill running down Isaac's spine. "So I should surrender myself to you then?" Archington held his hands up in mock surrender. "Call the police! Arrest this man at once, he's murdered ninety nine people in cold blood!" He eyed them carefully and smiled. "Except you know by now don't you? All those anonymous calls about dead bodies you make - you know they never get followed up and you know why. I have people in the police. People at the hospital. People in the council offices, people at the newspaper. Some are bribed of course, some are loyal followers, some are something in between. But the point is that I do have people everywhere because I am part of something which is everywhere."

Isaac decided to ignore Archington's attempts at unnerving them. "What is this box? What's inside it? The bleeding, it's an opening ritual right?"

Archington looked as though he couldn't be less bothered by them as he now went back to organising the sheets of paper on his desk. "Yes that's correct, well done. You know I meant it that time when I said that you're an intelligent guy. And you're right on track here, with what you're saying. Regrettably you won't get any further down those tracks."

"Why not?"

"Because not a single one of you will be leaving this room. Not alive at any rate." Archington's voice remained calm but the words were horrifying.

Out of the corner of his eye Isaac could see the others exchanging worried looks. He was beginning to wonder if this really had been such a good idea after all.

Archington looked up from the desk again and his eyes seemed to settle on Jack for the first time. "But who do we have here?"

"Stay away from him." Isaac warned sharply.

Archington snorted a laugh. "Oh he's your lover is he? I remember when you could be locked up for buggery." Archington said merrily. "The good old days." He winked at Isaac.

Isaac felt a new wave of confidence go through him - Archington's comments had just about annoyed him enough to give him the boost of courage he needed. "You're going to tell us what we need to know. What's the bad thing that's coming? What is this box you're trying to open? Tell us!"

Archington just folded his arms and laughed at them.

"A clever man like you and all you can do is laugh? Or are we getting a bit too close to something?"

Archington laughed again. "Oh Isaac my boy, you're nowhere near!"

Isaac was beginning to feel furious now. "Keep your secrets about the box if you want to, but there is something that you will tell us all about or I swear I won't be responsible for what happens."

"And what would that be?"

"Gabbi. You put something in her brain, something that hurt her more than anything, something dark and evil no doubt. And I care about her a lot. And whilst I don't agree with killing people, I think with supercilious bastards like you I might just make an exception."

"Ooh good word use." Gabbi muttered, almost silently.

Archington only laughed more.

"Stop laughing!" Isaac demanded, marching over to Archington. "Tell me what you did to my friend!" With that he shocked himself by punching the professor straight in the jaw. There was a audible gasp from those behind him. The worrying thing was that Archington barely moved. Isaac was certainly not overly strong but he would have thought that he had the strength within him to make an aging professor move slightly with a punch to the face.

He eyed Archington carefully and he saw the professor's eyes twinkling back at him. He then saw Archington's fist coming right at him but he was too slow to react - the next thing he knew he was flying through the air, the room seemed to spin and all he could hear was mixed screams from his friends. After a second in midair he landed with a crash at the very back of the lecture theatre. Every bone in his body ached instantly - his face stung like hell, it felt like it had been splintered into a thousand pieces. He put his hand to his forehead. There was blood.

"The reason I'm laughing Isaac, and you'll see why I have every right to laugh, is because I did absolutely nothing to Miss Gurtpasha. Absolutely nothing." Archington said in a smug kind of way.

Isaac got limply to his feet, using the lecture theatre seats to help him. Jack rushed up to him and the others followed.

"You must -" Isaac stuttered.

"I didn't do anything. I give you my word. Now killing ninety nine people, yes, I did that. But whatever happened to dear Gabbi, well, that's something else entirely." Archington smiled - his eyes sparkling like they always did. "I do wonder what it is."

"We need to get out of here, he's too strong," Isaac said quietly to the others. "The door, go, get to the door."

They ran down the side of the room and headed for the door. Archington moved quickly in the same direction to cut them off. They all reached the door at the same time and Isaac motioned for the group to get back. Archington advanced on them. Isaac couldn't think straight, he just knew they had to get out of there before things got any worse. He didn't know how though, and his head hurt so much!

Ben summoned up some courage and kicked out at Archington, landing his foot in the professor's belly. Again he barely flinched. Ben then went to punch him but Archington grabbed Ben's arm mid swing and grinned at him before throwing him clear across the room where he collided with the whiteboard.

"Ben!" Billie cried.

"Oh Miss Stamford, so considerate, so caring. I believe it must have been you who was the most hurt when I ordered the death of that freak of a psychic."

These words seemed to enrage Billie. "You bastard!" she screamed, and in a moment of pure resourcefulness she picked up a chair which was next to her and with all her might swung it towards Archington, knocking him in the face. He faltered ever so slightly at this latest attack and so she hit him again. In the mean time Laura had run at him and jumped on his back and started hitting him from behind.

Isaac could barely keep track of what was going on now, it was all happening so fast. Gabbi rushed across to see to Ben - Jack looked at Isaac and nodded quickly before joining Billie and Laura in their assault on Archington. They were rushing at him again and again now, constantly being knocked back, knocked onto the floor or into one another. Billie still had the chair and she swung it at him again, only now he caught it by the leg and wrestled it with relative ease from Billie's grasp.

"Chairs for that!" he said, still laughing despite being attacked by Laura, Jack and Isaac all at once. He swung the chair at Billie and sent her flying back into the lecture seats before elbowing Laura behind him, causing her to fly off and join Gabbi and Ben by the whiteboard. "And now it's just the sodomites." Archington announced looking happily at Isaac and Jack.

They both attempted to punch or kick him but with very little success. As Isaac threw another punch Archington grabbed his arm and held it, twisting it round so much Isaac was sure it would break. Isaac yelled out in pain and he saw Archington grab Jack's foot mid kick and by his hold on the foot alone he spun Jack round and caused him to soar across the room and land somewhere near Billie who was only just stirring.

"No!" Isaac yelled.

"I'd disagree with you there." Archington said, using his other hand to take a tight hold of Isaac's throat.

Isaac felt himself being lifted easily off of the ground, and he instantly began kicking and thrashing violently, struggling for breath - Archington was holding his throat so tightly! He couldn't die now! He couldn't could he? Could he? Someone would save him surely!

"NO!" He heard Gabbi scream at the top of her lungs. A blindingly white light filled the room and Isaac felt Archington's tight grip release before he fell to the floor in exhaustion and relief. He'd been saved alright- he just had no idea how.

Chapter Twenty Seven

When the bright light faded Archington was unconscious on the floor and Isaac was lying next to him. Everyone was stumbling or staggering towards them - nobody looked in a particularly good shape, but thankfully no-one looked seriously hurt either. Everyone was looking extremely disturbed however - no doubt utterly stunned by the mysterious rescue that Isaac had just received. Jack reached a hand down and helped Isaac to his feet.

Everyone was then staring at Gabbi, but they weren't stares of wonderment or amazement. They were stares of worry and confusion. Gabbi herself looked more worried and confused than anyone else.

"Gabbi what did you do?!" demanded Ben, clutching his sore arm.

"I, I don't know, I -" Gabbi sounded completely dazed.

"There was a light," Billie said, "I saw it, this white bolt of light. It was so bright, like impossibly bright. It exploded from her hands."

Isaac didn't understand it at all. "Like some kind of energy?" he said, looking across at Gabbi again - she did look utterly shocked and shaken. Then he happened to glance down at Archington and to his horror he saw the professor's arm move. He was starting to come round. "We need to leave." Isaac said suddenly, looking across at the others. "Home. Right now." He was as shocked and full of questions as the rest of them, but the questions would have to wait. He certainly wasn't going to chance another escape from near death.

They left the lecture theatre immediately and ran as fast as they could back to the house. Jack's leg was hurting, as was Ben's, but they ran as best they could nonetheless. Everyone was hurting somewhere on their bodies, but luckily none of it was quite serious enough to warrant a trip to the hospital.

As soon as they were all safely through the front door they all headed for the living room to sit down and try and figure out what exactly had just happened. Laura and Billie perched nervously on the edge of the sofa and Gabbi sat down gingerly on one of the armchairs. Ben sat in the other armchair whilst Isaac and Jack stayed standing, although Jack had to lean against the wall with his injured leg.

"Now I know we're all confused," Isaac began, "but since I was fading into unconsciousness at the time can sometime please just calmly say what happened just now?"

"I exploded. Like Billie said." Gabbi said quietly. "Kaboom." She looked more shocked than anyone. Isaac wasn't surprised. If he'd just shot energy bolts from his hands then he'd be shocked too. "I don't know what it was but it felt connected to whatever went into my head the other night. I just remember fearing for Isaac's life and getting really, really worked up and then I shouted no and it happened." Her voice was almost a whisper. "I had no control." She looked down at her lap. Gabbi was a tough person and this was the most scared Isaac had ever seen her.

"Control or no control - thank you." Isaac said, going over to her and giving her a big hug. "Thank you Gabbi, you saved my life. And I promise you we will figure out what's happened to you."

"What if it's bad Isaac?"

"It won't be. Okay? I promise, whatever it is we will deal with it. You'll be okay, you'll be fine - I'll make sure of it." Isaac smiled at her. She was as innocent in all of this as any of them were and it seemed that even though she received the least physical injuries she was the one who came away most hurt. Gabbi nodded at Isaac in agreement and he got up and stood over by Jack once more.

"Maybe it was witchcraft." Ben suggested. He received several doubting looks. Whilst Isaac fully believed in witchcraft, it didn't quite fit in here. "Well it looked like magical powers to me." Ben sniffed defensively.

It was clear that the group was about to erupt into arguments so Isaac got in there first with a plan that had just that second jumped into his head. "We don't know what it was. There's no way for us to know right now. So we can't start jumping to any conclusions. And unfortunately we still don't know anything about anything else either."

Billie sighed. "So it's square one again."

"Possibly." Isaac said. "But whether it is or not we need to move our square. We need to leave Monks-Lantern." Instantly there were shocked faces staring at him from around the room, telling him that his announcement hadn't gone down easily. It was something he had toyed with for a while, he'd been thinking what they would do if things got to a more dangerous level with Archington. He knew it sounded drastic but looking around the room at the various cuts, bruises and limps told him that the situation had reached just that - drastic.

"Leave?" Laura repeated.

"Yes. Leave Monks-Lantern right now."

"But we've got -" Billie began.

Isaac cut her off. "No. We need to leave. Archington knows where we live. We're not all pretending we're not involved anymore, he knows we're onto him. I wouldn't mind betting that the first thing he'll do is send someone round to get rid of us. He nearly got rid of me just now, bloody nearly got rid of all of us."

"Yeah but we should be safe shouldn't we? He wouldn't just kill six students, that'd be daft surely?" Laura argued.

"I'm really tired Isaac." Billie moaned quietly.

Suddenly Isaac was beginning to feel frustrated a bit. "Look I know the last hour hasn't been enjoyable but this isn't up for debate. We need to go."

Now Ben decided to weigh in. "I just don't -"

"Just don't what?" Isaac didn't understand why everyone was fighting this plan! "Was everyone in the same fight I just was? The one where our sixty something year old professor has superhuman powers? The one where we were all on the floor within minutes?"

"Okay." Ben conceded. "Okay. I understand we're not safe. But mate, how is running away going to lead us to knowing more? "

"Because I know where we need to run to." Isaac's idea for where they could go wasn't one that he relished the thought of, mostly because he hated bringing trouble to innocent doors and tried to avoid doing so whenever possible. But regardless of that preference the location he had in mind did seem like the most logical one. He looked across at Gabbi and caught her gaze. "I'm sorry sweetheart, I'm going to need to ask a favour of you. I would suggest somewhere else if there was somewhere else but short of just running into the woods I think a trip to Cowbrook might be our only hope."

"What's Cowbrook?" Ben asked.

"Small town, ten miles that way." Isaac pointed straight out the living room window without looking at Ben. He kept his gaze firmly on Gabbi. She looked sad and a little defeated, but she nodded in agreement at Isaac nonetheless.

"It's okay Isaac, I understand. And it is the safest place for us to go." Gabbi smiled but she was clearly not in the smiling mood. None of them were. Everyone else still looked uncertain as to what exactly was going on.

Isaac decided to put an end to the suspense. "Everyone, we're going to see Gabbi's dad. You'd all better go and get ready. We're leaving in fifteen minutes."

Chapter Twenty Eight

A minute later and Isaac was hurriedly getting changed in his room. Jack sat on the bed. Isaac had never been on the run before, he wasn't sure what to wear. He held up an orange hooded sweatshirt and a purple hooded sweatshirt before chucking the orange one to the side and putting the purple one on over his black t-shirt.

"I think you made the right choice." Jack said.

"I don't know, I think orange would maybe look better with my skin tone. Purple's better of blending in though isn't it? Doesn't stand out as much."

"I meant about the running away thing."

"I know you did. I was just trying to pretend for a moment that the most important choices in my life really were just choosing between colours of hoodies." Isaac sighed as he zipped his hoodie up. "I don't know Jack. I know it's the best thing to do to keep us all safe but at the same time I don't know at all if it is the right thing to do or not. My instinct says to run, but maybe that's wrong. Maybe we should stay and put up a fight. My head is still all achy and my face hurts, I might not even be thinking straight."

"I'm sure you are thinking straight. We're all hurting - physically and mentally. But what you said makes sense to me - we need to time to regroup and we can't very well do that if Archington is going to bash the door down any moment and crunch us down into talcum powder. I'm proud of you. You took control."

"Yeah well, we'll just see where it gets us. My last plan of confronting Archington didn't exactly go as I intended it to." Isaac pointed to the sore wound on his temple as evidence.

"But that doesn't mean that your plan now is going to be wrong. And confronting him was still a good idea, there wasn't anything wrong with the plan. It was just a shame that Archington turned out to be a super villain."

"I suppose." Isaac looked at Jack and hesitated before asking the question he knew he had to ask. "What are you going to do now?"

"Well that depends. What do you want me to do?"

"Stay here with me." Isaac answered the question honestly. "But you have work. I don't want to get you in trouble."

"Then here I shall stay. I'll just tell work I've got some terrible plague or something. I'll phone them now and then it will all -" Jack's phone suddenly sprang to life, and started ringing and vibrating. "Oh, wait, sorry it's my mum. I should probably take this, bear with me."

"Okay."

"I'll be two seconds." Jack left the room. The minute the door was shut Isaac slumped down onto the bed. Holding his head in his hands, he felt like he wanted to cry. What was he doing? Going on the run, had it really come to this? He breathed in deeply and stood back up. There was no point in moping about anything now - he'd just have to get on with it. A moment later and Jack returned to the room, looking troubled.

"What's wrong Jack?" Isaac asked, fearing more bad news.

"It's my mum, she's being taken into hospital." Jack looked shaken. "That was the ambulance guy who called. She's had a heart attack."

Selfishly, the first thought that flashed through Isaac's head was disappointment at the idea that Jack might now have to leave. "Oh sweetheart, I'm sorry." He walked over and gave Jack a big hug.

Jack hugged back tightly. "Isaac, I don't know what -"

"Go to her." Isaac said, even though really it was the last thing he wanted Jack to do. Jack looked confused. "You were going to say you don't know what to do right? Well I'm telling you. Go to her. And I'm the leader, so you'd better do as I say." Isaac smiled, even though inside he was crying. He was so upset that Jack wouldn't be with him now in whatever was about to happen, really he had to fight every urge not to grab him and tell him he couldn't leave. But that really would be selfish on an unacceptable level.

"But I told you that I'd be with you in all this."

"I know. But it's okay. You've helped me so much already, just by existing. Now go and help your mum."

"Thank you baby." Jack came forwards and they kissed.

Isaac made sure to enjoy it - he wasn't sure when he'd be getting another one or if he would ever have another one at all.

"I love you." Jack said after they broke apart.

"I love you too. And I'll call you when I can, once we're there safely or whatever."

Jack looked at Isaac seriously. "Are you going to be okay?"

"Of course. I'll be fine." Isaac lied.

"You'd better be." Jack bent down and picked up his rucksack, which he kept packed pretty much all the time during his stays.

"I will be, I promise. You be careful too."

"Yes the train to Yorkshire could well be dangerous." Jack smiled.

"Could be. Your leg I mean though, go careful on it."

"I will. It's feeling better already anyway."

Isaac nodded and held in tears. "You'd better go then, we'll be off in a minute ourselves."

Jack nodded and headed for the door to Isaac's room. "You will be very careful won't you?"

Isaac nodded. "Cross my heart, hope to die."

"Don't you dare." Jack smiled. "I'll see you soon yeah?"

"Yeah. Really soon."

"Good." Jack smiled one last time. "Bye Isaac." And with that he headed out of the bedroom door.

Isaac heard the front door slam a second later and watched out the window as Jack walked by. "Goodbye." he muttered. Refusing to allow himself to cry at such a critical time, Isaac opened his eyes wide and breathed in deeply several times through his nose. It had been the right thing to do. Besides, it was no good getting upset about it now. If they were going to figure everything out then getting emotional about Jack leaving wouldn't help at all.

Just then Gabbi appeared in Isaac's doorway. "Was that Jack leaving just now? Where'd he go?"

"His mum's had a heart attack. I told him to go to her."

"Oh." Gabbi looked at Isaac for a moment. "Are you okay?"

"Not entirely. But it doesn't matter." Isaac turned and looked out the window. The light of the day was rapidly disappearing. "Let's go."

Chapter Twenty Nine

The town of Cowbrook, where Gabbi's father lived and where Gabbi had grown up, was only small - not much bigger than a village really. It was about ten miles out to the west of Monks-Lantern and thankfully it was a big enough place to warrant a train station so getting there was easy enough.

Isaac had hoped that he might have caught one more glimpse of Jack when they got to the train station, but he noticed as soon as they arrived that a train to London had just left - carrying Jack away from him at high speed.

Trains to Cowbrook were frequent and they'd only just bought their tickets when one such train pulled into the station. The carriage they got on was empty which was fortunate, and whilst Billie, Laura, Ben and Gabbi sat in a set of four seats together, Isaac took himself off a few seats in front and sat in a two-seater by himself. He needed a few moments of reflection - everything had suddenly got very difficult. He gazed out of the window as the train pulled out of the station and started gathering speed. Offices and shops became houses and fairly soon houses had become fields and trees that started whipping past in a blur. He sensed someone approaching and turned his head just enough to see Gabbi slide into the seat next to him.

"Bit of a crazy few days Isaac." she said wearily but kindly. Always kindly.

"You're telling me." He turned to face her fully and gave her an exasperated smile. "Saturday evening it's all thinking positive and normal lives and parties, then two days later we've had brain attacks and super strength professors and blinding lights and now we're on the run." He paused and sighed. "Jack's had to run off, that all happened in a flash." He sighed again. "Oh dear. Too many sighs."

"You were wrong back at the house you know, it does matter if you're okay or not. It matters to me - it matters to all of us."

- 154 -

"It's you we should be thinking about Gabbi, I mean we don't have a clue what's going on with your brain."

Gabbi looked at Isaac seriously for a split second and then the very next moment she and burst out laughing. Really happy, giggling laughter.

"What?" Isaac asked, trying to stay serious but ending up breaking into laughter too. Gabbi's laugh was so infectious!

"Nothing," she said, still laughing. She had tears in her eyes where she was laughing so much. "Nothing, it's just the way you said that sounded really funny! I mean it's so ridiculous, what's wrong with my brain?" She clutched her stomach and laughed some more.

Isaac was laughing too almost as hard as Gabbi was. It did sound funny. The others must have wondered what was going on.

Gabbi sat up straight and calmed herself a bit, taking some deep breaths and fanning her hands in front of her eyes to get rid of the tears.

"Better?" Isaac asked, still chuckling a little.

"Yes." she said, letting out one more giggle before stopping completely. "But seriously, are you okay?"

"I think I will be. You know I've been obsessed for too long now, trying to convince myself that we could all have this picture perfect normal life. Me and my friends – fighting monsters, yes, but still having fun. It was so important to me to prove that we could still all be normal human beings. That we weren't just this."

"There's nothing wrong with wanting a normal life. But then what is normal these days? We aren't defined by the fact that we fight monsters darling, that doesn't make us abnormal. It's just part of our lives, same as punching holes in train tickets is part of a train conductor's life." She bit her lip and looked thoughtful for a moment. "Well maybe we're not exactly the same as a train conductor but it's similar."

Isaac smiled. "You're right. You know Jack said something very similar to me the other night – he said that it doesn't matter what your life involves, you just have to live it and love it for what it is. And I think that's what I need to do. I mean yes it's inconvenient, I'd rather not be running away but hey-ho, that's our life. That's normal for us. And it's time to accept it."

"Better than a poke in the eye with a sharp stick eh?" Gabbi asked with a knowing smile.

"Much, much better." Isaac said happily.

"Good. Now let's get on and beat the bad guys."

Gabbi held her fist out for a fist bump. Isaac obliged and bumped his fist against hers, but then looked at Gabbi a little uncertainly. Her expression mirrored his.

"Gabbi, let's never do that again."

Gabbi laughed. "Agreed."

About five minutes later the train pulled into Cowbrook station and by that time the sun had well and truly set.

Walking from the station, Isaac thought that it was a shame that they were all there in such dire circumstances as Cowbrook really was quite a pretty place. The station was at the bottom of a small hill and the slightly curved road which led up the hill served as the high street. A small stream ran down parallel to the road on one side and on the other there was a string of shops - some independent stores which had clearly been there for generations and other more recognisable high street shops. At the top of the hill there was a market square with an old church and the town hall, as well as several banks and offices. In the middle of the square there was a beautiful spring time flower display surrounding an old iron water pump, painted green and continuously pouring water into a decorative stone trough. It really was a very pretty town, but unfortunately they didn't have time to be tourists.

"Your dad won't be cross will he?" Isaac asked as they walked along briskly. "Us all turning up like this, I know it will be an inconvenience." Even as he spoke he knew it was too late to do anything about it now, even if Gabbi's dad would be cross.

Gabbi shook her head. "No, dad loves to meet new people who believe in spiritual things. And I think he'll be only too happy to help us. Obviously we'll have to explain everything but he'll believe us, don't worry."

"You're so lucky to have a dad like that Gabbi." Billie said a little sadly. "My parents are rubbish."

Ben sniffed loudly. "Mine too."

"Mine three." Isaac said.

Everyone seemed to expectantly look at Laura as though she were meant to chime in too. "What? Oh I'm meant to say mine four aren't I?" Laura smiled as she spoke.

"Yes!" Billie instructed. "Join in the having of rubbish parents!"

Laura laughed along with everyone else. "Okay, mine four." she said with a chuckle. "No bless them they're not that bad really."

"Maybe Gabbi's dad can just adopt us all." Isaac said. "You know, if we ask nicely. Four undervalued students in need of good home. Well housetrained, good cooks, able to banish demons. What's not to love?"

Gabbi laughed with them all. "I'm sure he'd love to adopt you all! Ben you could be the younger brother I never had!"

Ben looked at her and screwed his face up. "Uh-uh, no way. I'm not letting you braid my hair and put make up on me for fun. Do that stuff to your other younger brother Isaac!" Ben laughed. "His kind love that sort of thing!"

"Oi!" Isaac laughed, reaching over and smacking Ben on the top of his head. "Pack it in straighty."

They walked a short while down a cobbled side street and then they turned off to the left up an even narrower cobbled street which led up a hill. At the top

Gabbi guided them right onto a properly surfaced street which looked to be a dead end – this would have to be the place.

Three quarters of the way down the road Gabbi stopped outside a semi detached house, painted white with the bricks that surrounded the door and windows painted a deep burgundy colour. Isaac guessed the house was built in the fifties or thereabouts. It was starting to show its age and the front garden was overgrown, but it looked welcoming nonetheless. There was a warm light coming from the front window.

"This is it." Gabbi announced. "Home."

"After you then Gabbi." Isaac said, gesturing to the front door with a nod of his head. He prayed that inside they might finally get some answers – or at least be able to regroup and have a decent brainstorm session without fear of being attacked.

"Right. Here goes." Gabbi said before heading up the drive to the front door. There was no bell so she hammered loudly with the letterbox flap. Moments later the door swung open. "Hi dad."

Mr. Galal Gurtpasha was a thin and wiry looking man in his mid sixties. He was mostly bald on top of his head but he did have hair still in the form of a short and dignified grey beard which suited his angular face. His eyes were twinkling and inquisitive, not unlike Archington's, and he wore thick rimmed circular glasses.

He looked very shocked to see his daughter and a straggly bunch of strangers on his doorstep. "My Gabriella! I wasn't expecting you until next weekend!"

Isaac noticed immediately that Galal had a faint but definitely detectable Pakistani accent.

"I know. I'm sorry for not calling. These are my friends." She indicated behind her to Isaac and the others.

Galal looked at them with kind eyes and nodded in acknowledgement. Then it seemed he caught sight of Isaac's cut on his face as he began to look worried.

"We're in trouble dad."

"Then you must come in, quickly." He stood back and allowed them all to enter, ushering them in with swift waves of his hand. "Quickly now, please do come in."

Isaac stepped over the threshold behind Gabbi and she led them all through into the living room at the front of the house which was the first door on the right. The room was filled with piles of old books and any shelves or surfaces were covered in either photographs of Gabbi or ornaments. The décor was a clashing mix of asian themed styles and chintzy british bits and pieces. Isaac could smell incense and then spotted the stick burning away on the side dresser. Sandalwood. Another thing Isaac noticed was that everything seemed to have a doily underneath it, even the incense stick holder.

Gabbi motioned for them to all sit down as best they could, which meant most of them sitting on the floor. Only Billie and Gabbi ended up on chairs and they left the big armchair for Galal, who was still locking up the front door.

Several moments later he entered the room. He looked at the empty seat and then at Laura who was sitting on the floor. "My dear, you should take the seat. You look hurt. You all do."

"Oh no, please, it's okay. We've disturbed you like this, please, you sit down." Laura said.

Galal smiled in appreciation, but shook his head. "No, I insist." He walked back into the hallway and came back immediately with a wooden chair. He placed it on the floor and sat down on it. "See, I'm fine here. Please sit."

"Thankyou." Laura said, although she still didn't sound sure if she should be taking a comfortable armchair away from a relatively old man.

"Now Gabriella, you must tell me why you are all here." Galal turned to his daughter who was sitting just across the room from him and peering over his glasses he stared hard into her eyes. "What trouble are you in?"

"It's one of our professors dad." Gabbi started what would no doubt be a long and complicated explanation of their situation. "He's-"

"Professor Archington." Galal said the words with a weary sigh. Isaac was stunned - everyone else looked stunned too and instinctively all eyes snapped towards Galal. Apparently the explanation might not have to be that long or complicated after all.

"How do you know about Archington?" Gabbi asked.

"My darling Gabriella, I'm afraid I've kept things from you. But there were reasons. You must understand that there were reasons."

Gabbi looked at her father for what seemed like a long time, her face painted with worry. "What things daddy?" She sounded more like a little girl than a grown woman. A worried child. "Something's happened to me, some power, some kind of force - it did something to me. Is that involved too?" Despite the worry in her voice she still sounded so calm, so loving still.

Isaac admired her patience, if he'd had the shock she had just had that day he would have been tearing the place apart.

Galal nodded in answer to Gabbi's question. "For you to understand, for you to all understand, we must go back in time."

"What literally?" Billie blurted out. She sounded excited. Isaac had to admit that the same thought had popped into his head.

Galal smiled warmly. "No my dear, I'm sorry. Although such things are possible if you know how."

"Oh." Billie looked embarrassed.

"In order for me to help you and your friends Gabriella, I must tell you more about your mother."

Isaac listened intently. He didn't know much at all about Gabbi's mum, only that she had died from a heart attack when Gabbi was a baby.

"What about her?" Gabbi asked, sounding even more childlike now at the mention of her mum.

Galal looked pained for a moment, obviously struggling to say whatever it was he was about to tell his daughter. "She didn't die sweetheart." Galal's face was etched with regret and shame.

The words seemed to hit everyone in the room like a punch in the gut. Everyone's mouths had dropped wide open in shock - Isaac's included. He closed it slowly and looked across at Gabbi. She was the most shocked Isaac had ever seen her – he wasn't surprised! Her eyes were wide open and innocent, filled with confusion and worry. Her mouth too had dropped open a little and her bottom lip seemed to quiver a bit as she sat there staring intently at her dad, hanging on for his next words.

"She simply returned home." Galal breathed in deeply. He was obviously saving the biggest revelation until last. "Your mother was an angel."

Chapter Thirty

Professor Archington placed the telephone back on the receiver which sat on the desk in front of him. That had been a difficult phone call to make, but a successful one nonetheless. The wheels were now in motion for the plan that lay ahead - the plan that stretched out far beyond the opening of the box. He rested his elbows on the desk and placed his head in his hands. It still ached slightly from where he had been knocked unconscious. To make matters worse it was cold in the room as the guildhall no longer had a heating supply. The sooner they could start using the sacred space again, the better. Once everything with the box was over and done with, maybe then. Leaning back in his chair, he sighed loudly. He was getting old.

"You look tired, Robert." He knew the voice instantly. It was her again! Just out of the corner of his eye he could see her. There she was, barely in sight.

"I am tired."

"Then stop. Just stop and rest."

"I'm tired of this world. Tired of its arrogance, tired of its morality. I won't stop until every last sanctimonious wretched soul is ripped from the world, howling in pain."

"And what do you get from that?" she asked incredulously.

"I get the power, the power to stand apart from all others and watch as everything falls into oblivion. I get to see it end."

"Except you don't have the power Robert. You don't have the power at all - it does. And it's pulling your strings, manipulating you -"

"I don't care anymore, don't you understand that? I am doing what I am doing because I must do it. And when everything ends my ultimate reward is that I end with it, because I cannot stand to be a part of a creation that did what it did to you."

There wasn't a reply for a moment. He could see her there still, just visible. Did she look sad? "Then you've gone beyond my help. I'm sorry Robert, I can't help you."

"Rose -"

Just then Skarl burst into the office in a flurry of robes. "Imperator!"

"Hell's teeth Skarl!" Archington bellowed. "Is it beyond your simpering infantile comprehension to remember to knock!?" He stood from his desk as he shouted and raised a hand as though he were going to strike Skarl.

Skarl cowered and backed away. "Sorry Imperator! So sorry! I have news about the children!" he called as though pleading a defence.

Archington softened and sat back down in his chair. "Very well. What have you learnt?"

"I've sneaked and creeped all through their house, but the little things have run away!" Skarl cackled.

Archington sat further back in his chair and folded his arms. "So they've fled then." He paused and sighed deeply. "Gabbi will have questions about what happened to her. They'll want answers. And safety."

"Where have they run to Imperator? Tell me and I shall chase and tear them!" Skarl gestured a violent tearing motion with his hands.

Just then there was a swift knock at the door. "Imperator?" It was Elias's voice.

"Come in."

Elias entered and nodded curtly, his hard features set in an expression of contempt and concern. "The children Imperator."

"What about them?"

"Brother Valgar was passing the train station just now. He says he saw them boarding a train to Cowbrook."

"Then they've gone to the father. How typical." Archington tutted and shook his head. "Send my thanks to Valgar, Elias - tell him he can eat a baby tonight if he wants to."

Elias nodded. "Yes Imperator."

"Oh and Elias?"

"Yes Imperator?"

"Telephone our contacts at the council and the emergency services, get them ready. There'll be a dead student by morning and it will be a local one. I don't want any fuss made."

Elias nodded once more before leaving the room. "Imperator."

Skarl looked at Archington excitedly. "Shall I run then? Shall I chase the children?" Skarl sounded euphoric at the notion.

"Yes. They can't run from me, just like they can't run from what's about to happen. It's almost time for the final bleeding. Then the box will open. Then this world will scream."

Chapter Thirty One

Karachi; Pakistan: Twenty years previously.

"I think my Gabriella likes it here Galal!"

Gabriella was sitting on her mother's knee, gargling and giggling happily. It was night time and they were sitting on a bench in Hill Park, not far from where they lived.

"I'm sure she does my love. You can see so far from here. Although I expect you are used to seeing much further from your home."

"Beauty isn't defined by quantity. And I find it truly beautiful here. With you."

"I wish you could stay with me Luxlucis. With both of us. I thank the Lord for the time we've had together but I wish it could be longer. I need it to be longer."

"I would wish that too. But we knew how this would work. And I've been truly blessed to spend this last year with you and my little girl." Luxlucis looked across at Galal and smiled. "We will be together again. Have faith and believe in that."

"I do. I do believe." Galal choked the words through tears which had suddenly appeared. Today he had woken up next to his wife, tomorrow he would wake up alone. He was just so grateful that he would still have Gabriella. She would remind him always of Luxlucis.

Luxlucis turned Gabriella around so they were face to face and gave her a big cuddle. Gabriella giggled some more, completely unaware that her mother was about to leave.

"I'll always love you Gabriella. And I'll always be with you." She kissed her daughter on the forehead and then lifted her over to Galal who took her caringly. "Galal, I would wish that our last moment could be one of pure peace, but I'm afraid I must tell you some important things before I leave."

Galal was instantly intrigued. "Tell me."

"Our daughter's life will not be easy. There are things in her future. Bad things."

Galal was horrified. He knew that Gabriella, being half angel, would inherit some of her mother's supernatural powers when she came of age on her twenty first birthday, but this information he was hearing now was completely new. "What kind of bad things?"

"I can't be sure, it's just a feeling. It's a long way off as yet -and she's strong, she has strength from me that will help her. But it will be bad. Very bad."

"What can I do? How can I help her?"

"You must move Galal, you must move to England."

"England?!" Galal hadn't expected to have to move half way across the world.

"The city of Monks-Lantern, or near enough to it. Now whatever is going to happen will happen, you can't stop that. You mustn't try and hamper her or keep her restrained. Let her live her life and when the right time comes you will help her."

Galal had never heard of a place called Monks-Lantern, but nonetheless he trusted his wife absolutely. If it had to be done then it had to be done. "Okay, I'll do it. If it is what must happen. Should I tell her about you? About where she comes from?"

"No my love, not yet, not for a while. It would damage her more than it would help her. Wait until after her twenty first birthday. She will likely know herself by then, at least in part she will." Luxlucis grinned happily at her daughter. "She's a clever girl."

"I'll do exactly what you say. I promise you."

"I can help you just a bit more. There is a word. A name. It's significant to whatever is going to happen in the future."

"What is it?"

Luxlucis closed her eyes, obviously thinking deeply. "Archington." She opened her eyes once more. "That's all there is. That and a feeling of complete distrust. Look out for that man Galal. Be wary of him. It all starts with him." Luxlucis sounded deadly serious, and her expression of fear sat uncomfortably on her delicate features.

Galal had no idea how he would go about finding out more about all this but he knew that he had to. And if Luxlucis believed that he could, then he certainly stood a good chance of doing what was required of him.

Luxlucis stared up at the heavens and breathed in deeply. "It's time Galal."

Galal's tears came again. He knew the moment had been coming, it had always been coming but he still felt so unprepared for it. "I love you. I always will." he said firmly despite his tears.

"I'll love you across the stars my darling Galal. I'll never stop." Tear drops slid gently from Luxlucis's eyes and she lent in to kiss Galal. Gabriella was starting to get distressed and began crying.

Galal closed his eyes and kissed his wife for the last time. He felt the warmth of her lips and then a moment later it had disappeared. He opened his eyes. She had gone.

Chapter Thirty Two

"In most cases that you'll find, mortals and angelic beings aren't meant to have relationships. In the bible it's completely forbidden and the children of those pairings are hideous monsters."

Everyone sat enthralled at Galal's story. The childlike innocence was still on Gabbi's shocked face. Her cheeks were tearstained.

"Luxlucis and I weren't like that though. Once in a very long time there is a relationship that is truly based on love. Those stories from old times are based on lust, on a craving for the physical form. But Luxlucis and I truly loved one another, just our beings. God saw that and smiled upon it."

"How did it start? How did you meet her?" Gabbi asked, confidence growing in her voice again.

"She saw me from afar. From up in the heavens she saw me and was instantly captured." Galal laughed. "According to her that is. When I say it, it makes me sound rather egotistical. Like some sort of super-hunk." It was odd hearing words like that coming from an older man.

"But what then, did she just come to you?"

"She spoke with God and begged him for a chance to see if it was really true love or not. He gave her this chance and she came to me on earth. I already believed in other-worldly and spiritual things, so it wasn't scary for me to meet an angel, just a bit of a shock. But instantly I loved her. It was meant to be." He smiled dreamily. It was obviously nice for him to be reminiscing.

"But she couldn't stay? You said she had to leave on my first birthday?"

"Yes. God smiled on us, he certainly did. It's quite a rare occurrence for a relationship like that to be blessed, the last one previous to mine and your mother's was in the fifteenth century I believe." Galal spoke proudly as if he had just done well in an exam. "But despite it being blessed it could never be permanent. Just as a diver can explore the oceans for a small time but must then return to land, so too could Luxlucis live with me before having to return to the heavens."

"Weren't you angry? Angry at God?"

"Oh no, never. He gave us the time we had, and it was perfectly understandable that she had to return. Originally we were to have one year to be together on the earth, but when she fell pregnant we were told by a messenger that she could stay until your first birthday. So we were blessed further by being allowed to have more time together."

"Can I see her?" It was an inevitable question. She sounded hopeful as she spoke, even a little excited.

Galal looked pained before he answered. "No." He said the word as gently as he could.

The disappointment was clear to see on Gabbi's face – her expression dropped instantly.

"I'm sorry my darling, but you can't. That's just the rules."

"But why?"

"I don't know my dearest. It's not my place to question these things." He looked deeply into his daughters eyes. "How are you feeling?"

Gabbi looked uncertain for a moment, but then she looked as if there was some clarity in her eyes. "I'm okay actually. In a really strange way even though it's a shock it still sort of just feels right. It's like I'm shocked but then I'm actually not shocked at all. It's almost like I sort of knew all along but I'd just forgotten that I knew." She smiled, a real smile, not a forced one. "This morning I thought my mother was dead, and now I know she's alive. I've got no reason to be sad."

Suddenly, and quite unexpectedly, Ben spoke. "Well, maybe not a reason to be sad, but I think we've all still got reason to be worried." His words cut through the warm atmosphere that the front room had taken on during Galal's story.

Isaac knew instantly that Ben was right. As mind-blowing and amazing as Gabbi's heritage was, they still had an evil and rather psychotic professor to deal with.

Galal seemed to also be thinking the same thing. "Archington, yes of course."

"If you know anything," Isaac said, "anything at all. We're out of options."

"Then finally I can help you like Luxlucis said I would." Galal leant forward slightly on his chair, as if about to tell them an important secret that he didn't want the paintings on the walls to hear. "After I moved here I kept my eyes wide open for any person relating to the name Archington. I found nothing for a long time and then about five years ago he appeared at the university in Monks-Lantern. Professor Robert Archington. From that moment on I didn't stop researching, knowing that one day my Gabriella would need my help regarding this very man."

"And you found out some things about him? I mean we know a bit of biography but nothing about what he is up to right now. Except some kind of ritual involving a box." Isaac said.

"I found out lots. A life like mine you end up with a lot of contacts." Galal breathed in deeply, which Isaac now knew was a sign that something big was about to be revealed. "The Box of Infernos. That's the full name of the box you mentioned, although that itself is probably just a human name we've given to a much older object."

"What's inside it?" Isaac was eager to find out everything now, spurred on by the fact that they'd been there only half an hour and they already knew more than they themselves could find out in four months.

"A Djinn. A very old and powerful being trapped in the Box of Infernos millennia ago by the powers of light for its subversive and evil ways."

"I thought the Djinn could be good as well as bad?"

"Yes that's true, they can. But this one is undoubtedly one of the bad ones. Its name is, well, it doesn't really have one. But it has titles. The most famous one being the Abominable Nothing."

"Nothing as in what, it's invisible?" Laura asked.

"Nothing as in it leaves nothing left." Galal answered grimly.

Ben raised a hand. "Hold on, one second. What's a Djinn again?" he asked. "I know I've been doing this for a while now but some of it is still a bit confusing. Is it a demon?"

"Ancient spirits, immensely powerful, much more so than a mere demon." Isaac explained. "They can be good or evil, it's a choice they make themselves. If they choose to be good, that's great. If they choose evil, it's not so good. They're made of fire, or that's what legend says anyway."

Ben shrugged "Doesn't sound so bad." he said, very unconvincingly.

"It's from Djinn that we get the idea of Genies. It's the same root."

"You're a very clever young man." Galal remarked. It could have sounded patronising but it didn't. "And it's interesting that you mention the Genie, as there is some truth in that too."

"What kind of truth?" Isaac asked.

"The Abominable Nothing was trapped in there by God, or forces of God, and the intention was that it was to remain trapped in there for all eternity. However, followers of darkness conjured a way to release the Djinn. A ritual of soaking the Box of Infernos in the blood of a hundred souls."

"Wait, a hundred? So far there's only been ninety nine."

"Then they're almost finished." Galal said with a sigh. "All they need is their hundredth soul now, but that one has to be something different. The ninety nine can be any kind of person, nobody specific. But the hundredth has to be someone who is aware of the supernatural, aware of the Djinn - and most importantly someone who actively fights on the side of good."

Everyone looked around the room at each other. The same thought seemed to strike them all at the same time.

"Gabbi." Isaac said.

Gabbi herself looked suddenly shocked again. "Now hold on darling, you can't just assume that it's me. It could be any one of us."

"And if you'd said that to me yesterday then I would have agreed with you. But now we know about your mum and the fact that you're part angel. It just seems like you are the most 'side of good' one here." Isaac couldn't believe how quickly he'd adjusted to Gabbi being part angel, he was just saying it like it was normal now. Which of course, as he'd decided on the train earlier, it was. Abnormal was normal for them.

Ben decided to throw in some skepticism. "Of course we could all be being really bigheaded in imagining that it's any one of us. It might be someone completely different."

Isaac thought about what Ben said but ultimately he disagreed. Whilst they might sound rather conceited just assuming that they are the candidates for the hundredth soul, it did make most sense that they were. How Archington knew about them and how they were so close to it all - not to mention there seeming to be some destiny in all of them being together. It made sense.

"I agree with Isaac." Galal said.

"Me too." Billie nodded earnestly as did Laura.

Galal looked across at Gabbi. "I hate to think of my daughter in danger but as her mother warned me about it twenty years ago it does seem to make the most logical sense to me."

"Say this is all true then," Gabbi said, "and say the worst happens. What happens then? Dad you were saying something about Genies before we got sidetracked?"

Galal looked gravely at Gabbi, obviously not wanting to contemplate his daughter getting killed. "If the Abominable Nothing were to be freed then the one who freed it, Archington in this case, would be able to get the Djinn to do his bidding. Not quite three wishes but still it would be in Archington's service. And that's an awful lot of power to be in the hands of someone who is already immensely powerful."

"How come this is only happening now though?" Laura asked. "If it's been in the Box of Infernos for thousands of years then how come it hasn't been released before?"

"The Abominable Nothing has long been sought but only recently has it been discovered – the soldiers of God hid it well because they knew of its terrible power. Before now it existed only in old stories and legends, in children's rhymes. You know there were many of these powerful beings chained and trapped back in primordial times when chaos still reigned. They were scattered and buried, hidden in the loneliest of places. Some of them have been found and unleashed before, but never one as bad as the Box of Infernos.

The world won't be the same once it's opened and the Abominable Nothing is freed. The world as we know it will end. Undoubtedly."

As Galal spoke Isaac realised that the incense had burned out and the room had gone horribly cold. He knew the smell of sandalwood had been choking him but he wanted it back - it gave a warmth to the room which was now completely gone. The whole world could be changed, could be ruined, just by the small events which were happening right there with them. Isaac knew very well how important small decisions were. A small decision five years ago had cost three of his friends their lives. He wasn't going to let that happen again.

"We're going to stop it." he announced.

Galal looked at Isaac, surprised but impressed, and everyone else looked rather quizzical at his sudden burst of confidence.

"I think maybe we're supposed to. Those dead children in the library told us that we are meant to be together. Ben, you remember saying how you liked the idea of us having a destiny in all of this? Well maybe we do. Maybe we've got to stop pretending that we're just bystanders in these things, dabbling around a bit, and actually realise that maybe we can do something seriously to stop this thing."

"You're not just clever, you're wise too." Galal noted.

"No, I'm not. Thank you but I'm really not. I'm just trying to help. I've lost people before and I'm not losing anyone else. If the Djinn is released then we'll be in a really bad situation. Right now it's just us and Archington. That's what it boils down to right now and we can stop him. We've got Gabbi with her angel powers, we can defeat him!"

"Yeah how do my powers work? Can I do that lightning thing whenever I want?" Gabbi asked. She sounded positively confident about her identity now.

"No my darling, I'm afraid you can't." Galal said. "They will come to you when you really need them but you won't be able to force them. They will still help you in this fight though, it will all help."

A feeling of hope swelled around the room. It felt good to actually be in the know about something and be thinking positively about how to stop it. Isaac wasn't going to let Archington or any ancient djinns in ancient boxes take his friends away, not to mention the world in general. It was time for Archington to be stopped.

Suddenly the feeling of hope smashed with the shattering of the glass in the front door. Billie screamed in shock, Isaac looked for the nearest weapon and Galal leapt to his feet only to be knocked down to the ground by a hooded figure that came scampering into the room. Isaac recognised the intruder instantly as Skarl.

"Hello children." Skarl giggled.

"Dad!" Gabbi cried, jumping to her feet.

Everyone else stood up too, ready to either run or fight or do whatever was needed.

Just then another figure walked in behind Skarl. It was Archington, professorial as ever in appearance and wearing a warm smile on his face. "So this is where you are!" he cried. "I have been going out of my mind with worry!" He stood there smugly, his arms folded across his chest.

Isaac glanced at Gabbi beside him, she was straining in concentration with her hand outstretched, obviously trying to use her new powers but to no avail.

"Ah ah ah!" Archington said, shaking his finger. "There'll be no repeat performances of earlier this evening thank you Miss Gurtpasha."

Isaac glanced down at Galal who remained unmoving on the floor. Everyone stood rigid, waiting for someone to make the first move.

"Skarl, let's get what we came for." Archington said summarily.

Skarl hissed loudly and advanced on them.

Isaac instinctively stepped in front of Gabbi. "You're not going to take her!" he shouted.

Skarl laughed insanely. "Very well, as you say, I'll just eat her heart away!" He snorted at them and growled, his mouth wide open.

Billie grabbed a lamp that was on a table next to her and hurled it at Skarl. The lamp shattered and Skarl was knocked back slightly.

Ben then took the opportunity to rugby tackle Skarl to the floor whilst Laura grabbed a walking stick that had been leaning against her chair and started hitting the soul dweller over the back with it as he writhed on the floor with Ben next to him. All the time Archington just stood and watched.

"Take Gabbi and get out!" Ben shouted.

Isaac was torn as to what to do but keeping Gabbi safe had to be the priority. He grabbed her by the hand. "Come on!" he commanded and they headed straight towards the door that Archington was blocking. Isaac swung out with his right fist as powerfully as he could and although it collided with Archington's jaw the professor only flinched slightly.

Archington smiled, that same smile that had felt so warm and wise in lectures which now felt cold and deadly. "Is that all?" he asked before throwing a punch directly back at Isaac.

The room span and he felt pain all over him as he smashed into something. Then everything went black.

Chapter Thirty Three

Isaac's first thought was that he was still unconscious in Galal's living room as all that surrounded him was pitch black. Yet instantly he realised he was conscious as a wave of pain coursed through him. Also he realised that he was tied up on a chair, or at least his hands were tied behind his back around the back of the chair. His tried to move his feet but then realised that they must be tied to the legs of the chair too as he could barely move them at all. Wherever he was it was very cold too, and although he really had no way of knowing he sensed that the room he was in was quite big. And then another thought hit him, one that was scarier than all the others. He didn't exactly feel like he was alone in the room either. As terrified as he was he decided it would be best if he showed as little fear as possible. Then he might have a chance at surviving whatever was about to happen to him.

"Okay," he shouted. His head rippled with pain as he spoke. "I know someone's there." His voice echoed in the room, bouncing off walls he couldn't see. For a long moment there was nothing but hollow silence. He decided to shout again "Come on I know -"

The match ignited just centimetres from his face. He gasped in shock and saw that the tiny spark of light from the flame lit up the aging features of Professor Archington.

"Hello Isaac."

Isaac decided not to waste time with ironic pleasantries. "Where am I?"

"You're in the cellar beneath the guildhall."

"What did you do to my friends?"

"I killed them." Archington answered as plainly as if he were just describing what he'd had for breakfast.

Isaac's stomach turned over. He felt violently sick.

A split second later Archington burst out laughing. "No, I didn't kill them, I just wanted to see your reaction. They're alive."

The sick feeling went away a bit but not much. Then another disturbing thought entered Isaac's mind. "Why are you answering all of my questions?"

"Because I am going to kill you. And there's absolutely no way you can stop me."

The sick feeling returned with full force but Isaac was determined not to show it. As scared as he was he wasn't dead yet and until he was he wouldn't give up trying to stay alive. "So how long have I got?"

"Oh you've got a little while as yet. Not my choice of course, but there are a lot of rituals surrounding all this that need to be completed first."

"The Box of Infernos. Am I soul one hundred?"

"I wouldn't have picked anyone else."

"But Gabbi-"

"Oh no Gabbi would have been too easy. You're the one in charge. You're the one who started it all with your arrogant thoughts and your pathetic remorse of the past."

"How do you know about my past?"

"I have my sources."

The match suddenly burnt out. Isaac was amazed it had lasted that long.

"I think we can do away with the atmospheric darkness now. Let there be light!" Archington commanded with a theatrical voice and all of a sudden the room was flooded with dim but effective light from a few strip bulbs on the ceiling.

Isaac got his first clear glance of where he was being held. The room looked a lot like a cellar, with a main open part in the centre where Isaac was and then arched recesses all around the walls. There was a steep set of stairs leading up and out of sight just in front of him.

"See, just like God." Archington smiled from his crouched position just in front of Isaac.

"What sources?"

"I told you we have people everywhere. And the information I found about you Isaac, dear me that was tough reading. Toby, Lee, Matthew - all dead, blood everywhere."

Isaac felt a stab of painful guilt in his heart. "Stop it."

"You must have been terrified, fighting for your life alongside them. At least you tried though eh? You were there, you tried to save them, tried to stop them. Oh wait -" Archington grinned slyly.

Isaac avoided Archington's gaze. "I said stop it. Please."

"Oh I'm sorry does the truth hurt? You know if anything you should be saying thank you rather than please."

"Why?"

"Do you really think your little incident that night would have slipped by as quietly as it did without a few choice words whispered in the right ears? Three teenage boys brutally murdered - there should have been a media frenzy, a nationwide manhunt to catch the killer. Was there? No. You have my order to thank for that."

"There were journalists -"

"Hardly. A few men at your garden gate for a few days? Tell me, did you ever see it on the news? Did you ever read about it in the papers?"

Isaac was shocked at the realisation that his night of terror had been controlled by Archington's forces without him even knowing it. "So you knew about me even then?"

"Pay attention young man, I told you I just read some files on you - I wasn't there myself. No at the time of your mishap I was busy with other projects." Archington gazed at Isaac for a moment, considering him. "It still sits in you doesn't it? All the pain of that night, it's still there - open and raw like a savage cut on your soul that stings every time someone touches it."

Isaac didn't say anything - it was a rhetorical question as the answer was clear.

"You should care less Isaac. Let go of all your right and wrong arrogance, just let all that go. There are other ways Isaac, oh such infinite ways to go on. Forget about what's right and what's wrong and focus on the power."

Isaac remembered the man who had been talking to Inspector Ackley. Their power was everywhere, that's what he had said. "And that's what this Djinn will give you is it? Power? To do what?"

Archington smiled. "Oh it goes far higher than all that."

"How do you mean?" Isaac was intrigued. Higher still? He thought they'd reached the top.

"Hush. We don't speak of it yet."

Isaac decided not to probe any further. He didn't want to enrage Archington. Instead he decided to change the conversation entirely. "Are you a demon?"

Archington burst out laughing. "No!" he said, still chuckling. "Why on earth would you think that?"

"Well it's the superpowers to be honest. I mean no offence but you're old, you shouldn't be that strong."

"Ah no, that's just a gift."

"From who?"

"Hush." Archington looked at Isaac for a moment, staring into his eyes.

Isaac glanced away as it was uncomfortable. It was almost the look one would give to a lover.

"You know Isaac, I really did mean it when I said you were clever that time. I honestly think you are. You're just misguided, drowning in matters of right and wrong and good and evil. Come and drown in what I follow and I can promise you that you won't be disappointed."

"I'd rather die."

"Oh don't worry. You will." Archington smirked. "Why do you care so much Isaac? Because of that night with your friends is that it? But that was the past Isaac, you can't change that. What is it that you want now?" It sounded very much like the questions Pete had asked Isaac that first time they met.

Isaac told Archington the same thing he told Pete. "I just want to help."

"And you really think you know what's best-"

Isaac shocked himself by interrupting Archington mid-speech. "No I don't. I don't pretend to have the monopoly on what's right and wrong, goodness knows I've done enough questionable things that I'd be stupid to try and label everything. But some things - like killing ninety nine people? Some things when people are getting hurt, lives are getting lost or torn apart or both then yes, yes I do want to help and yes I do think I know what's best because there isn't anyone else."

Archington narrowed his eyes whilst still smiling at Isaac. "And there we have it in full view at last. The arrogance. The self-righteousness."

"If I'm out of line then I'll be punished in due course. In the mean time until the last breath leaves my body then there isn't any way you'll stop me from wanting to do the right thing." Isaac could see that his words had at least shocked Archington if nothing else.

However the bad news was that the sarcastic yet warm smile that Archington had been wearing had now been replaced with a frown.

"And what do you think is the right thing hmm? The problem with right Isaac is that it automatically means that someone has to be wrong. Right is only right when there's a wrong too. Religions in this world have used the defence of right and wrong for centuries to commit atrocious crimes. Love everyone but hate anyone that disagrees - that's the motto people like you live by."

In the strangest of ways Isaac agreed with what Archington had just said. "There is a lot of arrogance and ignorance out there. I know that from personal experience. I don't agree with any of that."

"You say all that. Very pious of you Isaac, very holy. But it's a front. You spew all of this love and care and right thing bile but you'd turn if you were pushed, you turned that night from your friends and you'd turn again, you'd turn just like the brothers did when-" Archington stopped as if he had gone too far.

"Brothers?"

"It doesn't matter."

"No come on, if you're going to kill me anyway then tell me."

Archington coughed a laugh. "The order I used to belong to in Scotland, before I found my much higher purpose with this order right here, they were supposedly good people. Supposedly they were in the right. Then one day, one warm midsummer evening when the fragrant smell of lavender hung in the air and blew in the breeze, they murdered my wife Rose. Rose Padley."

Isaac was dumbfounded. "What? Why?"

"She was a witch you see. She used to make potions and remedies from the herbs she grew in the garden. But several members of the order frowned upon her, frowned upon her activities. And they frowned upon me, a member of the order, having her as a wife. So they killed her. Stabbed her in the heart."

"Professor that's awful. I'm sorry." It was beginning to dawn on Isaac just how he could defeat Archington - and it certainly didn't involve fists or feet.

"That is the arrogance Isaac. And it's in all of you, deep down it's there. Maybe one day a witch might come to this town. Maybe she'll have heard of a boy here who kills demons and banishes spirits to realms of eternal torment - and maybe she'll think that's wrong and maybe she'll try and stop you. You'd kill her if you had to, you'd murder her just like they murdered my wife. And all the time, even as you stuck the knife inside her, all that time you'd be thinking that you were doing the right thing."

Isaac shook his head. "You're wrong."

Archington shrugged. "You might term me as being one of the bad guys but whatever that means at least I'm honest about what I'm going to do. Didn't I tell you quite honestly that I'm going to kill you tonight?"

Isaac wasn't sure whether to appreciate that honesty or not. He was actually beginning to feel sorry for Archington - he was clearly rather deluded and had obviously turned insane from the grief but in an odd way it was understandable. Isaac decided that since Archington was claiming to be in such an honest mood that he would try and find out as much as he could about all that was going on. "Tell me more about this order in Scotland."

"What do you want to know?"

"What do they do? Who are they?"

"The Order of Dunamis, or at least that's their name now. They're an ancient group - the second oldest order in existence. They're Christian now but the order itself has roots back though ancient Judaic times, back into the ancient religions of the near east and back and back and back to the earliest civilizations. They would try and keep that fact downplayed however - they do like to think of themselves as very Christian."

"And what do they do? How come I've never heard of them?"

"They are a secret order, emphasis on secret. Just like us really, they have to stay completely secret as their work is so important - to them at least."

"What work is that then?"

"They research and guard powers. Ancient powers. Some good, some bad - but one in particular."

"Which one?"

Archington just laughed. "I know you're going to die, but still some things remain a secret. Suffice to say though that I saw the benefit of that power where they only saw the negatives. And that itself led me to where I am today."

"Which is where exactly?"

"I said just now that The Order of Dunamis was the second oldest order in history. Someone has to be the first oldest." Archington smiled.

"Your order doesn't have a name then?"

"Of course we do, but we gave up needing to use it centuries ago. Our reputation precedes us you see. Our numbers aren't as many as they used to be, but as I've told you we still have followers everywhere. Don't be fooled by the members round here wearing their hooded robes - we have just as many who look as plain and ordinary as you do. Loyal servants all across the earth and all across creation. All of them waiting, all of them readying themselves."

"And what is it that you serve?"

"We follow that which the Order of Dunamis fears most."

"That one particular power?"

"Indeed."

Just then, another voice. "Imperator?"

It seemed to make Archington jump just as much as it made Isaac jump. Isaac looked across and saw that a figure had appeared on the stairs. He couldn't see it in detail but he knew from the voice that it was Skarl.

"Yes Skarl?"

"We're ready to drip, drip, drip, bleed the little boy dry!" Skarl squealed.

Hearing those words Isaac was certainly beginning to become more than just a bit terrified. All this time he had hoped that the others would turn up and save him but now he was starting to think it would be up to him to save himself.

"Very good. Go back up, I'll be along presently."

Skarl nodded and ran back up the stairs. "Yes Imperator!"

Archington sighed. "Insane demon. You just can't get the staff." Archington stood up now and looked down at Isaac. "Come along then Isaac. Let's go and change the world. Together." Archington ripped the cords from Isaac's hands and feet with great ease. He grabbed Isaac forcibly by the shoulder and pulled him to his feet.

Isaac struggled but it was useless. No, force wouldn't win this fight. He'd have to use words. "Professor, please just listen to me. You don't have to do this!"

"But you wanted to help didn't you?" Archington said as they headed for the stairs, "That's what you said. And by giving your life you are helping! With the Djinn released I will progress our work of ages and help to make this world what it should be - free of right and wrong! All shall be destroyed in equal measure."

"It won't bring Rose back!" Isaac cried.

"It won't matter. This world is past saving, none of it is worth even an ounce of mercy."

"So no-one on earth deserves to live because of what a few men did to your wife?"

"Open your eyes Isaac!" Archington exclaimed, pulling Isaac up the stairs with him. "Innocence is the ultimate human weakness. It's not just a few men, it's everyone. And it goes far beyond what happened to my wife. People will see that, when the Abominable Nothing is released and when our power rises, the whole world will see."

Archington swung the door open at the top of the stairs and led Isaac into a large room which Isaac guessed was the main meeting room of the guildhall. It was a dimly lit room and there in the centre was a large wooden table tilted ever so slightly forwards at the foot of that table on the floor was what Isaac guessed must have been the Box of Infernos. It wasn't a huge box, about two feet across. It was made out of a dark, rotten looking wood and it looked old, incredibly old. There was a single rusted metal clasp that kept it shut at the front and all over the surface were carved archaic symbols that Isaac didn't recognise at all. It also seemed to be covered in a deep black and dark red looking substance - dried blood. Vomit rose up in Isaac's throat but he suppressed it. Glancing quickly around the room he saw about twenty hooded figures, all grasping black candles. Fear swept over him again and again and again.

"Take him!" Archington commanded.

Before Isaac had time to resist two strong arms grabbed him and forced him over towards the table. He kicked and screamed, the reality of the situation finally setting in. There wasn't going to be a rescue. His words had failed him. He was going to die, and the world was going to end.

Chapter Thirty Four

The village of Vale; Northern Scotland: Eighteen years previously.

Robert was sat on his knees leaning forwards over the cold body of his wife. He wept continuously whilst cradling her head, staring deeply into her now vacant eyes that used to be the home of so much depth and life.

"Rose." he whispered. "Rose, please come back. Come back to me Rose." He heard the crying coming from the other room but he couldn't get up to go to it. Right now he couldn't, he just wanted her back. His thoughts were interrupted when he sensed movement in the open door to the cottage behind him.

"Brother Archington."

It was Brother Septimus, the leader of the order - Robert recognised the broad Scottish accent. Turning his head away from Rose slightly he saw Brother Septimus's stout frame standing there in the doorway, dimly lit by the dying sun outside. A pair of bumble bees flew past behind him, obviously attracted by the lavender in the garden.

"I am sorry that this was necessary brother." Brother Septimus said grimly.

"Necessary?" Robert muttered.

"Yes, necessary. A sad necessity, I'll grant you that. But a necessity all the same." Brother Septimus entered the cottage a little further. "You're rising in our order brother. Within a few years you could be answerable to none other than me. It was not right for you to be cavorting with one so -" Septimus eyed Rose's body carefully, "- inclined. Not right at all."

"Right." Robert said the word and it took on a new meaning. A new, wicked meaning.

"Witchcraft and devilry, it flies in the face of all that we as an order hold dear. It is against the will of God, Robert, and we work his will. We could no longer tolerate such as travesty of life."

Robert gently placed Rose's head down on the floor before rising from his knees and turning to face Brother Septimus who had now fully entered the cottage and was standing but a few feet away. "I see."

Brother Septimus offered a small smile. "You must understand that it's right."

Robert nodded. He could feel the blood pumping in his body, hear it in his ears. His brain prickled with fiery anger. "I see everything much clearer now brother."

"Good."

"It's just a pity that you won't."

"What do you -"

Before Brother Septimus had finished speaking Robert had grabbed a knife that lay on the small table to his side and leapt at Brother Septimus, knocking him back against the wall of the cottage and plunging the knife straight through his right eye. Brother Septimus screamed in unbridled agony as deep dark blood poured from the gory wound that was his eye, covering the right side of his face and dripping quickly to the floor within seconds.

"Brother Archington!"

Robert withdrew the knife savagely and then pressed it hard against Brother Septimus's neck.

"Hush now brother. Don't you know this is the right thing to do?"

Brother Septimus looked on in horror for one last moment through his remaining eye before Robert dragged the blade savagely across, opening Septimus's neck up from ear to ear. Blood poured. Septimus gargled but didn't scream. A moment later he collapsed to the floor, gasping like a landed fish for a few seconds before becoming still completely.

Robert now stood between two brutally murdered bodies. One who deserved it and one who certainly didn't. The crying continued in the other room but he still couldn't face it. His hands shook as he looked at them - they were covered in blood. Just then the air in the room got very thick and tight as though something even more uncomfortable than the two gory bodies were present. Robert felt for a moment like he suddenly wanted to run away, to just run out the door and flee down the road as fast as he could. Yet despite that instinct he stayed still, he stood there staring at the bodies either side of him and wondered what the odd feeling of dread was that now inhabited the room.

Suddenly there was a voice in the air, only it wasn't in the air at all - it felt like it was in his mind. And it wasn't even so much a voice as thoughts, thoughts being manifested in his brain.

"This world is old. It is diseased. Rotten."

"Who are you?" Robert called out.

"I am that which your kin fear most."

Robert felt his stomach clench. He knew what was in his mind now. "What do you want?"

"*You.*"

"Why?"

"*You possess potential. You have unrestrained hate in your blood.*"

"I'm not, I mean I'm -"

"*This world ridded you of your wife. Serve me and I shall rid the world of itself. All shall fall to emptiness.*"

Robert stood paralysed for a moment. Then he realised that his hands had stopped shaking ever since the thoughts had started. He knelt on the floor between the corpses and bowed his head. "I serve you. Master."

Chapter Thirty Five

The wood on the table felt rough as Isaac was forced down onto it. Harsh, biting ropes were tied crudely round his wrists and ankles so he lay face up, limbs outstretched, looking helplessly around him. He saw Skarl grinning happily to his left side and on his right he thought he recognised Elias, the man who had killed Pete.

So much death, Isaac thought. His least favourite thing in the world, the thing that had once taken his friends away from him and there was so much of it. And now his death would be one more.

He saw Archington approach him from the side carrying a rusted looking dagger. It didn't seem to have a handle or anything, it was just a dirty looking shard of sharp blade. It looked as old as the box.

"On this night," Archington bellowed, "the Box of Infernos shall be opened! The Abominable Nothing, the most destructive one, the scourge of light, shall be released!" Archington looked down at Isaac and smiled. "Isaac Jacobs, the extinguishing of your life signs the death warrant of this ancient earth. Congratulations."

Isaac knew he only had moments left, and he knew he only had three words left to say. "I forgive you." he said, looking Archington straight in the eyes.

The twinkle had gone from them. For a moment it looked like all the anger had left him and Isaac actually dared to think that he had managed to stop him just with those words.

Then Archington's face hardened once more. "Then you're even weaker than I thought." he said before raising the dagger.

Isaac shut his eyes. There was nothing left to do. He prayed silently and just waited. It would be over soon. Jack flashed through his mind, his friends, Gabbi. The things they could have all seen together, the things they could have done. All lost now, a future that would never happen.

Then his eyes flashed open. Not because the dagger had been plunged into him but because the main doors had just been broken open, he had heard them splintering!

"Isaac!" It was Gabbi's voice!

Wild un-tempered hope sprang up within him and relief washed through his mind like a tidal wave. He had been saved!

"Get them for God's sake, get them!" Archington shouted.

Isaac heard running and shouting and the sound of fighting but he could barely see anything from his position on the table.

Archington raised the knife again – a determined, mad look in his eyes now.

Wherever the hope had come from a moment earlier it returned there immediately. Isaac braced himself for what was coming, shutting his eyes once more. It didn't quite seem real, the whole situation seemed so surreal in a way that he didn't fully believe he was about to be sacrificed, although he guessed he would believe it soon enough when he lay there bleeding.

"Get away from him!" Gabbi's voice sounded closer now.

Isaac tried to twist and turn but he still couldn't see her.

"You won't stop him from coming! You may be part angel but I can still snap you like kindling you little whore!" Archington screamed.

"Want a bet?" Gabbi asked and a moment later there was a bright flash and then a bolt of the purest white energy smashed into Archington's chest and sent him flying across the room. Gabbi rushed into Isaac's line of sight at last. "Thank goodness that worked!" she cried, and immediately started undoing the ropes that bound Isaac. "And cheek of it, calling me a whore!"

Isaac could hear the fighting continue behind him. He smiled up at Gabbi. "Thank you thank you thank you!" he exclaimed, feeling unbelievable relief that for now at least his life had indeed been spared. He shook the ropes off of him as Gabbi untied them and sat up. He grabbed her face with his now free hands and kissed her forcefully on the forehead. "You're amazing."

Gabbi smiled and raised her eyebrows. "Duh!"

Isaac looked round and saw that about half of the hooded guys had already run off, obviously scared by Gabbi's powers. The rest were fighting Ben, Billie, Laura and Galal.

Isaac and Gabbi ran over and joined the fray. In comparison to the super strength that Archington had, these guys were relatively easy to deal with. Isaac saw that Galal had brought a gleaming sword with him and Ben was carrying a crossbow.

Several more of the hooded guys ran out of the front door. Soon they were more or less evenly matched with seven assailants to their six.

Billie and Laura were using planks of wood they'd found to batter two of the attackers into submission - Laura managed to knock hers unconscious with a blow to the back of the head and then went on to help Billie with her hooded man who had her on the ground and was attempting to throttle her.

Galal and Ben were fending off three of them with punches and kicks. One of them had found a sword from somewhere and ran up to Galal, brandishing the sword at the older man in a menacing fashion. Perhaps the attacker thought he was going for the easiest kill but if that was the case then he was sorely mistaken.

With speed and athleticism that shocked everyone and made even the remaining hooded villains stop and stare for a moment, Galal swung, ducked and twirled with his own sword in hand and within moments he had skillfully disarmed the attacking hooded man and held the point of his sword to the villain's throat.

"Leave now and leave with your life." Galal warned.

The figure pulled his hood down to shockingly reveal a pale face with black eyes and hollow cheeks with what looked like small horns growing downwards from his chin like a devilish type of beard. It was obviously a soul dweller like Skarl, but one who had lived in the body for so long that it had started to morph into a demonic form.

"Who do you think you threaten, human? I am Valgar, I'm a child of the Ar'kanak - I take children from their beds and devour them whole! Blades do not scare me!" Valgar rasped.

Galal looked horrified for a moment and then spoke. "Then you should have no fear of this!"

With that he swung his sword once round over his head and then with a single clean blow he struck Valgar's head from his neck.

Everyone gasped and jumped a little - even Billie who was still being semi-throttled on the floor.

The body of Valgar stayed standing for a moment, thick black blood pumping from the neck. Then it fell to the floor.

Isaac had been watching all of that unfold whilst trading blows with Elias. Elias seemed to have sought Isaac out personally, obviously wanting to settle the score from their last encounter. Suddenly from somewhere within his robe Elias procured a small knife.

"Time to cut you scum!" Elias spat.

Isaac stretched his arm out to try and grab the knife from Elias's hand but Elias was too quick and slashed the knife viciously across Isaac's open palm as it approached. Isaac groaned in pain as the hot sting of the cut throbbed in his hand. He looked down, the cut went right across his palm. Thankfully it wasn't that deep but it still bled a lot.

Elias grinned viciously, still holding the knife that was now covered in blood. "Now I'll finish what the Imperator started!" he announced.

"No!" Isaac yelled, diving for Elias as he realised what he was going to do, but it was too late.

Elias slipped past him and ran for the Box of Infernos, diving for it and slamming the knife into the top of it so that it stood there, its pointed tip buried in the wood. The blood on the knife ran down the blade, dripping onto the lid of the box.

Isaac looked on in horror. Surely it wouldn't be enough? Those few drops of blood, that wouldn't be enough! Would it? Isaac stared at the Box of Infernos, not taking his eyes off of it. For a moment it looked like nothing was happening but then slowly and very distinguishably it began to shake, the lid rattling up and down, straining against the metal padlock that held it shut.

Skarl, who up until this point had been watching the fight from a dark corner, now emerged and rubbed his hands together in anticipation. "The box!" he called gleefully. "The box, the box! Our box of treats is opening!"

Everyone seemed to stop their fighting and wrestling at this point and looked instead towards the box.

Isaac was pleased at least to see that his friends were mostly victorious now in their battle with Archington's minions, with only three robed figures still standing. Across the room in the other direction, Isaac saw Archington begin to stir.

Billie called out across the room having knocked her throttling attacker into unconsciousness at last. "Isaac, what do we do?"

Isaac didn't answer her, he couldn't think. He needed time to figure something out - this was all happening too fast.

"Imperator, look!" squealed Skarl.

Archington rolled over onto his back and then sat upright. Instantly he started laughing when he saw the box shaking. "You've failed Isaac! All of you have failed!" He looked at the box delightedly. "The Box of Infernos is open! The Abominable Nothing is free!"

With that last shout from Archington a bright orange light pierced outwards from inside the box. The padlock shook violently before snapping and landing with a clank on the floor. Then, with an unearthly roar like some kind of demonic waterfall, the lid of the box flew backwards and a great column of fiery light rose up and hit the ceiling.

Everyone in the room had to shield their eyes momentarily and take a few steps back from the light.

After just a second Isaac's eyes had adjusted and he looked more clearly at the fiery column. Inside it he could see that a great swirling creature had arisen. The Abominable Nothing! It looked like it was made out of the blackest smoke, with the smoke creating billowing robes and rags which were flying out in all directions. Isaac couldn't make out much of its actual physical body at all, if it even had one. All he could see were two piercing fiery eyes penetrating through the blackness of its smoky exterior.

It was suspended in the column of energy which had erupted from the box and seemed to hang there in the column about ten feet off the ground. Its fiery eyes darted all around, looking at each and every person in the room.

Elias started leaping about with excitement. "It's free!" he called, running round until he was standing in front of the Djinn. "It actually worked! I did -"

He was cut short as the Djinn roared and breathed a hot fiery blast down onto him.

Elias screamed but within seconds he'd been reduced to ash.

Isaac gasped. He heard Billie scream behind him.

The Djinn roared again.

Skarl shrieked and appeared to run off in terror into the basement where Isaac had been held.

The other members of Archington's cult stood back into the shadows, obviously fearing for their own lives after watching one of their brothers being incinerated.

"My lord Djinn!" Archington was now standing once more and was extending welcome arms towards the creature. "I am the one who released you! Serve me!"

"I am come to do my master's bidding!" The Djinn said. Its voice was just as smoky as its appearance.

"As am I my lord! Our purpose is the same!" Archington shook his hands for emphasis.

The Djinn seemed to gaze at Archington as if it were considering his words.

All this time Isaac's mind was racing, desperately trying to think of something to do, some way of stopping the Abominable Nothing before it was completely free. All the time it stayed in that column of energy Isaac figured he had a chance of just reversing it and putting the monster back in the box. He just had to figure out how.

The Djinn seemed to now gaze at its surroundings a little closer. "How long have I slept?"

"For over two ages. Humanity covers most of the planet now, the elder beings are in retreat. But we can change that."

The Abominable Nothing seemed disgusted at these words. "You are human!" it breathed, as if it were passing judgement on Archington.

"I am imbued with the power of your master. I work for him!"

The Djinn considered Archington a moment longer before speaking. "Then we will work together human. For him."

"No!" Galal's shout came unexpectedly and by the look on his face after he'd shouted it seemed that he'd surprised himself just as much as he'd surprised everyone else.

The Djinn whirled round in his column and looked at Galal and the others. "Who are these small things?"

"Sacrifices my lord." Archington said with a smile. "Burn them."

At this the Djinn roared with terrifying ferocity.

"Dad look out!" Gabbi screamed.

"Galal!" Isaac shouted, diving towards him and knocking him out of the way just as a hot blast of fire rained down onto the spot where Galal had been standing. They both tumbled to the floor at the feet of Gabbi, Laura, Billie and Ben. The idea Isaac had been searching for had just hit him - he just hoped it would work. "I've got a plan." he announced, looking up at his friends from his position on the floor with Galal. "It might not work but I think it'll be better than a poke in the eye with a sharp stick." Isaac paused for breath. "I hope anyway. I need you to keep the Djinn busy, all of you. Keep it distracted!"

The others nodded at this and Isaac helped Galal to his feet.

The Djinn looked at Isaac with those fiery eyes. "You." it seethed, its voice full of rage. "You would dare to rob a Djinn of its sacrifice?"

"Hey! Genie!" It was Ben. The Djinn immediately switched its glare from Isaac to Ben. "Where are my three wishes?"

"Yeah!" Laura shouted. "We helped open your box, what about us?" The Djinn roared again and everyone scattered.

Good work guys, Isaac thought. It was the opening he needed. He grabbed a little dagger he'd seen laying on the floor and then ran around the open Box of Infernos to where Archington stood, arms folded. He was so content watching the Djinn attempt to destroy everyone he didn't notice Isaac sneak up beside him.

"Sorry Professor." Isaac said, grabbing Archington's wrist as tightly as he could.

Professor Archington looked genuinely surprised at Isaac suddenly appearing like that and that moment of surprise gave Isaac exactly the opportunity he needed.

"I need a favour."

With that he slashed the blade across Archington's hand as quickly as he could, and then before Archington had time to grab him Isaac ran for the Box of Infernos.

"No!" Archington bellowed, but it was too late.

Isaac was by the box, directly next to the column of energy with the Abominable Nothing within. He threw the bloodied knife down hard into the fiery energy, straight down into the open box. "A few drops of blood from someone who's fighting on the side of good opens it. I wonder what a few drops of blood from someone who's doing the opposite will do?"

Archington looked furious, like he was about to fly off into an unfettered rage. "No!" he simply bellowed again, his face going red with anger.

The Djinn suddenly roared in anguish. It looked down and around from the others who were still distracting it and saw what Isaac had done. Then it gazed at Archington with a fury that matched Archington's own. "The last soul was not fully bled!"

Archington didn't say anything now. He kept swapping his angry stare from the Abominable Nothing to Isaac and then back again.

"You human fool! The last soul needed to be fully bled!" The Djinn howled and raged, its swirling shape turning and contorting, becoming formless in the column of fiery energy. With one last screech of anger it swirled and raged its way down into the Box of Infernos, the air in the room crackling and hissing, the column of energy almost exploding back into the box with the Djinn. When the last of the Djinn and the energy was back in the box the lid snapped shut and the air in the room was normal again.

Isaac looked at the box and was shocked to see the padlock back on the lid as if it had never broken off.

There was a moments silence and then it was as if everyone suddenly remembered where they were. The remaining members of Archington's cult who had been cowering whilst the Djinn was free began their attack on Gabbi, Billie, Laura, Ben and Galal once more and Archington took an angry step towards Isaac before seething at him through squinted eyes and then turning on his heel and running towards the basement.

"Gabbi!" Isaac called, "I need to follow Archington, can you hold these guys back?"

"I think so. After that monster they'll be easy!" she said with a smile, kicking one of them in the face as he attempted to get up off the floor. "Are you going to be okay?"

"Yeah." Isaac replied. "I think I know what to do!"

He turned and ran, flinging himself down the flight of stairs at the back of the room and when he got to the bottom he saw Archington standing in the centre of the room with his back to Isaac and his arms outstretched.

"Tribuo mihi vestri vox! Tribuo mihi vestri vires! Tribuo mihi vestri vox! Tribuo mihi vestri vires!" Archington shouted.

The basement shook violently. Isaac looked up at the ceiling worryingly as the glass in the some of the lights shattered and rained down onto the floor. Isaac knew a bit of basic Latin and as far as he could understand Archington was asking for power and strength from somewhere. He figured it was the same power that Archington, his minions and the Abominable Nothing apparently followed - the same one that had been feared by the Order of Dunamis.

"Professor!" Isaac shouted over the noise of the building shaking. Archington lowered his arms and turned around so they were facing each other. "I'm sorry for cutting you just now! But you don't have to do this! You don't have to be this way!"

"How do you know?"

"Because it's wrong! I don't know everything, I honestly don't. But this, what you're doing right here, what you almost did tonight, hurting people, this is wrong!"

Archington just stared at Isaac. "It's all there is Isaac. All there is for me."

"No it's not! You were hurt once, when those murderers killed your wife. You know how much that hurt. How can it be right to bring that hurt to others?"

"Others deserve it. This whole world deserves it."

"You don't believe that. Not the intelligent man that taught me in lectures, he wouldn't believe that!"

"Wouldn't he?"

"No! It's this thing, this power. Whatever it is that you follow, the thing that the Djinn mentioned, that you work for, this is just what it wants. It's tricking you! Tricking you into opening the Box of Infernos and goodness knows what else! Be the clever person that you are - don't let it!" Isaac shouted desperately.

Archington appeared to be on the brink of a mental breakdown, and if he was mid-way through summoning something dark and powerful Isaac certainly didn't want him to finish. For the first time Isaac looked into Archington's eyes and saw a real flash of uncertainty.

"She tells me the same thing you know."

Isaac could barely hear him over the shaking of the room. "Who does?"

"She comes to me sometimes, in the corner of my eye. I think she's just in my mind, I'm sure she can't be real. But she tells me the same as you just have."

"Rose? Does she speak to you?"

Archington suddenly sounded very sad. "But which voice do I trust? I've had voices in my mind for so long now, oh such voices. Which is better than the other?"

"Hers is!" Isaac shouted. "Of course her voice is better!"

"I miss her so much Isaac. I'm doing this for her! This world, this horrible, stinking world where everything is twisted and diseased - this world did that to her!" Archington shouted. "And I don't want it Isaac, don't you understand? I don't want it anymore! I want it gone."

"I've lost people too Professor, you know that. My best friends, they died whilst I watched. I remember that, every day I remember it and every day it kills me. But you go on, you try and make things better. There is good out there Professor, I promise you there is!"

Archington shook his head. "It doesn't matter now. Good, evil - it all becomes blurred. You go far enough and everything turns to grey. And the power Isaac, you don't understand. The power I have now - I can't let it go. It's in my blood, it's right there in my soul. I can't let it go." There was actual vulnerability in his voice now, it sounded disjointed.

Isaac began to hope that he may well have just broken through. "You can. I believe that you can! Just be brave, think of Rose and be brave. Be brave and just let it go. Just let it go!" Isaac begged.

The room still shook violently and plaster and dust now started falling from the ceilings and the walls.

Suddenly Isaac felt like his heart had leapt into his mouth in shock as the next thing he knew he was being strangled from behind - someone or something had jumped on his back. He heard the rasping breath in his ear and knew who it was - Skarl. He must have been hiding down here ever since he'd got scared by the Abominable Nothing.

"You must not stop the Imperator sneaky boy!" Skarl screamed. "I'll feast on your yummy eyes and drink the blood from the empty holes before I let you interfere!" Skarl bit down hard on Isaac's ear.

Isaac screamed as the sharp teeth bit into him. The pain was sharp and intense and seemed to reach right into his brain. He jabbed backwards furiously with his elbow, trying to knock Skarl off but it was no good. Isaac looked up was amazed to see Archington running straight towards him with an expression of determination and anger on his face. But he wasn't looking at Isaac - he was looking at Skarl.

"Get off of him!" Archington bellowed as he ran over.

"Imperator, no!" Skarl whimpered, releasing Isaac's ear.

It was too late. Archington had reached them and with all his strength he pushed Skarl off of Isaac, sending the demon backwards into several crates which were stacked in one of the arched recesses. The force of the push caused Isaac to fall backwards onto the floor and he landed on his back with a hard thud. He lay there for a second, recovering from the shock of the sudden attack. The room had finally stopped shaking and Archington stood over him.

"Here," Archington said, extending a hand.

Just then Isaac heard new footsteps hurriedly approaching down the staircase that led into the basement. Isaac looked over and saw the athletic shape of Ben appear at the bottom of the stairs.

"Get away from my best mate you bastard!" Ben shouted, raising his crossbow. He had a wild look in his eyes - he was obviously running on pure instinct and emotion.

Archington continued to outstretch his hand to Isaac.

"Ben, no!" Isaac called out desperately as he saw Ben's finger move but it was too late.

Ben fired.

Archington fell.

Chapter Thirty Six

The bolt had landed firmly in Archington's stomach. He crumpled to the floor and lay there breathing heavily.

Isaac suddenly found his eyes full of tears. This couldn't be happening! He had just got through to Archington!

Ben stood a few feet away, looking utterly bewildered.

Isaac put one arm around Archington's shoulders and the other across the professor's chest.

"I don't, I don't understand!" Ben stuttered.

"He was helping me!" Isaac cried, his voice choked with emotion. "He was helping!"

"Oh god. Oh god what have I done?" Ben clasped a hand to his mouth.

Archington groaned in pain.

Isaac held his hand out to Ben. "Ben -"

"I've killed him." Ben whispered. He looked as broken as Archington did. "Oh god what am I?" With that he dropped his crossbow and fled back up the stairs.

Isaac looked down at Archington, whose breathing had now calmed down. He looked peaceful. Isaac then glanced down at the wound. Dark red blood was blossoming quickly through Archington's shirt.

"Don't worry," Isaac said. "We'll get help. You'll be fine okay? Professor you'll be fine." Isaac tried to sound convincing but he realised it sounded anything but.

"It's okay Isaac. The things I've done, I don't think it would have been good for me to go on anyway."

"Don't be silly. You just saved my life."

"I tried extinguishing it earlier. What kind of a man does that make me?"

"It makes you a brave one." Isaac took the hand he had across Archington's chest and used it to wipe tears from his eyes. Fresh ones took their place. "Professor you can't die. You could help us, we need you."

"You don't need an old murderer like me." Archington gave a small laugh but then instantly winced with pain. "Besides, like I said, you're clever. Just now you figured out how to put the Djinn back in the box, right there and then. As furious as I was it was still very clever."

Isaac said nothing, he just tried to force a smile but it barely appeared.

"Isaac, I don't have long, I need to tell you something. Just now you showed me great kindness. You showed me love."

"I just did what I thought-"

"You'll need to be stronger than that to defeat what's coming." Archington's expression turned cold and solemn. "Because it is coming Isaac. Something is coming. I'm so sorry but it is and there's nothing you can do." Archington himself sounded full of fear.

A powerful man like that being afraid made Isaac absolutely terrified. "What is it? What's coming?! Please tell me!" Isaac shook Archington just a little as he spoke.

Archington opened his mouth to reply but he was stopped. He stared deep into space for a moment.

Isaac looked at him confused. "Professor?"

Archington suddenly looked immensely pained, as if the worst tortures in the world had just been inflicted upon him. He screamed.

"Professor!" Isaac shouted but Archington just lay there screaming and writhing.

The building started to shake again. The air around them filled with a pervading sense of dread and terror which made Isaac's stomach twist over and over in knots of fear and made every bone in his body want to flee as fast as he could. The space surrounding them started to crackle and hiss with energy - it swirled around them faster and faster until it was as if they were in the centre of a hurricane. Isaac looked all around him - he couldn't see the rest of the room anymore, he could just see this crackling blue and black energy moving faster and faster. He held the professor tightly, trying to comfort him in the midst of it all.

Suddenly the energy rose up above them and condensed into a single ball before shooting directly down into Archington's chest.

Archington lay silent. He had stopped moving.

"Professor?" Isaac asked again. "Professor!" He shook Archington but it was useless. The building stopped shaking once more. Archington had gone.

Isaac leant over him and let several tears fall. They'd failed. They'd stopped the Abominable Nothing from being freed completely, but they'd still failed. It had all been in vain.

Chapter Thirty Seven

When Isaac returned to the main room upstairs he found all of his friends alive and generally unharmed except for some minor cuts and bruises. He immediately noticed that Ben wasn't among them.

"Hey!" called Billie as Isaac wandered slowly over towards them, stepping over an unconscious body on the floor on the way. "What happened?"

"I'll tell you later. For now I'll just say that Archington's dead."

"Oh." Billie said. She was clearly unsure as to how to react. "Is that a yay for us or a -"

Isaac shook his head solemnly. "Where's Ben?"

Laura indicated to the main doors with a nod of the head. "He said he needed some air. I think he was a bit exhausted after the fighting and the almost burning." she explained.

Isaac looked over towards the door. He should go out and check on him. "Yeah."

"I still can't believe we did it." Billie said. "I mean things seemed so bad after you got taken Isaac but we thought about what you said about being able to stop this before it gets any further and I don't know, suddenly things just clicked into place."

"Yeah," Laura agreed, "It's like when push came to shove and we got here and everything happened we all just knew what we were doing."

"Maybe we really are all meant for this. Maybe tonight was proof that there is some power in all of us being together." Billie said wistfully. "Destiny makes me hungry though, I fancy ice cream when we get in."

Isaac smirked despite his sadness. "Well there's certainly power in a two by four." he said, looking round at the various unconscious bodies. "I'm not going to be pissing either of you two off anytime soon." He then looked across to Gabbi who was busy talking to Galal. A moment later he saw them hugging.

After they broke apart Galal came over to them. "I'm proud to have my daughter with you all. For twenty years I've been waiting, knowing that a day like today would come. And now I'm glad that although there's been tragedy we have managed to stop evil from prevailing." He looked once more at Gabbi. "Your mother must be very proud Gabriella. Proud of all of you."

Isaac wasn't so sure about that, but he smiled in appreciation nonetheless. "Thank you." Isaac said. "For all your help with everything."

"Don't mention it, please. If you ever need my help again, I pray for your sakes that you don't but if you do, you know exactly where I am." Galal smiled. He turned once more to Gabriella. "I'll see you next weekend then my darling?"

"Yes dad, of course." Gabbi said with a smile, hugging her dad one more time.

Galal nodded at them all and turned to leave the guildhall, slowly walking towards the doors.

Isaac hesitated for a moment and then ran after him, leaving the others behind for a moment. "Galal?" Isaac called.

"Yes Isaac?" Galal asked, stopping his walk for a moment.

"Professor Archington, the Abominable Nothing and all these hooded people - they're all working for something. Archington died just now but before he did he warned me that something was on its way. He said something was coming. Do you know anything about that? Anything at all?"

Galal shook his head sadly. "I'm sorry my boy, I don't know anything."

"But you knew about the Box of Infernos and the Djinn -"

"All of that was very lucky research. And the information I had on Archington took years to compile and even then I only heard rumours about a religious group of sorts that he once belonged to."

"The Order of Dunamis."

"Ah, see? You already know more than me." Galal smiled softly. "There is a feeling in this world that some kind of vast shadow is gathering. What it is I can't tell you. But whatever it is it seems that for now it wants to stay hidden. Hidden doesn't mean it's not dangerous though - in fact it means quite the opposite."

"So what do we do?"

"You stay together, you stay strong." Galal patted Isaac warmly on the shoulder. "And if you need any help at all you come and find me."

Isaac nodded in agreement. "Okay." In reality he had no intention of involving Galal again unless it was absolutely necessary. He was an aging man after all and he'd already almost died once tonight. Isaac certainly didn't want to make a commodity out of him.

"Good. Take care Isaac." With that Galal turned and walked out of the front doors, walking with a slight hobble which reminded Isaac again that they shouldn't endanger Galal again without it being absolutely necessary.

Isaac turned and walked back to Gabbi, Billie and Laura.

"Everything alright?" Gabbi asked.

Isaac nodded. "Yeah, I just asked your dad if he knew anything more about what this thing is that Archington was working for. The master he mentioned."

Laura looked hopefully at Isaac "Did he know anything?"

"No." Just then a thought popped into Isaac's head. "I suppose the question is now what do we do about our friend smoky?" He looked over to where the Box of Infernos had been but he was alarmed to see it was gone. "Oh."

"Two of Archington's lot took it when they realised they weren't winning." Laura explained. "We tried to stop them but they got away." She looked at Isaac apologetically. "Sorry."

"Don't be silly, it's fine. I don't think they'll try opening it again - they'd probably need to start the whole ritual from the beginning again with soul number one. We should be safe." Isaac said, hoping that he was right and that they wouldn't be seeing that box again anytime soon - or anytime ever for that matter.

"What do we do about everyone here though?" Billie asked, indicating to the various unconscious bodies on the floor. "Do we phone the police? An ambulance?"

Gabbi looked back towards the stairs that led down to the basement. "Yeah and what about Professor Archington's body?"

Isaac looked back at the stairs sadly. "I think we're just going to have to leave him. It's in the bad guys' interests to keep this all quiet as much as it's in our interests. Like Archington said, they have contacts in the emergency services. I'm sure if we just leave then everything will get tidied up. One way or another." Isaac did feel bad just leaving Professor Archington in the basement but he couldn't see an alternative. It was the same sort of problem they had when Pete had been murdered.

Just then his ear suddenly stung and touching it he remembered that Skarl had bitten it. He thought for a moment as to whether he should go down and try and banish Skarl or destroy him like Galal had destroyed Valgar. Something inside him told him not to however - there had been enough fighting and destruction for one day. He hoped that he wouldn't live to regret that decision and he hoped that like the Box of Infernos Skarl would just slink back into the shadows and not bother them again.

"I should go and speak to Ben." he said, suddenly remembering that Ben was outside still. "Give me a few minutes with him and then we'll leave."

"Okay well hurry up!" Billie said, warning him with a shake of her fist. "I really want a cup of tea and some ice cream!"

The late night air was refreshing as Isaac stepped outside the guildhall. He suddenly realised that he had no clue what the time was, but he guessed it must be after midnight. He looked out across the courtyard and he couldn't see Ben. He went right up to the footpath by the road and Ben still wasn't anywhere to be seen up or down the street. Isaac sighed – he had probably gone straight home after shooting Archington with the crossbow. Isaac knew Ben well enough to know that despite his manly and lad-like exterior he was really quite a sensitive person inside and he took things easily to heart.

"Oh Ben." Isaac whispered to himself. "It wasn't your fault." He pulled his phone out of his pocket and tried phoning Ben. It rang and rang – for a moment Isaac was sure it would go to voicemail. Then –

"Hi mate." Ben sounded anxious, nervous, distracted.

"Oh thank goodness, I was worried about you. Where are you?"

"I'm almost home. Sorry, I couldn't stay, I just couldn't. God I just murdered -"

"You didn't murder anyone."

There was a pause on the line.

"Ben? You didn't murder anyone okay?"

"I thought he was attacking you Isaac. I thought, I don't know – I just saw him standing over you. It all happened so fast."

"I know."

"I never wanted to kill anyone. I'm not, I mean he was a person -"

"You didn't kill him, not in the end. He was alive still – then some kind of force came and finished him off."

"Oh yeah as if he would have lived."

Isaac knew in his heart that Ben was right. Even if the mysterious force hadn't killed Archington he would have still died. There'd been so much blood.

Ben continued to talk before Isaac could respond. "I know he was a bad person, I know I should just shrug and say he deserved it. Bastard got what was coming to him. But I can't say that."

"That's because you're a good man Ben."

Ben coughed a laugh. "Yeah." He paused a moment. The line buzzed. "I started helping you because I liked the idea of helping people. All the stuff with the demons and the ghosts, it was exciting! And Susie had said about me having a destiny, I don't know – in some goofy way I thought I was continuing her work. Keeping her legacy alive I guess."

"And you are doing that!"

"By killing another human? Because that's who I am now Isaac. I'm a killer. You've never killed anyone and neither has Gabbi or Laura or Billie. But I have, just now. Whatever else I do that won't change. We can all try and move on from it, maybe even try and forget it, brush it under the carpet – but I will always have that in my mind. I'll be reminded every day, every time I walk past that building or hear someone at uni mention his name. I killed him. I'm Ben the killer. Forever."

"Okay, I know it's bad. But you're panicking. You need to take a breath okay?"

Ben didn't say anything.

"Would you feel like this if he had have been attacking me?"

"No. But that isn't the point really. And I lied just now as well – the main reason I started helping you was actually because I liked you. I liked you and the girls. You were so different to my normal friends from before uni – you were more like family." Ben chuckled sadly down the phone. "Ha, I never said soppy crap like that before hanging out with a stupid gay like you."

Isaac laughed. "You'll catch it if you're not careful."

"Yeah you wish."

"We are family though Ben, you know that. And families stick together and they work through things. We'll be home in a bit and then we'll chat properly yeah?"

Ben paused, as though he were thinking something he wasn't saying. "Yeah."

"But you're okay now? I know the situation isn't good and I know you're not happy with what you did – but you're okay?"

"I will be mate."

"Okay. Well we won't be long. I'll see you in a bit."

"Isaac?"

"Yeah."

Another hesitation, this time as though he were summoning up the nerve to say what he wanted to say. "I love you." Ben said the words meaningfully if a little embarrassedly. Then he hung up the phone immediately after.

Isaac smiled to himself and slipped the phone back into his pocket. Ben really was a soppy character deep down. He went to turn back towards the door of the guildhall but as he did something caught his eye across on the other side of the street. He was sure the whole area had been deserted but now there was a figure standing just across the road from him..

A girl in a pink dress stood there on the opposite pavement, just staring at him. The girl was about his age he guessed with wavy blond hair down past her shoulders. Her dress was a very pretty pink colour and it was ruffled and flowing, reaching down to just past her knees. In one hand she was carrying something, something that sparkled slightly. Was it a crystal? It was only small whatever it was.

As he looked he noticed the girl was really staring at him and it wasn't in an absent minded kind of way - it was as if there was something meaningful and purposeful behind it. Her eyes burrowed into him intensely, so intense in fact that it gave Isaac a cold chill. He felt the skin on his arms tingle with goose pimples. It was such an intense stare she was giving him - the kind of stare you gave someone if you knew them, if you knew them and knew they needed help desperately. Isaac had never seen her before in his life, he racked his brain to think if he recognised her from university or from anywhere but he just didn't. Still she stared at him from across the road. It really was the kind of stare you gave someone when you knew they were in danger and you wanted to warn them with nothing more than a look.

"Hey." Isaac's train of thought was interrupted by Gabbi, who had come up behind him "You okay? Where did Ben go?"

Isaac turned to face Gabbi. "He's gone home." He turned his head back round to look across the road. The girl in the pink dress had gone - vanished completely. "Did you just see -"

"What darling?"

"There, just across the road? There was a girl in a pink dress, did you see her?"

Gabbi shook her head. "No, no I didn't. But then I wasn't looking across the road." Gabbi looked puzzled. "Was she important?"

"I don't know, no probably not. It's just she looked at me like there was something wrong, like she knew me. I don't know."

"Oh. Should we look for her do you think?"

"No, no. Like I said, it probably wasn't important." Isaac looked at the spot where the girl in the pink dress had been and frowned. "It was probably nothing."

Gabbi rubbed Isaac's shoulder warmly. "How come Ben went back without us?"

"He's quite torn up over the fact that he killed Archington."

Gabbi gasped. "What?"

"Well, sort of killed him anyway. He thought Archington was attacking me so he shot him with the crossbow."

"He wasn't attacking you?"

"No, he was helping me. I managed to get through to him in the end. It was all quite tragic really, the whole story. I'll explain it all to you properly when the others are here." Isaac sighed loudly. "But Ben didn't know so he fired. Archington fell and he was dying I think, but then at the very end it wasn't the crossbow that killed him."

"Then what did?"

"Some kind of force came, an energy in the room. I don't know what but I wouldn't mind guessing that it is something to do with whatever Archington had been working for. Anyway that's what killed him in the end. Just as he was about to give me some information too."

Gabbi sighed and tutted sadly. "Always the way." She reached out and took Isaac by the hand. "We did good tonight Isaac, despite the tragedy. You know that don't you?"

Isaac nodded. "I know."

"We saved the world." Gabbi said brightly, a big smile on her beautiful face.

"Do you think if we just tell that to all our professors at uni they'll just give us firsts?" Isaac asked wearily. They had their final exams coming up and he wasn't in the mood for them.

"We could try." Gabbi smirked. She started swinging his hand happily from side to side.

"I love you Gabbi." Isaac said, brightness finally penetrating his sad mood a little. He felt the brightness grow a little more and reached out and grabbed her in a tight hug. The sad dark clouds in his mind pushed back fully now and the brightness shined as he nuzzled his face into her shoulder. They were alive, and they did it! They stopped the Box of Infernos from being opened! Isaac even found himself laughing a little now – god this had been a mad night for emotions!

Gabbi hugged back just as tightly. "I love you too darling." she said, her voice happy but strained by how tight the hug was. After a moment they broke apart. "Hey I wonder if I'll get super strength as part of my new angel upgrade?"

Isaac smiled widely at her. "You never know. How're you feeling about all that anyway?"

"You know it's like what I said at dad's earlier. I mean it's weird but at the same time it's not weird at all. Like I don't feel freaked out by it, not really anyway."

"A bit though?"

"Well yeah, a bit. I mean I woke up this morning being a hundred per cent human Gabbi, now I'm going to go to bed knowing I'm half angel and my mum isn't actually dead so much as just back up in heaven. She's up there right now with wings and a harp and all that other angel stuff -"

"A halo." Isaac suggested.

"Yes, yes I bet she's got one of those. I mean it is a bit mad isn't it?"

"It is. But then as we discussed on the train earlier - that's our lives now." Isaac blew out his cheeks loudly and turned to see Billie and Laura emerge from the guildhall. "Come on everyone, let's go home."

Chapter Thirty Eight

On the walk back home Isaac got everyone up to date with what exactly had happened between him and Archington – both before and after the release of the Abominable Nothing. The story seemed to leave everyone in a state of mind where they weren't quite sure what to think – whether to feel bad for Archington or not. The way Isaac looked at it, it was a tragedy regardless of whether Archington was good or bad in the end. And you can't help but feel bad when there's a tragedy, whatever the circumstances.

"I think we should still feel really happy though." Billie said after they had pondered Archington for a while. "We did just do something amazing. Everyone's going to wake up tomorrow, safe and sound because of us." She seemed to think on for a moment. "We're like superheroes!"

Isaac burst out laughing along with the others. "Superheroes?!" he asked in disbelief. "Can you imagine? Us lot, running about down misty alleyways wearing luminous lycra outfits? Capes flying out behind us?"

"We'd look amazing." Billie insisted.

Laura raised her eyebrows. "You won't catch me in lycra – skinny jeans are tight enough thank you very much!"

"Oh Gabbi you could have a white one!" Billie enthused. "And you could like throw your halo like a frisbee to knock out demons! Or if you had a little harp you could fire arrows with it!"

Gabbi laughed. "Well that's this years Halloween costume sorted!"

Laura laughed too. "Oh Billie love you do need a cup of tea to calm you down I think!"

Isaac was laughing along with them when he heard his phone ring in his pocket. He pulled it out and saw it was Jack calling. "Oh it's Jack - I'll just hang back a little bit."

"Okay darling." Gabbi smiled.

Isaac slowed his pace down and hung back from the others before picking up. "Hello sweetheart!"

"Hey." Jack said in a tired but smooth voice. "What's happening? Are you with Gabbi's dad?"

"No, it's all over. With Professor Archington I mean."

"Oh god already? What happened? Are you okay?!" Jack was suddenly more awake and alert.

"I'm okay. I wasn't for a moment but the gang turned up and we made it through. Well, just about anyway. We're good."

"How do you mean you weren't okay for a moment?" Jack sounded worried.

Isaac didn't want to go into all the details again, not tonight - he really just wanted some kind words with his boyfriend. But since Jack had asked he felt he had to be honest. "Archington was going to kill me in order to open up the box and let loose the Djinn that was trapped inside. That's what was in there, a powerful Djinn. But it's okay, the guys turned up and saved me with the help of Gabbi's newly found angel powers. I mean the Djinn did end up getting released for a bit but it wasn't properly. We stopped it."

The phone line went silent for a just a moment. "Angel powers?!" Jack shouted down the phone in shock.

Isaac had forgotten that Jack didn't know all about that yet. It had all happened so fast that night. He chuckled a little down the phone. "It's a long story. Basically her mum is an angel." Isaac said the words rather plainly and it struck him that it was such amazing news he should have been telling it with great wonderment. It just seemed all so normal already!"That's unbelievable!" Jack sounded momentarily impressed but then obviously remembered what they had been talking about previously as his tone instantly lowered. "Wait hang on, rewind a bit. You nearly died! You nearly died and I wasn't even there to save you or help at all." Jack sounded distraught now. "I've only just found you, I can't lose you now - I won't!" .

"It's okay, I'm not going anywhere I promise." He knew it wasn't a promise he could really make but he made it anyway. "You'll never lose me okay?"

"I'm coming back." Jack sounded defiant. "I'm coming back to Monks-Lantern, I have to be with you. I should never have left in the first place."

"Sweetheart your mum, you must have only just got to her! She needs you now."

"No, I'm coming back. And mum's okay, the doctors say she is out of the woods. I need to be with you so I can help get you out of the woods you're in."

Isaac smiled down the phone. "Thank you sweetheart." It brought him great comfort to think of Jack coming back down to him, especially knowing that something worse was still ahead of them. "You'd best bring a torch mind, the woods down this way look like they're going to get pretty dark indeed soon."

"I'll make sure I have one packed."

They spoke for a few moments longer before saying goodbye. Isaac jogged a little to catch up with the others. They all greeted him warmly again as they turned the corner of Elsbridge Hill Road and started to walk back down to home.

Laura looked like she had a question she wanted to ask but didn't want to at the same time. "So what're the chances of things getting better round here anytime soon? All that talk of something bigger, something else coming – that's going to be worse than all this has been won't it?"

"Boo!" Billie cried defiantly.

"I think it's safe to say it won't get better." Gabbi said with a sigh. She looked across at Isaac as they walked and looked him in the eyes. "It will get worse, I can feel it. I don't know whether I picked up some of these higher frequencies we keep hearing about, but I can feel it. It's like Archington told Isaac before he died. Something's rising alright. Something is coming."

Isaac nodded slowly in agreement. It was sad to think about it after being happy in their part success that night but they couldn't ignore it. "Something bigger than Archington, something Archington and the Djinn were working for, something that has been hiding from us and from everyone all this time." Isaac didn't want to be over dramatic but at the same time didn't want to make the situation seem less serious than it actually was. "I imagine when it decides to come out of hiding we're all going to feel it." Isaac sounded scared, he knew he did. And that's because suddenly he was.

"What do we do then?" asked Billie.

"We keep going." Isaac answered. "We keep fighting. Together." He looked around at his friends as they walked the last few steps to the house. His brave friends who he loved so very much. And somewhere deep inside of him he realised that they really were supposed to be exactly where they were. He looked across at Gabbi and she smiled at him. Despite everything, she smiled. Their guardian angel. "We're meant to. I know we are."

Once through the front door everyone breathed audible sighs of relief. What Isaac wanted to do straight away was to talk to Ben and convince him not to feel bad. He needed that man just as much as he needed the girls or Jack. Ben had given Isaac so much over the last months that he wanted to make sure that Ben understood one hundred percent how much he was needed, wanted and loved.

"Ben?" he called out to the house. No reply. "Must be in his room." Isaac said, heading for the stairs.

Everyone else wandered into the living room and kitchen.

"I'll put the kettle on!" Billie cried. "Ask Ben if he wants one!"

"Will do." Isaac said as he ascended the stairs.

Despite the tragedy of the night and the terrifying news of what was to come he still felt a sense of hope, a kind of buzz of happiness that he had his friends and together they could sort it all out. It would all be alright, he just knew it would. Everything would be fine.

"Ben!" he called as reached his friend's bedroom door. It was shut. Isaac imagined Ben laying on the bed, staring wistfully at the ceiling. He knocked twice and then walked straight in, just as Ben always did with him. "Hope you're not naked -"

An empty room greeted him.

Isaac's eyes darted to the wardrobe, its doors open. Clothes gone. Then on the floor he noticed Ben's gym bag – also gone. A rising tide of panic swelled up from inside him. He felt clammy, nauseous. He looked this way and that, hoping to find Ben hidden in a corner but he wasn't there at all!

"No, no, no, no -" he found himself muttering to himself. "No this can't be happening!"

Just then he looked down on the bed and saw a piece of paper that had been torn badly from a writing pad. Ben's untamed scrawl was on it. Isaac snatched up the paper, reading the single line in the dim light from the landing.

I can't be this forever. So sorry mate. x

Isaac felt his strength leave him. His mouth was open in utter despair and the first he knew of the tears falling from his eyes was when heavy splashes landed on the paper he still held in his hand, making the ink smudge a little. He dropped the paper and clasped a hand to his mouth to stop himself from bursting out into loud uncontrollable tears. He felt himself shake – his shoulders, his hands, his legs – they all shook as the pain and sorrow burst through him in waves. He couldn't believe it, he couldn't! He needed Ben, they were friends! Ben called him a stupid gay and he called Ben a homophobe – he needed that! It was all happening again – Pete had said there would be a few to lose and this was it! The more he thought he more he wanted to cry, the more he wanted to scream with sadness. His tears had soaked the hand that he had clasped to his mouth by now. He removed it and looked round at Ben's empty room once more.

From somewhere downstairs Billie called up. "Hey what are you gays doing up there? Tea's ready!"

Isaac stared onwards in disbelief. "Please." he begged quietly to no-one in particular. "Please no."

Epilogue

"The Imperator betrayed us and now he's dead." spat the low voice.

There were about ten of them in the dark underground room, the dim glow of distant torchlight bouncing and dancing on the stone walls.

"What are we supposed to do now? Continue to try and open the Box of Infernos?"

"No." Skarl said forcefully, slinking out from behind a rough stone pillar. The air in the room was thick - claustrophobically so. "No more time for opening boxes!"

"Then what?" demanded the first voice "We do nothing? Our brotherhood has been working towards these events for millennia! Are we going to just let them end now?"

"No, no, no!" Skarl said, waggling a finger. "I've heard the master sing to me, such a pretty song. We must keep stepping forwards on our stepping stones. On and on and onto the next one!"

A third voice sprang up from amongst the group. "But we need the Imperator for that!"

"No. We need a dear old friend. A lovely friend who can do it all for us!"

"Who?"

"Someone who hates the Isaac boy, someone who is ever so good at ripping pretty boys' lives apart. Someone who wants to see their insides hung as lovely decorations!"

"But who!?"

"Bring him!" Skarl commanded.

From out of the gloom there came the noise of wheels, and soon a cage was brought into the low light that surrounded the group of hooded figures. All of them recoiled ever so slightly at what they saw in the cage.

"But he was banished!" cried one of the startled voices.

"Our power brought him back." Skarl informed them. He turned to the cage and addressed its inhabitant. "Verk'an-gorek! We have released you from the place of dust and bones. Will you help us in our destined task?"

Verk'an-gorek growled from behind the bars of the cage and laughed roughly. "I will."

The story continues in
The Chronicles of Darkness:
The Unknown Portal

www.chroniclesofdarkness.co.uk

Lightning Source UK Ltd.
Milton Keynes UK
UKOW040106140613

212209UK00001B/204/P